"Actually...." Ballard trailed off, uncharacteristically uncertain. She glanced at Jeffers, her brows arching in a silent question.

He grimaced and gave a little shake of his head, and then rolled his eyes and shrugged before taking a breath and looking at me.

"We were planning to track you down later."

"And here I thought I'd hid all my murder victims so well," I deadpanned.

"You do realize you cause yourself most of your own trouble, right?" Jeffers asked.

"It's a talent."

"You got a minute to sit?" Ballard said, gesturing toward the collection of bistro tables in the nook beside the coffee kiosk.

Color me flabbergasted. "Sit? With you?"

Jeffers made a scornful sound. "This is idiotic. Let's just go."

"And do what?" Ballard asked, ever the calm one of the two. "We're out of leads and time isn't doing us any favors."

PUTTING THE ICE IN NICE

EVERYDAY DISASTERS
BOOK THREE

DIANA PHARAOH FRANCIS

BOOK VIEW CAFE

Putting the Ice in Nice
Everyday Disasters: Book 3

Copyright 2023 by Diana Pharaoh Francis
ISBN: 978-1-944756-16-1

Published by Book View Café in conjunction with Lucky Foot Press 2023

Production team:
Cover illustration and design by Lyn Forester
Beta read by Patricia Rice
Copyediting and proofreading by Tiffany Trent
Ebook design and formatting by Jennifer Stevenson

www.bookviewcafe.com
Book View Café edition September 12, 2023
in conjunction with
Lucky Foot Press

To my family.

CHAPTER ONE

I was cursed.

Again.

I had to be. No one could possibly *not* be cursed and still get a ticket, have a flat tire, *and* spill her triple espresso mocha all over herself and her car before eight in the morning.

I gripped my steering wheel hard, tapping my foot as I waited for the cop to do whatever he was doing. Probably jerking off. He'd taken my license and registration and retreated to the squad car parked behind me, lights flashing red and blue. Cars whizzed by on the highway, some honking gleefully at me. I snarled, tempted to give the last one a flat tire. Or two. Or all of them. I could send a quick zap of magic and the assbite would be hating life at least as much as I was at the moment. I resisted the urge, silently congratulating the lucky bastard on getting away.

Sighing, I tipped my head back against the headrest, closing my eyes and trying to relax. I *had* been speeding. No point arguing. Of course, I'd also been wildly squirming in my seat as hot coffee broiled my thighs and crotch. Good thing sex wasn't on the menu any time soon; I probably had ninth degree burns on my cooch.

If the cop was any kind of a decent human being, he'd have at least considered letting me off with a warning. As it was, he'd barely hidden his laugh when I'd jumped out of the car and performed the hot coffee shimmy and shake, loudly cursing all the while. Now I had to sit in wet pants and underwear as I waited for my ticket. If I did the little nose twitch thing (that's not really how magic works, incidentally) and was suddenly dry, he'd probably be a little curious. Maliciously so.

That was not the way to cut the timer on this particular humiliation.

Another sigh and a little smile.

Officer Smug had fast lost his little urge to laugh at me when Ajax had leaped out my open door. He came up to my waist and weighed a good buck-fifty and I could still feel his ribs just a bit when I pet him. He also resembled a wolf. Some even said he was a wolf. I didn't see it. He was a giant, snuggly teddy bear. I'd rescued him from a seriously abusive situation, and we'd been close to inseparable since.

Upon Ajax's sudden appearance, Officer Smug had back-pedaled fast, nearly tripping over his own feet. He'd managed not to fall on his ass, so he had no real reason to be pissed. What kind of a man couldn't take a little justified cackling? Anyway, I hadn't turned him into a frog for finding my hot-coffee dance amusing, so he should return the favor and let me go without the ticket.

Though to be fair, he'd have to know of my largesse and telling him I was a witch would probably have him calling the little men in white coats to take me off to the nuthouse. That or he'd have corrected me and said it was spelled b-i-t-c-h.

Asshole.

I dug my fingers into Ajax's ruff and scratched his neck. He gave a little moan and leaned into the caress, lifting his head to give me better access to a particularly itchy spot. I obliged the silent demand, watching Officer Numb-nuts clamber out of his car in the rearview, my left foot tapping impatiently.

I hated being late, even if I'd rather eat a jar of live scorpions rather than have breakfast with my mother. My real mother. The woman who'd I'd grown up calling Mommie Dearest had turned out to be my aunt. She'd kidnapped me as an infant. Twenty-seven years later she'd been murdered and suddenly I had a new mother and a huge sprawling dysfunctional family, not to mention a witch community and culture that was about as bizarre as a twelve-legged cat. Not that those exist. I think. Wouldn't bet my life on it, though.

Anyhow, now my mother wanted to get acquainted, and I'd reluctantly agreed. It wasn't her fault her sister kidnapped me and then spent my entire life using me as her personal torture doll. It also wasn't her fault that she closely resembled Aunty Mommie. Nevertheless, just looking at her tended to make me first recoil and then want to kill her. At least a little.

Still, I felt a little sorry for her. She'd never had any more kids, and thanks to the birthing contract, my father had taken my two siblings (I was a triplet) and she'd never seen them again.

I made a face. Birthing contract. The witch community managed their magical bloodlines like horse breeders. They negotiated birth contracts between families, giving the studs and broodmares absolutely no say in the matter. Neither love nor lust nor like nor respect entered into the equation. Basically it came down to pimping out the family chromosomes, not to mention uteruses, dicks, and vaginas.

Despite my adamant refusal to be a part of that whole baby factory thing, my father (who I'd also just met) had determined that I belonged to him and therefore would fuck whoever he wanted me to and have whatever babies he'd contracted for. Bonus—I wouldn't even have to raise them!

Excuse me while I vomit.

"Here you go, Ma'am."

The cop passed my registration and license through the window. He was an older guy, maybe around fifty, with a shaved head to cover up the fact he was bald on top. Silver threads shot through his brown mustache and goatee.

"I'm going to give you a warning this time," he said.

"Really?" I hadn't seen that coming. "Why?"

"Call it extenuating circumstances," he said without cracking a smile, but the corners of his eyes crinkled slightly.

"That's...." I shook my head. "Thanks."

"Your dog licensed?"

I frowned, shifting into momma-bear mode. "He is."

"He doesn't have a collar."

"The fuckers who had him before me kept him on a chain. When we rescued him, he was starved, covered in bruises with broken bones and his collar had worn a bloody infected trench into his neck. I won't force him to wear one again."

At my description, his face turned to granite, his upper lip curled, his nostrils flaring. "Tell me you reported the assholes."

"It was a hostage situation. You probably remember. Happened not too long ago. A month or so, maybe. Out in north of town in the hollows. Father was a mean son of a bitch who beat the wife and girls. Wife ended up shooting him and then trying to off the girls. They hid in the doghouse with this big guy."

I scratched Ajax's ears, my throat knotting with emotion. He'd been determined to protect the little girls despite being close to dead himself. He'd weighed maybe sixty-five pounds and had broken bones from getting kicked who knows how many times. I still couldn't quite believe that Lorraine—one of my best friends and an incredible veterinarian—had managed to put him back together. She was a miracle worker. "Not sure what happened to the mother. Prison, I hope. No idea what happened to the girls. They weren't a lot better off than Ajax here."

He muttered something under his breath.

"Sorry?"

He shook his head. "Do me a favor and keep it to the speed limit."

"I'll try."

He quirked an eyebrow. I shrugged.

"You try pouring a raging hot cup of coffee on your twig and berries and not stomping down on whatever pedal you've got your foot on."

The corner of his mouth lifted. "I'd just as soon take your word for it if you don't mind."

"And even if I do mind, right?"

He smirked. "I like to think I'm smart enough to learn from other people's mistakes."

I tucked my registration back into my glove compartment and slid my license into my wallet. "Is this where I tell you thanks for the break and wish you a nice day?"

He stepped back and nodded. "Drive safely. I'd just as soon not see you again."

"And here I thought we were falling in love."

He smirked. "My husband would have my balls."

"My boyfriend might have something to say about it too," I said with pretend regret.

The mention of Damon made my stomach twist. I hadn't heard from him in days and I didn't know if I should be worried about him, worried about our relationship, or if I was being an emotional idiot. We hadn't been seeing each other long, and I didn't have any relationship experience to work from. I was totally in the dark and feeling like a fifteen-year-old with a crush on the high school quarterback and having a lot of what-the-fuck issues over him liking me back. Or loving me. Damon said he loved me. I was still trying to come to grips with how I felt about that and about him and now I was wondering if he really did or if he'd been having a stroke.

Definitely an emotional idiot.

Damon had been gone a couple of weeks now after receiving an emergency call. Apparently, it had something to do with his family, though he hadn't given me any details. I hadn't asked.

My new cop buddy patted the top of my roof. "Have a good—" He grinned. "A better day."

"You're a surprisingly nice cop."

"That's what everybody I don't give a ticket to says." He chuckled and returned to his vehicle.

"And now on to the next disaster," I muttered as I put the car in gear. I was still driving a Highlander. Not fancy or sexy, but it carried a lot of stuff and people, and I had a fluffy bed in the back for Ajax, along with a pile of old towels for when he took a dunk in the river where I generally ran, or at my secret cove.

I knew better than to even hint the universe might have another disaster in store for me, though it was inevitable. My whole life was ruled by Murphy's Law and Mercury was in permanent retrograde, while at the same time I must have busted so many mirrors in another life the bad luck had carried over to this one. At least I had managed to avoid the emergency room for a while.

I headed back to my house to clean up. I waved to Joseph the gate guard as I drove in, circling the looped driveway and parking at the front. I drew a long breath and let it out, fortifying myself. With a silent groan, I got out, Ajax hard on my heels.

The place looked like a French chateau with sweeping front steps and two wings angling off the main house. Stone gargoyles of various sizes perched along the roofline front and back. I scowled at them. Auntie Mommy had imprisoned them, forcing them to swear a blood bond to guard the house and property and all its denizens forever. My Uncle Mason had been able to break the spell that kept them bound in stone, except if their protection was needed. Now they stayed during the day and came alive at night. I'd promised to find a way to release them, but so far hadn't had any luck.

Actually, I hadn't tried all that hard. I'm a highly untrained witch. I have a lot of power and determination, which allows me to do a lot of stuff, but I hadn't wanted to let Auntie Mommy know I had power, so used it very sparingly. Stupid, since it turned out she knew exactly what I was, but I hadn't known that. I had no training and no clue how to begin to free the gargoyles. I'd tried, but I needed more than a seat-of-the-pants approach. Damon had started teaching me witch language and basic spells, but then he'd left town.

Taking a deep breath, I steeled myself to go inside, my body tensing, my stomach churning. I hated it here. This is where Auntie Mommy had spent years torturing me. I'd sworn I'd never come here willingly, and now I was living here. The universe has a crappy sense of humor. A psychic—Lindsey, who I'd saved from her evil aunt's ghost—had made a very vague and ominous prediction promising that trouble was coming, and then she'd written out an enormously complex spell all over the walls of an indoor gym. I had no idea what the spell did nor why it had been so important that Lindsey had been whipped into a frenzy to write it out. She had no idea either. Not what it meant or why.

I'd taken pictures to send to Damon, but they disappeared off my camera as fast as I could take them. I'd tried copying onto paper, but it disappeared again. Then it faded off the walls so that the only copy of it was seared into my brain. Nobody else who'd seen it could remember it, including Lindsey.

More than a little unnerved, I'd moved into the house. It had magical protections along with the gargoyles, though I hated the idea that they might have to protect me. I needed to find a way to free them before that became a potential issue.

I had a lot of enemies, most of whom I didn't know, most of them wanting me for my magical DNA. Apparently, I was the Serena Williams of broodmares. I came from two of the most powerful magical families of the witching world. They had an electronic server that disseminated emails to every witch, and I'd promptly sent everybody a message to fuck right off and that I wasn't interested in birthing no babies, but someone had already tried to kidnap me for my womb. He wouldn't be the last. Likely my father already had a kidnap squad or ten planning my capture.

I had nightmares about being put in some kind of catatonic state and popping out babies two or three at a time for as long as my body held up. With magical healing, it could be a long time. Bile flooded the back of my tongue and I swallowed. It didn't matter how many times I declared I was never going to let that happen. The cold hard reality was that if someone got a hold of me, they'd give me a lobotomy and turn me into an EZ Bake oven for whoever wanted to put a bun or three inside me.

I'd tried to convince my three best friends—Stacey, Jen, and Lorraine—to move as well, but they just hugged me and assured me they weren't targets. I had to admit that while worried about them, I hated to be alone in the mausoleum. Not that I was really alone. I had servants.

That fact alone was enough to make me vomit. I disliked the concept of servants. I didn't like people waiting on me and cooking for me or opening the door for me or doing my laundry. I'll admit, not having to clean the toilets or scrub the floors was nice, but I'd gladly go back to doing them for a little privacy. Unfortunately, when I'd inherited the house, I'd inherited the servants, too, and I wasn't about to put any of them out of a job, so I was learning to live with having people constantly around.

I jogged up the steps, Ajax leaping ahead. I hadn't reached the top when the door opened.

"Hey, Linus," I said, striding past the butler. Ajax made a beeline for the kitchen where he was bound to get treats. I smiled. Spoiled dog.

"I didn't expect you back so soon, Miss Beck."

"Just Beck," I said yet again. "I spilled my coffee."

"So I see."

I shot him a sideways glance, pretty sure he was laughing at me. His expression remained as bland as ever. It was a goal of mine to get him to break control and laugh.

"I hope I didn't interrupt your morning orgy."

"Not at all."

"I haven't been gone that long. You might want to get some blue pills to help your stamina."

"I'll keep that in mind for the afternoon orgy. I'll have another coffee prepared while you change."

"Thanks."

"Of course, Miss Beck."

"I know I've told you to drop the Miss thing and just call me Beck."

"Yes, Miss Beck. You have."

"And you're just going to keep doing it anyway."

"It would appear so."

"Maybe I should start calling you Mister Linus."

"That is your prerogative."

"Did you like Aunty Mommy? Like working for her?" The questions shot out of me before I knew I was going to ask it. I'd been wondering about it since I was a kid but never wanted to chance asking in case Aunty Mommy retaliated against him or whichever servant I asked.

"One does not judge one's employer."

"Did you know what she was doing to me?" Another question I'd been holding back. I wasn't sure I wanted the answer. What would I do if he *had* known? He couldn't have done anything. Aunty Mommy would have turned him into a cockroach if she didn't kill him outright.

"It was apparent she was abusing you, yes."

I couldn't be sure, but I thought his gaze hardened with the acknowledgement.

"She hurt any of the staff?"

"No. She would not." He said it with perfect certainty.

"I suppose it's hard to get good help." Especially those who'd conveniently ignore her nasty torture habit. Resentful anger sparked in my chest. I knew what she was capable of and that crossing her was dangerous, but I couldn't help wondering what would have happened if one of the servants had called her out or reported her. Maybe she wouldn't have killed them. Maybe someone would have stepped in.

Right. Who? The only ones who could have were witches, and she'd done an excellent job of hiding from the witching world. Who knew what sorts of spells she might have used on the staff to keep them from reporting anything?

I sighed. It's not like it mattered. It was all over. I just needed to get over it.

"I'd better get changed."

I heard a quiet, "Yes, Miss Beck," as I hurried off. So much for making him laugh. Maybe next time I'd try talking about the Holocaust or slavery or something equally amusing.

I'D CHANGED INTO A PANTSUIT AND WAS COMING BACK DOWN THE stairs when my phone beeped and then rang. I checked the ID screen. Stacey.

I smiled. "Hey! What's going on?"

Silence.

My stomach clenched. "Stacey? Are you there? What's going on?"

A soft groan. "I may or may not have fallen and I may or may not have broken my leg. Maybe some ribs too. Can you come take me to the hospital?"

I catapulted down the last of the stairs and sprinted for my car. "Where are you? Do you need an ambulance? Did you call 911?"

"Phone's dead. Can't call anybody but you, thanks to that little spell you put on it. Thank goodness for that or I'd be seriously fucked."

I could hear tears in her voice and the little gasps that told me she was hurting a lot worse than she was trying to let on. Plus she was talking in that peculiar voice people get when they're speaking through held breaths while keeping themselves braced against the pain.

"Where are you?"

"Well, that's part of the problem." Her laugh quickly turned into a whimper. "Ow ow ow. Fuck me, that hurts."

"Where. Are. You?"

"I don't know."

"Excuse me?" My pulse had leaped into high gear. I wrenched open my door and started the engine, setting my phone down as the car picked up the signal. "Can you hear me still? I'm in the car."

"I can hear you. I took my bike out to the bluffs. Decided to do a little cross country. Hit a rock or something and took a header. Crashed into a little ravine. Crap, Beck. It hurts like a dinosaur chewed me up." She let out a short litany of curses and then went silent except for what sounded like deep breathing.

"I'm on my way," I told her, stomping on the gas pedal,

my tires squealing. "Which parking lot? Did you go north or south from it?"

"Parked up by Ghost Creek Trail. Took the lower side and went off-trail maybe three or four miles in. Was trying to reach Schism Point."

Before I could respond, I heard some bumping and shuffling and then a loud clatter.

"Fuck! Beck, I dropped the phone. I can't reach it." Stacey sounded scared and close to crying.

"It's okay. I'll find you."

"Beck? I can't hear what you're saying!"

I heard sounds like the scrape of rocks and then a loud cry of pain and then crying. My hands clenched on the steering wheel and I jammed my foot to the floor. Stacey didn't cry, which meant her injuries were serious.

I wondered if I should call for help. Call the cops or the Park Service. I shook my head. I wouldn't risk the connection to Stacey. Anyway, I could find her faster. That's when I realized I'd left Ajax at the house. Should I go back? Maybe he could track Stacey. But no. He wasn't trained. I'd find her myself. Dierdre would take care of Ajax and make sure he was spoiled as he deserved to be.

"I'm coming! Hold on, Stacey! Keep talking to me!" I shouted the words as loud as I could, negotiating a curve and nearly going up on two wheels. Times like these I really missed my Thunderbird. It cornered smooth as butter at high speed. This Highlander was more top heavy.

"I hurt, Beck. I can't... Just please get here fast. I think I'm going to pass out."

CHAPTER TWO

I found Stacey's car in the north lot of the state park that stretched miles along the river. I screeched to a halt in the space beside her Honda and sprang out. I popped the Highlander's hatch and dumped out the bag where I kept a couple extra pairs of shorts, tee shirts, socks, and my running shoes. I quickly changed out of my silk pantsuit, ignoring the people around me. After tying my shoes, I rifled through the pile to find the first aid kit, a towel, protein bars, and a couple bottles of water.

I reloaded those into the bag and grabbed my phone and dialed 911. The operator answered.

"This is Beck Wyatt," I said. "I'm at the north parking lot of Spires State Park near the Ghost Creek trailhead. My friend went off trail and crashed her bike somewhere between here and Schism Point. She's in a ravine and badly hurt. You need to send searchers and medical help. I'm going to look for her. Hurry."

I didn't give him a chance to reply. I hung up and tucked my phone into a pocket. Next, I found a small gray pebble. I held it in my palm and focused on what I wanted. I gathered my magic and dumped it into the makeshift spell. The pebble flared bright green. I tossed it in the air.

"Take me to Stacey."

It darted away, heading up Ghost Trail. I followed, falling into a ground-eating run. Everything inside me urged me to go faster, but she had the advantage of a bike and I had no idea how far she'd managed to get before crashing. I had to pace myself. Once I headed off-trail, I'd be forced to slow down.

Luckily, Aunty Mommy had kept me super fit and had turned me into a long-distance runner as well as a rock climber. I could run a marathon without a lot of difficulty. Course that was with a huge calorie load, stretching, and a lot of water.

The sun shone brassy against the cloudless sky, and scents of mesquite, dried grass, blackberries, oaks, and other trees filled my lungs. At barely nine o'clock the shade still held in the night's cool air, but the day was swiftly heating up.

As I ran, I wondered if I should have called Jen and Lorraine. Not much they could do, but they'd want to know. Not to mention Officer Mikey and Stacey's stepbrother Luke. And the rest of her family. Unlike me, she was close to her family, even though they tended to be a little smothering.

I stopped and pulled out some water, drinking as I typed a text to the girls and then put my phone away again. They could pass the word. The green spark hovered, waiting for me to get going. I followed it another half mile before it veered off to the left. I found myself on what probably started as a deer track and had now become an off-road trail for bicycles.

It wound around brush, trees, and boulders, plunging

up and down and making twisting turns. I slowed to avoid twisting an ankle or falling. That wouldn't help Stacey one bit.

I made myself pause to rest a couple times, swigging water from one of the bottles. The other I was saving for Stacey. I had no idea how far I'd actually come, but the pebble didn't show signs of stopping.

"Where the fuck are you, Stacey?" I asked the little clearing where I'd stopped to stretch my hamstrings.

I didn't bother shouting for her since I had the pebble to guide me and I didn't want to waste my breath. I just kept telling myself she'd be okay and to hurry.

A couple times I had to detour, since the pebble wasn't that concerned with whether I could fly or not, and it brought me to escarpments I couldn't easily climb or gullies I couldn't jump that were too deep to climb down and back up.

It was almost eleven o'clock. I had dozens of mosquito bites and my clothes were drenched with sweat. I slowed to eat a protein bar when up ahead, the pebble went past some scrub bushes and scraggly oaks and disappeared. Bright green light flared like the beacon it was. I dropped the remains of my protein bar and raced forward.

"Stacey? Stacey, are you there?" I shoved my way through the bushes and found myself standing at the top of a rocky ravine. It appeared to have been carved by storm runoff and was currently bone dry. The glow emanated from somewhere at the bottom. A little way to my left, a clump of blackberries lumped up to block that side of gully.

Brush, wildflowers, star thistle, and dried grass obscured my view, but the pebble's green glow glinted off something metal. Stacey's bike. It lay twisted over a dead log that sprawled crosswise, its roots frozen in the air like octopus tentacles.

"I'm here," came Stacey's shaky voice.

Some brush moved and I realized she must be underneath it.

"Okay, I'm going to figure out how to get down there. But first...."

I popped open a location finder in my phone, took a screenshot of the GPS coordinates and texted them to Jen and Lorraine, ignoring the several dozen texts and missed calls from them and a number of others. I added a note telling them to relay the co-ords to Search and Rescue. I didn't know if I'd be able to get Stacey up by myself; moving her could really do physical damage. More physical damage. I didn't want to risk using magic to get her out. I wanted actual real medical personnel on hand.

"Hurry," she begged and I could hear her fear and pain.

"Sure," I said. "I'll just jump down on top of you. You can soften my landing."

"You're a witch. Can't you do better than *that*?"

"You've been watching *Practical Magic* too much. Or maybe *Hocus Pocus*. Anyhow, I don't have a broom or a pointy hat."

Her snicker ended on a sob. "I know what you're doing."

"Do you?"

"You're trying to distract me."

"Nope. Just trying to deal rationally with an irrational woman."

She made a raspberry sound. "I'm very rational for someone who can see her leg bone."

"Fair," I said, shuddering. I could handle shit happening to me, but not to my friends. Anger spurted up inside me that Stacey was going through this kind of suffering.

By now I'd figured out that I needed to walk down the edge of the ravine and find a place with some handholds. I found a spot about twenty-five feet down. Making sure my pack was secure, I sat and rolled onto my stomach, lowering myself slowly. I scrabbled for footholds, and finally found the protrusions I'd been banking on.

"Did you have to pick such a deep hole?"

"Go big or go home, right? Anyway, you're a master rock climber. If there's such a thing."

"Hate to break it to you, but you're not going home. You're going to the hospital."

"Was that supposed to be a joke? Breaking it to me? Because I've had enough breaking for one day, thank you very much."

"You know, when they say 'break a leg,' it's not meant to be literal," I said, spidering my way down. Stacey was right. I really was an expert rock climber and the wall of the ravine wasn't exactly Everest.

I dropped the last couple of feet and hustled to Stacey's side after pushing aside the bicycle.

"You look like shit," I said, squatting down beside her and doing my best to ignore the piece of bone protruding out her shin. Blood oozed from the wound and stained the ground beneath her. The rest of her was laced with bloody scratches and splotched with bruises. Her clothes were torn and her broken leg was swollen and a livid red. Tear streaks cut through the caked dirt and blood on her face.

"Like you should talk. Should we review your raw hamburger look after you tossed yourself into the river? Or maybe when you rescued the gargoyle females? All barbecued up? I didn't tell *you* you looked like shit."

"Actually, you did."

"At least I waited until you cleaned up first."

"To be fair, I was cleaned up on the first one before you saw me, so that one doesn't count."

She lay on her back between a bush and stub of rock. It's a miracle she didn't break her back. I quashed a spike of panic as the possibilities started running through my brain. I'd managed to avoid thinking about them until now, but I had a feeling I wouldn't be sleeping well for a while. Blinking back tears, I fished out the bottle of water, popped the cap, and then hesitated.

"You shouldn't move. Your back could be broken."

"It can't break any worse," she said, eyeing the bottle longingly.

"That's not true."

"Okay, but I've wiggled around a bit to get comfortable, so if there's damage, I've already done it. Give me the fucking water before my tongue snaps in half."

I slid my hand under her head and helped her lean up enough to drink.

"That might be the best tasting thing I've ever put in my mouth," she said after several swallows.

"I think I'm insulted."

"After your cooking, of course."

"And margaritas."

"Of course. And chocolate. Coffee. Salted-caramel ice cream. Girl Scout Cookies. Sometimes even a really nice dick." She started to chuckle, but it morphed into a whimper of pain. She breathed slowly. "I think I'm dying."

"You just *wish* you were dying," I corrected. "Help should be on its way."

"Help? I thought you were the cavalry." Stacey's eyes had closed and she sounded sleepy.

"No napping," I said, fear tap-dancing across my heart. "You could have a concussion."

"I wish it were only a concussion. I feel like someone took a crowbar to my skull."

"Good thing you're hard-headed."

"Like you should talk."

Stacey's eyes drifted shut again.

I brushed my fingers over her hand, trying to keep her awake. "Don't sleep, Stace."

She opened her eyes. "You're annoying me. You realize I've been napping on and off since I fell down here, right?"

"Humor me."

She sighed. "Fine, but you have to entertain me."

Just then my phone buzzed. I pulled it out. Jen. I answered.

"Hey."

"How's Stace?" Thank goodness I'd spelled her phone, too, along with Lorraine's. They could always contact me whether their phones were dead or broken. I doubted I'd have any signal down here.

"Hurting. Hope help gets here soon."

"We gave them the coordinates you texted. They said they weren't far."

"I'm going to take a picture of Stace and send it to you so the paramedics will know what to expect."

"Good idea. Let us know when they get there and take care of our girl."

"I will." I hung up and sent the picture, making sure to get a good view of her broken leg.

"How long before they get here?" Stacey asked, sounding like she could barely muster the energy to speak.

"Soon," I said, giving her another drink.

Soon turned out to be almost an hour. I'd done my best to help make her comfortable, using my magic to create a cushion of air underneath her, and after about five tries and a lot of swearing, I managed to wrap her in a cocoon of numbing magic. It didn't take away the pain by any means, but it dulled it enough to give her some relief.

I talked non-stop to keep her from falling asleep and made her drink all the water I had left. She was pale beneath the blood and dirt, though, and her body tremored like she had palsy. Why she hadn't gone into shock yet I didn't know, but it looked like it might be starting. I lifted her unbroken leg and set a rock under it, hoping that would help.

"Cold," Stacey whispered.

I concentrated on winding heat through the numbing spell. A few minutes later, Stacey heaved a relieved sigh. I silently urged the search and rescue team to move faster.

Finally, I heard sounds of crunching footsteps and the swish of brush on legs.

I jumped up and hollered. "Hey! Down here!"

Things moved both too slowly and very quickly after that. The rescue team's descent into the ravine seemed to take forever as they anchored ropes and rigged up rappel lines and a pulley system. I was glad of the preparations they'd made when three two-person rappel teams dropped down. The two paramedics assessed Stacey's condition as the other team members lowered medical boxes and a litter.

I whispered an apology to Stacey as I removed my spells so the medics could get an accurate understanding of her condition.

They took her blood pressure and pulse and checked her eyes and examined her head for other injuries, rapid-firing questions at me. What's her name? Is she allergic to anything? Medical conditions? Pregnant? What drugs does she take? How old? Recent surgeries or injuries? Addicted to anything? Reactions to penicillin? What about morphine?

As they received answers, they continued working. The put a foam collar around her neck and carefully got a brace board underneath her in case her back was injured. They started an IV and injected it with painkillers before lifting her into the stretcher and strapping her in. Within twenty minutes Stacey had been lifted to the ravine's rim. Grabbing a handy rope line, I quickly climbed up after her, ignoring cautions, questions, and offers for climbing belts or other offers of help.

"I'm not your patient," I reiterated for the billionth time. "She called me and I came looking for her. When I found her, I sent the coordinates so you could get her to the hospital. I don't need any help."

"You're good at climbing and cool under pressure. You should think about training for our volunteer search and rescue team," a stocky man with graying curly hair said. "Always looking for quality recruits." He handed me a card. "Call me about it. That over there is Kelly Barstow," he said, gesturing with his chin. "She'll be needing your information."

The paramedic in question—short dark hair, cedar-brown skin, and ropey muscles, squatted beside her opened medical cases, quickly sorting everything back where it belonged and snapping them shut. All around us, rescuers in their brown pants and yellow shirts with Ride County Search and Rescue picked out in green block letters wound up ropes and gathered the rest of their equipment, all of them chattering like squirrels.

Kelly caught my surprised look. "Always a good day when you get a rescue and not a recovery," she said as she stood. She handed me a water bottle out of her backpack before shouldering it and motioning me to follow her as she fell in behind the four men carrying Stacey.

"Your friend's lucky. Injuries like hers usually mean shock and death. Good thing you found her so quickly. She wouldn't have lasted the night. I'm surprised her organs hadn't started to shut down."

A shudder ran through me. "She's going to be okay though, right?" Just having to ask the question made me want to vomit.

"No guarantees, but I've seen people in worse condition recover just fine. They'll take good care of her at the hospital. They've got a great trauma surgeon and orthopedic staff. I hooked her up to fluids for hydration and some morphine to keep her comfortable. She didn't seem to have lost all that much blood, which might be what helped to delay the shock. My bet is they'll operate soon as she gets to the hospital. After that, it's just waiting for it to knit up. As long as nothing else was seriously damaged."

"Are you being straight with me or sugar-coating it?"

"No sugar."

"Anything important you're leaving out?"

The corner of her mouth quirked up. "You must be a lawyer."

I shook my head. "I just have trust issues."

Her smile widened. "We've got a chopper waiting for her at the top of the bluff." She pointed vaguely upward. "It's small. Won't be room for you. Someone can drive you to your car or take you to the hospital."

"Hospital," I said.

She nodded as if she'd expected the answer. "I'll need you to fill out a form with your name and number. We'll need Stacey's next of kin, too. I'll let them know at Emergency to expect you."

It wasn't long after that that I watched them load Stacey into the blue and white helicopter and a couple minutes later, they'd flown out of sight.

The curly-haired man I'd spoken to before came up the trail just as the helicopter rose. Though I'd stayed well out of rotor-range, bits of dirt and debris stung my face and a cloud of dust floofed out, swallowing up everybody else in the clearing. I coughed and drank from the bottle Kelly had given me, swishing the water in my mouth before spitting it out.

"I'm John. I'll give you a lift if you want," the curly-haired man said, tossing his gear into the back of a pickup truck.

"Beck. And thanks," I said, climbing into the passenger side.

He got behind the wheel and started the truck and put in gear. "Nice meeting you, Beck. Hospital or your car?"

"Hospital, please."

"You've got it."

He flashed me a little grin and grabbed a magnetic red and blue light from his dash. A cord trailed down to a place out of sight on the left side of his dash. He rolled his window down and set the light on the roof before flicking a switch. He pressed a button on the steering wheel. A siren sounded.

"Now we can speed."

"You a cop?"

"That a problem?"

"Only if you think I murdered someone."

He eyed me. "Did you?"

"Nope."

"Pretty specific comment to be random."

"That is true."

He went silent for a minute as if waiting for me to clarify. When the silent pressure technique didn't work, he shifted to direct attack mode.

"You going to explain?"

"And ruin the fun of hunting the story down yourself? I may be an asshole, but I'm not that much of one. Besides, you're being nosey."

He laughed. "Cops get paid to be nosey."

"Aren't you off the clock?"

"We're never really off the clock."

"Sounds exhausting."

"You're trying to change the subject. You going to give me a clue?"

"Murder suspect wasn't enough?"

He shrugged. "There are a lot of murder suspects out there. Until they're not. Doesn't really narrow the search much."

"Maybe you need to practice your cop skills."

He gave a little shrug of concession. "Maybe I do."

A few minutes later, he pulled into the Emergency Department's circular driveway. "You shouldn't be far behind the chopper. Go through those doors and someone will get you where you need to be."

"Thanks. And thanks for coming to find us."

"It's what we do. I hope your friend heals up quick."

Tears burned in my eyes as it suddenly hit me how close I'd come to losing Stacey and the realization punched me in the gut. I didn't know if I'd ever be able to catch my breath again. I'd spent most of my life protecting Stacey, Jen, and Lorraine from the cruelty and rage of Aunty Mommy. She leveraged their safety against me so that I would agree to take whatever torment she wanted to throw at me. When she was murdered, I'd started thinking they were safe. I was still staring down the threat of the witching world, but they were finally out of the crosshairs.

Except they weren't safe. Life wasn't safe. Stacey'd been riding her fucking bicycle and she'd almost *died*.

"Hey." John's callused hand gripped mine in warm strength.

Both mine were knotted into fists on my thighs as I tried to breathe down the inferno of panic that swept through me.

"She's going to be fine," he said, his eyes steady on me. "I promise."

My lips moved in an attempt to smile. "You can't promise that. You don't know."

"Maybe so, but I refuse to allow the worst into my head until I have to. In the 'what-if' game, the house always wins, so don't play it. Whatever will be will be, but until you know for a fact that it's bad, choose to believe it's good."

"You sound like one of those TV doctors."

"Probably about as qualified too," he said, patting my hand and sitting back. "But I've been around a lot of blocks and seen a lot of people when hope is in short supply. Choosing hope over despair is always better. Now, you got anybody you can call? Someone to come be here with you?"

I nodded and sniffed, annoyed to realize I was crying. I hated to cry. I swiped my hands over my cheeks. "Our friends—practically sisters, really—are on their way. And Stacey's family."

"Good. Go on, then."

I opened the door and slid out of the truck. I turned back before I shut it. "I'm Beck Wyatt. Check with Detectives Ballard and Jeffers at the local PD. I'm sure they'll give you an earful."

"I'll do that. And if I can help you with anything, let me know. You've got my card. Remember what I said about training for Search and Rescue. You'd be an asset."

I pulled his card out of my pocket and glanced down at it. "John Bowen. Department of Fish and Game? You're a game warden?"

"They call us wildlife officers now."

"A lot of animals out there committing crimes, are there? Bears shaking down the squirrels for their nut stashes?"

He grinned. "I tend to focus on the two-legged criminals. Plenty of those to go around."

I shoved the card in my pocket. "Thanks for the rescue and the ride. And don't worry. I'm not the criminal you're looking for. At least not today. Tomorrow could be a whole other story."

"I'll be sure to keep you on my suspect list."

I grinned. "You won't be the only one."

CHAPTER THREE

I pushed through the hospital's double-glass doors into a small lobby area. On the left flowed a wide path leading to another set of extra-wide double doors heading back into the treatment area. On the right were several stations containing desks with computers and behind those, shelves and storage areas. Just inside the door was a corral containing a dozen different wheelchairs, a small army of IV stands, and an assortment of other equipment. I saw a number of nurses and hospital staff in various colored scrubs, but most of the people were some variety of cop or other first responders either filling out paperwork or talking with patients' families.

A few of the families had small children or babies. The kids either sat scared, clinging to each other, a parent, or some other adult, or they squirmed and wiggled while playing with their toys.

"Can I help you?"

A tall nurse in light blue scrubs approached. He wore a cap over his hair and a stethoscope around his neck, along with a lanyard with his hospital ID and a set of keys.

"My friend was brought in on the Lifeflight. Her name is Stacey Wade. How is she?" My words came out like machine-gun fire.

Before he could respond, Kelly pushed through a door I hadn't noticed. Beyond it, I could see a kind of staging area/locker room.

"Oh, good. You got here. I'm on my way out but wanted to touch base and tell you Stacey made the flight just fine. Doctor's evaluating her now. They'll do some scans and take X-rays to ascertain the extent of her injuries. In the meantime, Dave here will take good care of you."

She stretched out her hand and gave mine a firm shake.

"Thanks for your help," I said.

"It's my job. Is there anything else you need from me? Otherwise, I'll leave you to Dave."

I shook my head. "I owe you."

She flashed a grin. "No, you don't."

"All the same, expect some chocolate and flowers at the least. Maybe a case of wine and a small house."

She chuckled and walked away. "Just an FYI: I'm a sucker for chocolate chip cookies," she tossed over her shoulder.

"I'll keep that in mind."

"Come have a seat," Nurse Dave said as Kelly departed. He waved toward a cubicle with two chairs facing a beige metal desk. I sat in one and he went around to the other side, tapping on his computer keyboard and scanning the monitor.

"You said your friend's name was Stacey Wade? Ah, here she is. I'd like to ask you a few questions if I may."

I nodded, wishing I had a gallon of coffee. All my remaining energy had melted away when my butt hit the seat of the chair. I felt like a comatose jellyfish. "Whatever you need."

He nodded. "Does Stacey have a living will?"

I shook my head. "I don't think so."

"What about a medical POA?"

"POA?"

"Medical power of attorney. Someone who can make health decisions on her behalf if necessary."

Panic jolted me. "Why do you think she needs that?"

Dave looked up and gave a reassuring smile. "It's standard to ask. Just something the hospital likes to have on file. Does she have one?"

"Not that I know of. Her parents, maybe?"

"What are their names? Do you have their contact info?"

I answered his questions the best I could, fidgeting the entire time. I didn't know what medications she took beyond birth control pills. I didn't know her primary doctor. In fact, I didn't know a whole lot and that lit a guilty fire in my belly. I *should* know. A good friend *would* know. Would make it a point to know in case of an emergency.

I drew in a breath and let it out slowly. She was going to be fine. What medical science couldn't fix, magic could. I didn't know how to heal, but my Uncle Mason or my friend Ben who was also a medical student no doubt could. Damon certainly could, but I didn't know when he'd be back in town. It had been a few weeks since he left to help handle a family emergency, and so far he hadn't mentioned coming back. In fact every conversation had grown shorter and more cursory with every passing day.

A fine needle of hurt slid through my heart. Inwardly, I berated myself. Damon couldn't help it if he was busy. He'd already upended his life to be with me here. Besides, he'd said he'd rather work the long hours so he could come back as soon as possible. All the same, I couldn't help missing him, and that was unfamiliar territory, which only unsettled me more. He was my first boyfriend, my first crush, my first adult romance. I had no idea how to navigate our relationship, or how I really felt. Or wanted to feel.

All of which had absolutely nothing to do with Stacey and showed just how much of a selfish asshole I could be, focusing on my own stupid shit while she'd had serious trauma.

After asking all his questions, Dave pointed me in the direction of the waiting room where Jen and Lorraine had already set up camp. Upon seeing me, they jumped up and peppered me with questions, even as Jen thrust a large iced coffee into my hand.

"There's no news," I told them after reporting everything that had happened. They are evaluating her and after that, probably surgery." And by probably, I meant there was no possible way on the planet that she'd escape without it. If she did, it would be a miracle.

"Sit down," Lorraine said, pulling me down into a textured plastic chair beside her. "Tell us what happened."

Jen pulled a chair around to face me.

"Better drink some of that before you get started," she said, gesturing at the iced coffee. "You look like whoever ran you over backed up a couple times."

"Thanks," I said and took a sip, closing my eyes as the cold, bittersweet liquid slid down my throat.

"Don't get me wrong," Jen continued. "You look tons better than when your Auntie Mommy would have a go at you."

"But you still look like crap," Lorraine said. "Are you hungry? I can go get you something."

I shook my head. "I'm not sure I could keep anything down."

Neither commented on the fact that I wasn't having any problem with the coffee. In fact, if I'd had trouble drinking it, they'd have had me hospitalized. If I ever said anything like 'I don't like coffee' or 'No thanks, I don't want coffee,' that would have been taken as a red flag that I'd been kidnapped, an alien had taken over my body, or I was dead.

"What happened?" Jen asked.

I explained getting the call from Stacey and going to find her.

"Good thing you put that spell on our phones," Lorraine said, her expression pinching like it did when she tried to mask her emotions. Of all of us, she was the softest-hearted.

"I need to add a tracking spell," I said. "And make it possible for the phones to call anybody and not just me."

"So, start your own magical cell phone service? No batteries or actual cell towers needed?" Jen teased. "You could make a mint."

I could tell she was trying to keep things light. All four of us dealt with loneliness, fear, and pain in the same way, which was to joke until the bad feelings passed or we couldn't ignore them anymore. It appeared I dealt with my romantic feelings the same way, but I'd have to figure that out later. When I couldn't ignore them anymore.

At least I'm consistent, if emotionally stunted.

"With Aunty Mommy dead, I have more money than King Midas, and anyhow, if I'm going to use magic for retail, I'd want to do something actually worth doing, like making ice cream that doesn't need a freezer to stay frozen, or making some kind of instant mocha latte cup that fills on command."

Lorraine nodded. "Or tampons that self-clean, never leak, and also provide orgasms on demand."

Jen cackled. "I was going to suggest pockets big enough to hold a cow but appear to be normal-sized, but orgasms sound like an excellent idea. Clean, non-leaky tampons? That's a winner."

Lorraine shook her head. "More women would go for the pockets-of-holding. Wouldn't have to carry a purse, and if you made it so it didn't weigh anything, they could carry a buttload of stuff."

"They could travel without any luggage!" Jen clapped her hands. "And always have snacks on hand."

"Maybe a bicycle, too?" Lorraine suggested.

"Okay, enough," I said. "If I ever go into retail, pockets of holding will be my first product, but since hell hasn't frozen over, how about we get back to freaking out about Stacey?"

"Or we could freak you out by reminding you that her family is on the way—her very large, rambunctious, and insane family—and you will be their center of attention until they can get their hands on Stacey. Maybe you should drink some more caffeine."

Jen nudged my cup, her grin pure evil.

I blanched. Stacey's family was enough to populate a small city and incredibly diverse in their... quirks. "Oh, fuck me. I need to hide. Quick, stab me so I can get admitted."

Both Lorraine and Jen smirked and shook their heads.

"Not going to jail just so you can avoid getting interrogated by Stacey's family," Lorraine said. "I have animals to care for. Besides, if you were in the hospital and we were in jail, Ajax would be very sad."

Fine. If they weren't good enough friends to maim me, then the better part of valor was to run away. "I've got to find a bathroom," I said and jumped to my feet. I was half-running when Lorraine called out behind me.

"There's one just around the corner."

The sound of Jen making chicken noises nearly drowned her out.

"It's out of toilet paper," I said over my shoulder, lifting my hand to flip the bird in their general direction. "Or being cleaned, or out of soap, or there are snakes in the toilets. Can't use it. Got to find a different one." Maybe in Mongolia.

I fled out through the doors leading into the rest of the hospital and made a beeline down the hallway.

Because Woods Community Hospital serves as a trauma center and hub for a lot of specialists, its campus sprawls across more than a dozen acres and included at least that many buildings. I was in the main and largest of those, which meant I had a decent chance of getting lost. The place had accreted many additions over the years, so the layout was generally nonsensical and convoluted. You had to a have a map, a compass, and a guide-dog to nego-tiate it.

Perfect.

I jumped into an elevator and pressed a random button—twelfth floor. Another half dozen people shoved inside, each pushing buttons for their various destinations. For once I wasn't impatient with stopping at nearly every floor as people got on and off and sometimes the door opened to a vacant landing. If I'd thought of it, I'd have done the kid thing and pressed all the buttons.

A gray-haired man with sagging jowls and spidery red veins across his cheeks and wearing green scrubs had punched the fifteenth floor and I decided to ride up with him, the better to waste time.

The elevator door opened and he stepped out and turned left, tossing me a curious look over his shoulder. I got off, wrinkling my nose at the peculiar hospital smell of disinfectant, some kind of fruit scent, and coffee.

I glanced up at the signs directing me to different offices on the floor. I rolled my eyes at myself. What did I care where I was? I just needed to avoid the Emergency Department.

For the next hour I explored various floors and whenever someone stopped me, I claimed to be looking for the cafeteria, or a coffee stand, or a particular department. I'd follow their directions and then keep going. It was just bad luck when I stopped for an iced mocha with four shots of espresso that I ran into Ballard and Jeffers, the two cops who'd investigated my mother's murder.

"If it isn't Beck Wyatt. What did you do to yourself this time?"

I didn't see them coming, so Jeffers's question made me jump. I turned to glare at him.

"What do you mean what's wrong with me? There's nothing wrong with me. And don't sneak up on people."

Ballard's brows rose and the corner of her mouth lifted in a smirk, though whether it was aimed at me or her partner, I don't know.

The two of them wore their usual suits, though as always, Ballard looked refined and elegant, while Jeffers looked like he'd slept in his clothes. Or more likely, had spent the night with someone and was wearing the same clothes as yesterday. Ballard had a lean athletic build with smooth dark skin, high cheekbones, and a no-nonsense set to her chin. Jeffers was taller than Ballard, lean-waisted, with wide shoulders and a broad chest. He was good looking, if you liked a cleft chin and a crooked nose, and he'd nailed the bad-boy attitude. Or maybe he was just an asshole. Or, more likely, both.

"Usually your hospital trips include a lot of blood loss and stitches," Jeffers pointed out. He cocked his head, his gaze running over me. "Though you don't look too beat up. Maybe it's internal injuries?"

"Because I left my hospital bed while my liver was hemorrhaging and my brain was liquifying to come get a coffee." I rolled my eyes. "Maybe you should go back to detective school."

"In fact, you *would* leave your hospital bed and crawl on your stomach if it meant a coffee," he pointed out, not bothering to acknowledge my dig. Clearly he'd come to know me well.

"But would I change out of my fancy backless hospital gown?" I took my coffee, smiling at the barista. "Could I have three marionberry scones, too, please? Oh, and a bottle of orange juice and a chai latte, extra syrup, extra hot." Jen and Lorraine would need sugar and caffeine reinforcement, too. "Add whatever these two want." I gestured at Ballard and Jeffers.

"Thanks," Ballard said, speaking for the first time, then turned to Jeffers. "Don't even think about accusing her of bribing us." She smiled at the barista. "I'll take one of those scones and an extra-large black coffee, please. What does bring you here, Beck?"

"Stacey was in a bike accident."

"Sorry to hear it. She okay?

"Broke her leg and maybe her ribs."

Up until this point, I'd manage to avoid thinking about Stacey. I'd firmly told myself there was nothing I could do and it would be awhile until the doctors said anything. If they did say anything, Jen and Lorraine would text me. The magic spell I'd put on their phones didn't rely on a cell signal. I could be fifty thousand feet deep in the ocean and they could reach me.

"Sounds painful," Jeffers said, taking his order from the barista.

I ran my card through the credit machine, then tucked the orange juice bottle under my arm, gathered up the bag of scones, and picked up the cardboard drink holder bearing the chai and coffee. "It was pretty bad. They had to Lifeflight her in."

"She must've really done a number on herself," Ballard said. "Send her my best wishes."

"I will." I checked the time. "I guess I'd better get back. I'm sure her family has arrived."

I sounded as gloomy as I felt. Much as I liked Stacey's family, it was like being trapped in a funhouse with every Jack Nicholson and Jim Carrey character either had ever played, a circus full of clowns, the Animaniacs, and a convention of rabid raccoons, all starring in their own family soap opera. The drama and theatrics was hugely entertaining but equally exhausting.

That I'd abandoned Jen and Lorraine to that clusterfuck made me a ridiculously bad friend, but then again, they'd warned me so that I'd have a chance to collect myself. I'd needed a chance to emotionally armor up, not to mention stuff down my residual panic from the entire rescue scenario.

"Actually...." Ballard trailed off, uncharacteristically uncertain. She glanced at Jeffers, her brows arching in a silent question.

He grimaced and gave a little shake of his head, and then rolled his eyes and shrugged before taking a breath and looking at me.

"We were planning to track you down later."

"And here I thought I'd hid all my murder victims so well," I deadpanned.

"You do realize you cause yourself most of your own trouble, right?" Jeffers asked.

"It's a talent."

"You got a minute to sit?" Ballard said, gesturing toward the collection of bistro tables in the nook beside the coffee kiosk.

Color me flabbergasted. "Sit? With you?"

Jeffers made a scornful sound. "This is idiotic. Let's just go."

"And do what?" Ballard asked, ever the calm one of the two. "We're out of leads and time isn't doing us any favors."

"So, we shouldn't waste any on Crowe's bullshit."

"You know Detective Crowe, correct?" Ballard asked me.

"Officer Mikey? He's been trying to get into Stacey's pants since forever and he has a stick up his ass sideways. What about him?"

"He's a detective, not an officer," Ballard said, looking at me curiously. "How do you know him?"

"Like I said, he's got a thing for Stacey," I said, deliberately keeping the explanation vague.

In all actuality, he'd got sucked into parts of my life he had no business knowing about. Specifically, the magic parts. Stacey had asked for all our help when the estranged husband of a coworker had stolen the poor woman's cats and threatened to kill them if she didn't come back and put up with his abuse. This after months of harassing her and driving her out of jobs. In the middle of Project Help Lydia, we'd gotten sidetracked into rescuing some new friends of mine from a psycho-bitch ghost.

Mikey had witnessed all of it and had been the one who

arrested Lydia's ex after the bastard attacked her. When we had begun our misadventures, he'd despised me, Jen, and Lorraine for corrupting poor Stacey. He thought she was as pure as water from God's ass and he thought we'd been convincing her to do illegal and immoral things. If only he knew. Nine times out of ten, Stacey was our ringleader. He wanted—and probably still did—for her to be the sort of sweater and pearl-wearing girl that she'd probably vomit all over given the chance. In particular, he wanted someone more staid and interested in marriage and motherhood. Stacey was neither of those things.

By the end of our adventures together, Mikey and I had arrived at a detente. He'd backed off insulting Jen, Lorraine, and me at every turn, and I'd decided to have a wary respect for him, while otherwise ignoring his existence unless and until I was forced to acknowledge it.

Apparently, I was being forced to.

"What do you want to talk to me about? I'd really like for these drinks not to get cold." I nudged my chin toward the cup holder and bag of scones in my hands. "Plus, I want to see if there's been word on Stacey."

"Have a seat," Ballard said, gesturing toward a table.

I shook my head. "I need to get back."

"Fine. We'll walk with you," she said, falling in beside me.

She was an annoyingly good cop and didn't have an ounce of give-up in her. Normally I admired that. Today it was a pain in the ass. "Whatever blows your dress up."

"We caught a case a couple weeks ago," she said as Jeffers fell in on my other side. "We think it's a murder-kidnapping."

"You think? You don't know?"

"It's a weird scene."

"It's a weird case," Jeffers corrected.

"It is." Ballard nodded. "The whole department has been working on it. Anyhow, we've run out of leads and the clock is ticking on the kidnapped victims."

"What's so weird about it? And what does it have to do with me?"

Jeffers winced, his next words grudging. "We were tossing ideas around this morning and Crowe pipes up with a suggestion that we talk to you. Said you might have some insight. Wouldn't say anything else."

"Why didn't he talk to me himself?"

"We're the leads on the case."

As if that explained everything. Not that I cared all that much.

"What kind of insight does he think I can give?"

Duh. Magical, of course. The scene was weird, so that must mean magic was involved. Couldn't just be some strange set of ordinary circumstances. I gritted my teeth. This felt like a set-up. What was Officer Scrotum's game?

"He wouldn't say," Ballard responded. "He did say we should tell you that he's not screwing with you." Her brows rose in a question.

"He thinks Jen, Lorraine, and I are the reason why Stacey won't go out with him. That she's some princess and we're the evil trolls trying to turn her into one of us. And yet he still made detective. Amazing, given he obviously has shitty detection skills. Anyway, he would like the three of us to drop out of Stacey's life so he can have her to himself."

"On what planet does he think that will happen?" Jeffers asked, looking gratifyingly confused. "You girls are practically hooked together at the hip."

"Exactly," I said. "Clearly he's a moron."

"Men are stupid creatures," Ballard said.

"Hey!" Jeffers protested. "Don't lump me in with him."

"If the shoe fits," I said.

He glowered and started to say something, but Ballard cut him off.

"Got any idea why he'd tell us to find you?"

"Because he's a dick?"

"He's a professional dick, though," Ballard said. "He might mess with *you*, but not with us. He seemed sure you'd have something to contribute to the case."

"Maybe he's got a fucked-up sense of humor. Scratch that. Clearly he has a fucked-up sense of humor."

"I don't know," Ballard said. "I find him rather lacking in that department."

"That's fair," I admitted grudgingly. "Whenever laughs, he takes a chance that the stick he's got jammed up inside him will perforate his colon. So, he wasn't joking. Maybe he was having a seizure. Or has that STD that melts your brain. What's it called?"

"Syphilis," Ballard offered.

"Yeah, that one."

"He doesn't strike me as the type, and anyhow, syphilis hasn't been a thing since penicillin."

"Okay, then maybe he's just an idiot."

Ballard pretended to consider. "Except he's not."

No, he wasn't. Asshole. I sighed. "Why don't you ask him?"

"We're asking you," Jeffers said. "And since you're dodging the question like a pro, my guess is he's right."

He'd gone into detective mode, and I had his full attention. I wasn't done dodging, however.

"So you tracked me down here to the hospital? Just because Officer Scrotum said I might have insight?"

"*Detective* Scrotum," Ballard corrected without cracking

a smile. "And we were already here. Meeting you was just lucky."

Yeah, bad lucky.

"Shoulda expected it, though," Jeffers said. "Hospital seems to be your natural habitat."

I didn't have a good comeback for that one.

We'd just about reached the Emergency Department. I stopped to look at them both. "Whatever you want from me will have to wait until Stacey comes out of surgery and I know she's okay."

Ballard frowned. "That could take hours."

"Probably."

"We don't have time for that," he said.

"Too bad. I'm busy"

"We got three missing people. One of them is only ten," Jeffers said. "Make time."

My mouth pinched together as I wrestled with what I should do. Stacey, Jen, and Lorraine would all tell me to pull my head out of my ass and go help the cops, as all I'd be doing here is waiting for news. Lives were on the line. Still, leaving felt like abandoning Stacey.

I didn't really have a choice.

I blew out irritated breath. "Fine. What exactly do you want from me?"

CHAPTER FOUR

I agreed to go with them on the condition that I found out any news on Stacey first, and that we stopped and picked up Ajax. It pretty much went without saying that they'd have to provide coffee, but just in case, I told them so.

First, they had to survive Stacey's family.

When I went through the doors into the Emergency Department lobby, I stepped into chaos. The place was packed and most everybody gabbled loudly. A few people who weren't Stacey's family sat wide-eyed in chairs, watching the chaos, afraid it could spill over onto them. The staff was starting to circle like riot police.

Jen and Lorraine stood in a corner, trapped by the frothing mob. I could tell they were being peppered with questions, but nobody listened for answers. Another knot surrounded someone in scrubs who looked like a panicked rabbit about to be run down by a herd of stampeding yaks.

I kept to the outermost fringes as I eased my way toward Jen and Lorraine. I didn't get very far before someone noticed me. My name bounced through the crowd and suddenly they turned and surged at me. I resisted the urge to put some kind of magical wall around myself.

Jeffers swore softly and stepped a little closer, though whether it was to protect me or use me for a shield, I couldn't tell. My bet was on the shield, though.

They surrounded us. I scanned faces. I recognized most of them—I'd been to enough of Stacey's sprawling family barbecues and holiday celebrations to actually get acquainted with many of them.

Most of these people were not related by blood. Some were stepsiblings, stepaunts or -uncles, stepcousins, step-parents, half-siblings, or foster brothers and sisters, and who knew what else. The family was like a big sponge: it absorbed anybody in its path and it took a lot of effort to escape. Most people never made it out.

Both of Stacey's parents had been married multiple times. Her mom was on her fourth husband and her father had recently finalized his fifth divorce. The freakish thing was they not only still got along well with each other and were good friends, but the same applied to all their other former spouses.

Jen, Lorraine, and I were like distant cousins, since the four of us had tended to go off on our own. Not that Martin and Louise hadn't tried to pull us into their maelstrom at every possible opportunity. I'd always envied Stacey for having such loving parents and tight-knit—if sprawling—family.

I stood patiently as they crowded around. Within seconds they'd shoved between me and my two escorts. I was surrounded by frantic faces, all peppering me with questions. I waited, wondering if they'd quiet down enough for me to answer anything.

A loud whistle pierced the noise. I looked for its source,

finding Jen. She stood on something I couldn't see and swept a glare over the collected family.

"If you don't shut up, you can't hear the answers to your questions," she declared, hands on her hips. "At the rate you're going, the hospital is going to have you all arrested for causing a riot. Now back the fuck off and give Beck some breathing room."

"You heard the lady," came a deep voice from near the front doors.

Luke Galloway, one of Stacey's stepbrothers. For once I was glad to see him. Or hear him.

A stirring in the crowd and he pushed through to stand in front of me, followed by Officer Mikey, aka Detective Scrotum. Talk about signs of the apocalypse. I'd never have thought I'd see the two together actually looking reasonably friendly.

Both wanted into Stacey's pants, and thus far, neither had had a snowball's chance in hell. Well, not entirely true. She'd have screwed Mikey's brains out if he wasn't so hung up on the whole make-a- future-together thing. Stacey had zero faith in happily-ever-afters and wasn't going to set herself up to fail. Given the success rate of her parents' marriages, I couldn't blame her.

Luke, on the other hand, was all about being a slut and didn't mind sharing the tales of his conquests. Mistake on his part. When his dad and Louise got married, Stacey was eighteen and he was twenty-two. They'd never thought of each other as siblings, so dating wasn't cringe-inducing as far as the whole incest thing goes, but Stacey had no intention of starring in one of his sexcapade stories. The idiot had shot himself in his foot. He might have had a chance if he didn't insist on telling the world all his slut-stories.

I lifted my brows, glancing at Mikey and then Luke.

Both were magnificent specimens of male beauty. Mikey was a hair taller than Luke with short brown hair and a square jaw. He carried himself with a military bearing and had a preference for cowboy boots, Wranglers, and western shirts.

Luke had dark hair with gray eyes and had an ease about him like nothing could upset him. He had clothing made especially for him, but didn't flaunt his wealth, which he made doing secret tech stuff for the government. Apparently, he was good at it because the man was rich. He was also down-to-earth and generally unimpressed with his money.

Just at the moment, both men looked tense, Mikey radiating hot fury, while Luke's was about as cold as one of Neptune's moons.

"What happened?" Mikey demanded, glaring at me like I was responsible for Stacey's injuries.

My hackles rose. So we were back to that bullshit, were we? I gave him a death stare before focusing back on Luke. Louise now stood beside him, and Martin was next to her. The two clutched each other's hands as they stared at me, clearly starved for information.

Stacey had got her ringlets and curves from her mother. Her father gave her her blond hair. Both were kind, generous, and loving people, which Stacey also was, but then she'd open her mouth and say something outrageous and snarky, and they'd look at her like she was a space alien. She, Jen, Lorraine, and I fit together like LEGO pieces. Or as Stacey would no doubt say, dicks and vaginas.

I handed off the drinks and scones to Jeffers, who passed them to Lorraine. She and Jen had wriggled through the crowd and stood between the two detectives. I stepped closer to Louise and Martin, tensing when they both reached for my hands and clasped them tightly.

"She's fine," I told them firmly. "She was up on the bluffs and ended up in a ravine with her bike. I was able to find her and call for rescue. They flew her here and are taking care of her now. She had a broken leg and maybe a broken rib or two, plus some scratches and bruises. She was conscious and coherent when I found her."

I spoke succinctly because details weren't going to help, and I spun the news as positively as I could.

"Why'd she call you and not 911 for help?" her cousin Celia asked. She was in her early twenties. Her eyes were red and her nose sounded stuffy. She'd clearly been crying.

"*I* was the help," I said, keeping my voice even. It's not like Celia was wrong. If I wasn't a witch, then calling me would be utterly stupid. I could hardly explain that, or that Stacey's phone could only call me because I'd spelled it to work even if it was dead or broken.

"But—"

"Does it matter?" Luke said before she could argue the wisdom of calling me rather than 911. "Beck found her. The doctors are taking care of her. I, for one, am beyond grateful to Beck."

Without warning, he grabbed me away from his parents and pulled me into tight hug. He pressed his lips near my ear.

"Thank God you're a witch," he murmured. "I owe you more than I can say."

I gave a minute shake of my head. "Nobody owes me anything."

He loosened his grip and stared down at me, expression more serious than any I'd ever seen on him. "My future was looking fucking bleak without her in it. You probably saved my life. So if there's ever anything you need, anything I can do no matter how big or small, you've got it. No questions asked and I don't care how illegal it is."

He held me there until I nodded.

"Good."

After that, it became a hug-Beck-fest. I got passed around like a rag doll. There was no dodging the kisses and fervent thank-you's and promises of all sorts of rewards, from food and drink to car-repairs and countless other services and goods. Whatever businesses they ran, I would always be welcome and my money would never be good.

The noise level rose again as everybody started talking. Or wailing, as a few relatives had begun doing. Dramatic much?

By the time the last family member mauled me—one of Stacey's stepaunts who was probably in her forties and wore heavy raspberry-colored lipstick and a thick layer of too-sweet perfume—I was covered in a rainbow palette of lipstick and glosses, spit, and who knows what else. All I knew for sure was that I desperately needed a shower and maybe a bleach bath. Definitely a bleach bath.

The only person I hadn't yet been subjected to was Detective Scrotum. He'd joined Jeffers and Ballard as they waited for everyone to finish manhandling me. Jen and Lorraine talked with Luke and some of Stacey's cousins, while Martin and Louise and most of their former spouses as well as Louise's current spouse tried to pry information out of the hospital staff.

Ten or eleven security guards came striding in, no doubt summoned to handle the riot in the Emergency Department waiting room. I hated to tell them, but this was as subdued as they got. I doubted it would be long before they decided the family needed protecting and switched sides.

The family had a habit of doing that sort of thing. If I didn't know better, I'd say it was magic.

I wasn't going to get to see how it played out, however. .

"Is your tetanus shot up to date?" Lorraine asked with a repulsed look.

Jen just shuddered and handed me a half dozen restaurant wet wipe pouches from her purse.

I started tearing them open, paying no attention to Ballard and Jeffers who'd come to join us, with Mikey tagging along. He no longer had that accusing look, but that didn't mean I'd forgiven him for having it in the first place.

"You about ready to go?" Jeffers asked after watching me clean up.

I'd used every wipe and still felt like I'd been drooled on by a giant St. Bernard before getting rolled across a public bathroom floor.

"Go where?" Jen demanded.

"A crime scene," I said, giving Mikey a blistering look. "Apparently some idiot asshole told these two brilliant detectives that I could give some insight into the crime."

Detective Scrotum didn't even have the grace to look apologetic. "That's right." His brows arched as if daring me to explain why.

I rose to the occasion. "He thinks I'm a witch and I have magical powers." I wiggled my fingers like I was casting some kind of cartoon spell and made whoo-whooing noise. "Isn't that right, Officer Mikey?"

The corner of his mouth twitched. "That's right," he said laconically. "She's absolutely a witch."

Of course the way he said *witch* he really meant *bitch*. No mistaking it. I'd have kicked him in the balls, but the look in his eyes said he was teasing. Mostly. He was having fun trying to make me squirm. Challenge accepted.

"Can we stop off and pick up my pointy hat and broom? Oh, and the sparkling red shoes."

"No wand?" Jeffers asked.

I rolled my eyes. "Oh, please. Wands are so yesterday."

He smirked. "I stand corrected."

"Do you want one of us to come with you?" Lorraine asked, frowning.

Since she and the girls knew that Mikey wasn't joking about the witch thing, he actually thought magic was involved in the crime, and so she worried for me. My last experience with a magical criminal almost got me murdered.

All the same, I couldn't help feeling responsible. If magic had been used, then Ballard and Jeffers were way out of their league. I was too—I'm not a closet Nancy Drew or anything—but at least I know a bit about magic. And as far as I knew, the only witches around here were either friends, family, or enemies, and if one of them had done it, that made me all the more responsible.

"Stay here with Jen. I'll get back as soon as I can."

She gave a reluctant nod. "Just be careful."

"And you three make sure nothing happens to her," Jen added with a scathing look at all three cops.

"I wasn't invited," Mikey said.

"You are now," Jen said. "Unless you want me to tell Stacey you got Beck sucked into an investigation and didn't bother to have her back."

He scowled. "That's blackmail."

"It's non-negotiable," she shot back hotly, and I realized that this was about more than this crime. Jen was worried about Lindsey's psychic prediction that trouble was coming for me.

My stomach knotted and I took a deep breath to relax it. It was entirely possible that Stacey's accident had been the trouble Lindsey had been talking about. Possible, but not probable. That had happened to Stacey, and if the looming evil was about that, why hadn't Lindsey warned her instead of me? Nor did the fear and desperation—not to mention nearly dying—that Lindsey had exhibited while trying to get the prediction to me seem justified by a mere awful bike accident.

It didn't pass the smell test.

I hadn't actually let myself think a whole lot about the creep-show prediction. How could I even prepare for it? Never leave the house? I'd probably end up getting sucked halfway down the toilet drain somehow, or trapped in the clothes dryer, or something equally humiliating and impossible. Well, impossible if magic wasn't involved, but it was clearly going to be, since along with the prediction, Lindsey had provided a bonus by way of a massive indecipherable spell.

She'd been in a fugue sort of state and had written the whole thing out on an enormous canvas, aka the bare walls in Luke's indoor basketball court. It had all been meaningless to me, but I'd filmed it and sent it to Damon, who'd received a blank recording: nothing but white walls. When I went to look at the video on my phone, all traces of the spell writing had vanished from the video and all the still pictures. It also faded off Luke's wall.

Of course, every squiggle, loop, and line of it was etched in my memory. I could close my eyes and literally see the whole thing in my mind's eye. I'd tried drawing part of it out for my Uncle Mason, but it always faded to nothing about as fast as I drew it out. The whole thing was a lesson in frustration and aggravation. Thus, the only way to properly deal with it was to shove it out of my head and pretend it didn't exist. That only worked if nobody else pulled it out of the trash and held it up like a trophy.

But this sort of thing is what Jen lived for. She didn't let anybody shove shit under the rug. At least not for long. She was one of those annoying people who liked to face reality head on and made sure that everybody around her did the same. Well, at least most of the time. She, Lorraine, and Stacey hadn't forced the issue with me when I was dealing with Aunty Mommy and her persecution of me. They'd recognized I couldn't or wouldn't talk about it and hadn't pushed. Of course, once she died, all bets were off.

The upshot was that Jen didn't like me going anywhere near danger without someone with me. Never mind that the danger would undoubtedly be of a supernatural bent and three non-magical cops were about as likely to have a chance living through a nasty encounter as I would have surviving a throw-down with Godzilla.

Nevertheless, Jen wasn't about to let Mikey refuse, especially since he was responsible for getting me dragged off to a murder scene.

"The sooner we go, the sooner you get back," Ballard said.

"Has there been any updates on Stacey?" I asked Lorraine and Jen.

They shook their heads. "Reception just said it would be a while and a nurse would update us when they had any news," Lorraine said.

Of all of us, she was the most calm and relaxed. That came from being a veterinarian and knowing how much had to be done to prepare for surgery, plus actually performing it. While we worried about what was happening, she knew better than to get her panties in a wad every time someone wearing scrubs or a white coat appeared with a clipboard. We wouldn't be getting any kind of an update for possibly hours.

Which meant I'd lucked out running into Ballard and Jeffers, because I wouldn't have to stay here and do nothing but stew. That and chat with Stacey's family, which sounded like a fate almost worse than death. I like them, but they were exhausting even when I was in a good mood and not stressed from having one of my best friends—a sister, really—in surgery.

"Let's get this over with," I told Ballard.

IT WAS QUICKLY DECIDED—WITHOUT ANY INPUT FROM ME—THAT Ballard and Jeffers would drive and Mikey and I would sit in the back. Mikey looked like he'd eaten slugs, and I smirked the entire time.

They took me home and I took a quick shower before changing into jeans and a tee shirt. Meanwhile, Dierdre, the housekeeper, served snacks to the three detectives. Her definition of snacks was a buffet of cold pastas, cheeses, fresh bread, fruits, and vegetables, as well as hot dill potato chips.

Aunty Mommy had kept a full staff including four chefs who worked on rotation so that one was available and preparing food twenty-four hours a day, seven days a week. They kept a bounty prepared and I insisted that the staff eat it or take it home or else donate it to the local shelter, since there was no way I could possibly put a dent in what they cooked, even if I had a sudden dinner party for twelve.

After the three stuffed their faces, we loaded up. I invited Ajax along and the look on Mikey's face was priceless when he realized there would now be three of us in the back, one of whom was a giant wolf dog with a lot of hair.

I'd adopted Ajax after helping Lorraine rescue him from a horrifying situation. He'd been terribly neglected and abused, and yet had protected two little girls from their abusive father.

I had a way with animals. Lorraine called me an animal whisperer, because I could calm most any animal and usually get them to do what I wanted. I figured it had to be magic, and I was more than happy to help her with scared or violent patients. Most of the time they'd been mistreated and if I could reassure them and show them a little kindness and love, it made me feel like I was on the moon.

Ajax had physically recovered from his ordeal thanks to Lorraine and some healing magic and had regained his thick fur coat and fluffy tail. He weighed a little over a hundred fifty pounds and was still gaining. Given his size, Lorraine predicted he'd eventually top out somewhere between one eighty and two hundred pounds. Another indication he wasn't actually dog but a full wolf.

I'd finally had to admit he might be when the girls threatened a DNA test. I didn't actually care, but Ajax acted like *such* a dog. He snuggled, followed me everywhere, slept with me, loved tummy skritches, and he practically danced a jig whenever I brought out the brush. Lately he'd learned to get it himself and bring it to me. Still, I supposed he had the right coloring, not to mention a habit of dropping his head low and looking at people from underneath, which was totally wolfy.

Ajax leaped into the back seat, pausing a moment to look at the detectives, then promptly sat in the middle of the back seat next to Mikey. I got in and fastened my seatbelt, and Ajax flopped down on my lap, his body flowing across the seat and up onto Detective Scrotum who glared at the oblivious dog.

"A crime scene is no place for a dog," he said.

"And yet he's coming with us," I said. "Of course, if you hadn't thrown me under the bus, Ajax and I wouldn't even be here."

Jeffers glanced over his shoulder from the passenger seat. "Thrown you under the bus?"

"That's what I said."

"But what did you mean?" Ballard asked, pulling out onto the street.

"I mean that Detective Scrotum here is awful free about throwing around my secrets. Makes me wonder if I should do something about it."

I cast him a sidelong glance, catching his flinch. I grinned at him so that he'd know I'd seen and that he'd taken my words exactly how I meant them. If he ended up with an incurable case of crabs or warts or a house full of cockroaches, he'd know why and how.

Low and out of sight of the front seat, I flicked a few sparks up off my fingers. Parlor tricks, but the tightening of Mikey's lips made me feel a little better. Sometimes I'm petty that way.

He turned away and I heard him mutter. "At least she got the detective part right, this time."

I snickered. Sometimes Mikey was all right. Too bad it was like a quickly-cured case of diarrhea. Before you knew it, he was cured and back to being an asshat.

CHAPTER FIVE

Ballard and Jeffers didn't say anything about the case as we drove, and Mikey might as well have been a mummy. I spent the time petting Ajax, who spread himself full length across my lap, the seat, and across Mikey's lap, depositing hair all over Detective Stick-Up-His-Ass's pristine charcoal slacks.

We ended up in Blue Oaks, an older neighborhood containing an eclectic mix of housing styles, from Victorian to Craftsman and everything in between. Once upon a time this had been a very wealthy neighborhood that had aged into stately gentility. Many of the homes had been restored with white picket fences and colorful flowers. Wide greenways with huge trees, many of them the blue oaks that gave the neighborhood its name, ran alongside all the streets. The trees formed graceful arches over the roads. The whole vibe smacked of an old thirties or forties movie. I found it delightful.

Ballard parked in front of a brick Queen Anne complete with a turret on one corner and a wide porch that skirted the front of the house and curved elegantly around the turret. The upstairs windows had forest green awnings over each of them. The trim was painted the same color of green with cream-colored accents. A wide set of brick steps led invitingly up to the green front door. The top of it was rounded, making me think of hobbits.

"So why am I here again?" I asked, standing in front of the steps and looking up at the house. My fingers tangled in Ajax's ruff.

"I have no idea," Jeffers said. "Care to enlighten us, Crowe?"

"Tell her about the case," Mikey said, not bothering to look at me.

The two other detectives exchanged a questioning look, like they hadn't already made this decision back in the hospital. I rolled my eyes.

"I can wait in the car."

Finally, Jeffers shrugged in capitulation. "We don't have any leads."

Ballard blew out a breath and nodded. "All right, then. This is the home of the Chapman family. Matthew and Arthur Chapman are married and have two children: Melissa and Toby, both ten. Twins. Two weeks ago, a worried neighbor called for a well-check. Seems one of their cars was missing, the other hadn't moved in more than a week, and she hadn't seen any signs of the family. They have a pool and generally spend every afternoon and evening swimming. Nobody answered the phones when the neighbors called.

"A group of neighbors had gone over to check on them and found the doors locked from the inside and all the shades drawn, both of which were unusual. One of them had a spare key, but it didn't work."

"But it worked later," Mikey said with a meaningful glance at me.

I rolled my eyes. If he brought me there because of that, it was one of the dumbest things I'd ever heard. There were a ton of a reasons a key might not work once and then work later.

Jeffers and Ballard watched our exchange with hawk eyes; I could practically hear the gears in their brains spinning. They had questions and were getting impatient for answers.

"What happened then?" I asked, starting to feel like a bug under a microscope.

"Like I said, when they couldn't get in, they called the cops for a well-check. Nobody answered the door. The key still didn't work. The officers who answered the call radioed our department and we were asked to contact the Chapmans' employers who said the two men had not been heard from for almost a week, which was unusual. Repeated calls to them went unanswered. At that point the decision was made to break in. We found several unlocked windows, but none would open, so we tried the key one last time. At first it didn't give at all, then suddenly, the bolt slid back smooth as butter.

"Between the cops and the neighbors, they must've tried the lock a dozen times. Didn't even get a wiggle," Mikey clarified. "Everyone was shocked."

"And yet these brilliant people are allowed to drive cars." I shook my head but could not so easily shake off the creeping unease I felt. I wasn't ready to say magic was involved, but I was beginning to get the awful feeling that Mikey was actually right, *and* I might have to tell him so. He'd be insufferable.

So, really, no changes whatsoever. Maybe I should have

left him with Stacey so I didn't have to hear the 'I told you so.'

Ignoring my comment, Jeffers continued. Ballard just watched me, not saying a word.

"Once inside, we didn't encounter any smells of body decay. We made a search of the first floor and that's when it got weird." Jeffers exchanged an unreadable look with Ballard who gave a nearly imperceptible shrug.

"Weird, how?"

"We found an adult male body lying on the floor just outside the kitchen. We'd still not smelled any decay and the body looked fresh."

He chewed his lower lip.

"And?" I prompted.

"Went to check his pulse and the creepiest damned thing—" A shake of his head and a grimace at Ballard.

"As soon as we touched the body, something bizarre happened," Ballard said matter-of-factly. "Straight out of a bad horror movie. We got a blast of warm air and we were swamped in the stench of decay. The body just sort of... melted? I don't know how to describe it. The skin turned mottled green and foam bubbled out the nose and mouth and it started swelling up like putting air in a balloon. It's like it went from a minutes-old corpse to one that had been dead for more than a week."

"Sounds unbelievable," I said and didn't look at Mikey. I could feel him smirking his triumph at me.

Asshat.

"Yeah, we got a lot of shit tossed our way at the precinct," Jeffers said sourly. "All kinds of jokes about ghosts and zombies. After we found the body, we did a check of the house. The rest of the family had pretty much evaporated. Nothing missing that we could tell, and no signs of foul play. Except that the cell phones were still here, along with toothbrushes, tablets, keys…"

"Everything you'd expect someone leaving on their own to take," Ballard said. "Autopsy didn't give us much. Said it looked like Arthur Chapman, our DB, spontaneously stopped breathing. No toxins, no signs of an attack of any kind, nothing. Course the decomposition meant they could have missed some things."

I noticed he didn't try to explain the sudden and rapid decomposition right in front of their eyes.

"When did they say he died?"

It took Jeffers a long moment to answer. "Around two weeks, given the state of decay."

I nodded. Yep. This was definitely looking worse. "Anything else?"

"One thing." Ballard took out her phone and skimmed through her pictures, pulling up one. "This was on the outside of the back door, right under the handle. Crime scene techs found it. Looks like there'd been one on the front door, too, but it was too smudged to tell. Found them on all the downstairs windows."

"On the *inside*," Jeffers added.

The picture confirmed my suspicions and Mikey's assessment. It was spell-writing, no doubt keeping the door locked. Smudging it had destroyed the spell and allowed the police to open the door. It appeared to have been written in chalk, which meant it had been intended to delay entry, not prevent it entirely.

"Curiouser and curiouser," I said, the creeping unease I'd been feeling morphing into a full-on 'Danger, Will Robinson!' drumbeat in my head. Now the question was: who'd done it and why? Aunty Mommy would have been the first name on my most-likely-to-kill-and-kidnap list, but she was already dead and if she was going to do the poltergeist thing, she'd have already been torturing me.

Unfortunately, while I couldn't imagine the motives, I could imagine that many of my new-found relatives—starting with my sperm donor—would easily be capable of murder and kidnapping. But again, the why of it totally escaped me. Not that they needed a reason. I wouldn't blink to hear one of them had done it just for fun.

"Now what I want to know," Ballard said with a narrow look at Mikey, "is what you thought Miss Wyatt might add to the investigation? You certainly aren't suggesting she's the killer, are you?"

I glared at Mikey. That one hadn't occurred to me, but it should have. He thought me, Jen, and Lorraine were responsible for Stacey being...well...Stacey. So, his opinion of me was already low. Had he put two and two together and decided that since I could do magic, and magic was clearly in use here, I must have done it?

"Yes, you certainly aren't suggesting I'm behind this, are you?"

He gave me a cool look before answering Ballard. "I'm not suggesting she's involved," he said. "I *am* suggesting she might have a useful contribution to make."

Now Ballard and Jeffries looked at me for answers.

"You're an asshole," I told Mikey.

"But I'm right, aren't I?"

I flipped him off and clomped up the stairs.

"What are you doing?" Jeffers demanded as I shouldered past. "What's she doing?"

"I'm going to look inside. Isn't that why you brought me?"

Jeffers made a growling sound as he followed me. "I

don't have a clue why we brought you here. Grasping at straws is what we're doing and wasting time."

I sighed. "You're not."

I turned the handle of the door, but it didn't open. I was tempted to open it with magic, but shockingly, I decided to be cautious. What if using magic triggered something bad? Like a curse trap or something? I chalked my uncharacteristic caution up to exhaustion from finding Stacey and not fear about that Damocles spell Lindsey had scribbled all over Luke's walls.

"Who's got the key?"

Ballard unlocked the door and pushed it open. "It's still a crime scene. Don't touch anything, and the dog has to stay outside."

It took some work, but I convinced Ajax to wait outside. He wasn't a fan of the situation and made sure we all knew it, letting out a long howl when I ducked under the crime scene tape and walked inside.

"Can't you shut him up?" Jeffers groused. "He's worse than a siren. Neighbors are going to have a fit."

"Of course I can. Let him inside." I smiled saccharine-sweet at him and he muttered under his breath.

I stopped in the foyer to gaze around, appreciating the airy brightness, amber wood, and cozy comfort. The place had been renovated but kept a lot of the original charm. The fixtures were antique, and the furniture was as well, though upholstered with modern fabric using modern techniques. Wallpaper had been used judiciously, along with warm neutral paints. They'd installed a cast iron wood stove insert into the fireplace. The wall art was mostly floral or cityscapes.

The place was clean with the typical clutter of families: a

sweatshirt draped over the arm of a chair; shoes kicked off behind the door; books and magazines piled on the coffee table; a cereal bowl holding a spoon; a pile of mail; charge cords; a couple of coffee cups; some pens; folded throw blankets; a program from a local play. Smudges of black fingerprint powder decorated the light switches, door handles, doors, tables, knick-knacks…pretty much any surface that might have been touched and could hold a fingerprint.

I chewed my bottom lip and then made a decision.

Magic is mostly wanting something to happen and then having the power and focus to make the change. Spells involve building up pieces of intent and locking them in, then taking the different pieces and putting them together to create the larger focus, then giving the whole thing the power it needed to do the job. I didn't yet know how to make spells—though Damon was starting to teach me before he left—but I have a lot of power, thanks to my fucked-up heritage. I'm one of three in a litter bred for power, kind of like racehorses are bred for fast running.

I didn't need much for what I wanted to do now.

Ignoring my companions, I drew magic into my hand. I imagined the power as tiny grains of sand flowing in streams around my fingers.

I drew a breath and blew it out, snapping my fingers outward as I did. Sort of like a chef's kiss. Motes of magic rose in the air and puffed outward. They floated throughout the house, settling wherever magic had touched, and lighting up bright pink with each discovery.

It was a bit theatrical, but the physical reinforcement of my intent helped me tighten my focus and keep it sharp in my mind. Anyhow, there's nothing wrong with a little harmless theater.

"What the fuck?" The words startled out of Jeffers like he'd been poked with a cattle prod.

Spots of pink glimmered on all the windows, highlighting the glyphs drawn on each and confirming that magic had been involved in the crime. I walked through the front sitting room. No pink here, except for the windows.

"Would someone tell me what the fuck's going on?" Jeffers demanded, hot on my trail.

"I'd like to know, too," Ballard said in a glacial voice.

I knew Mikey wouldn't say a word. They'd think he was nuts. I wasn't ready, either. I continued into the dining room and then kitchen, stopping on the threshold.

"Crap."

Every surface was pink, even the ceiling. A rectangle on the floor shone extra bright, no doubt where the spell had kept the body looking fresh. I had no idea why the killer had wanted to make it look fresh for discovery, but let it fast-forward decompose once the spell was breached. Then again, it wasn't my job to know, and anyway, who said the killer had to be logical? Or sane?

"All right. Enough. I want to know what's going on and you'd better tell me in small words so I understand," Jeffers growled, hands clamped on his hips exposing his side arm on his right side.

I was pretty sure he was holding on so tight so that he wouldn't grab his gun and shoot me. He looked more tempted than usual.

I rubbed my fingers over my lips, thinking. Telling Mikey had been sort of accidental. Sometimes I can turn into a cloud and go through solid objects. Or around them, anyhow. I couldn't control the ability. It seemed to trigger when I was pissed and sort of trapped.

That night with Mikey I'd been sitting in a booth between

him and Jen. He'd pissed me off so bad I'd needed to get up and away from him before I twisted his head off. My body-cloud ability had kicked in and I'd gone from sitting behind the table to standing in front of it. I hadn't had a whole lot of fucks to give—I still didn't, to be honest—so I'd just laid out the explanation. He hadn't wanted to believe me. No, he *hadn't* believed me, that is, until he saw more evidence. Apparently now he was a walking billboard advertising me.

The asshole in question now leaned a hip against the counter, arms folded as he watched me. He wasn't smiling, which probably saved him from me turning him into an ant and stepping on him. Or a dung beetle. Definitely a dung beetle.

"Well?" Jeffers demanded.

I gave an inward shrug. "It's magic."

Both detectives stared at me like they were waiting for a punchline. Mikey semi-successfully bit back a grin, but since it was directed at his colleagues, I decided to let it pass for now.

Jeffers exchanged a look with his partner and then lasered in on me again.

"Do you think that's funny? We've got two children and their father missing, not to mention their other father is dead, and you decide it's time to start wisecracking?"

"You've got to be some kind of shitbag to tell jokes while standing where a man was killed," Ballard said, icy cold instead of livid hot like Jeffers. "And you," she said, targeting Mikey, "I hope you enjoyed being detective while it lasted. You'll be busted down to parking enforcement by lunch."

"I had pretty much the same reaction when I found out," Mikey said, sounding sympathetic. "Unfortunately, she's the real deal and if all this pink is what I think it is, then magic was involved in the murder and kidnapping, and you're fucked without her help. If you want to find your two kidnap victims, you need to fight fire with fire."

Ballard's jaw clenched like she was fighting not to spew some harsh words. Jeffers had gone red and his eyes had started to bug out with the force of his fury. I decided to save him from stroking out.

I made a ping-pong sized ball of light and flicked it into the air between us, followed quickly by a dozen more. I then proceeded to send them spinning and bouncing in a snaking line. It turned vertically in a ferris wheel circle, then horizontally in a carousel circle, and then I started making random patterns and made some of the balls started flashing different colors. I spun them over Jeffers' head like a halo, then called them back to my hand and let them dissolve.

"What the fuck?" Jeffers had a dazed look like he'd been brained with a cast iron frying pan.

Ballard kept more of her cool and the only indication she was unsettled was the flex of her jaw muscles and a visible swallow.

"Do you believe me now, or do you want another demonstration?" I asked.

"How did you do that?" Jeffers said, scrutinizing me from head to toe. Looking for wires or maybe a holographic projector...if those existed.

"I guess that's a need-more-proof-question," I said. I sent tendrils of magic to open and close all the drawers and cupboards all at once, and since I'm petty, I picked Mikey up into the air and flipped him upside down, holding him a foot above the floor.

He yelped and kicked, scraping his fingers across the floor. "Beck! Put me down! On my feet," he added.

"Not yet," I said. "First I need to convince your fellow detectives that I am, in fact, a witch."

Jeffers made a choking sound at that last word.

"Magic isn't real," Ballard said in a tight voice. "It's not."

It sounded like she was trying to convince herself.

"Of course not," I said. "This is all explainable. Mikey and I broke in yesterday and wired the house up so we could hang him upside down, and we've got light projectors hidden in the ceiling lights. Wait 'til you see what's next."

"Beck," Mikey said warningly. "Be patient. It's going to take a few minutes for them to wrap their brains around this. Meanwhile, put me the fuck down. On my *feet*," he clarified again as I contemplated dropping him on his head.

"You got me into this, so you can do your part to show these two that magic is real."

"Christ on a cracker! Put me the fuck down."

I gave an exaggerated sigh. "Fine." I whipped him upright and dropped him back on his feet. The malicious part of me hoped he got whiplash.

I dusted my hands together. "Now that we're all on the same page, I'm going to look around."

"It's still a crime scene," Ballard said. "You can't go blundering around."

Seriously? She was going to go there? I didn't have a lot of patience at the best of times, and today it was especially low. She clearly didn't want me there and I was done trying to convince her and her partner. I mentally dusted my hands together.

"Well, since I definitely don't want to trespass on your

precious crime scene, I'll just go call and Uber and go check on Stacey. Good luck with your case."

I stomped away back toward the door. Not that I was leaving. Or if so, I'd have to come back and break in. Officer Scrotum was correct; now that I knew magic was involved, I had to help find the kids and their father. I couldn't sit by and let some witch abuse them. If they were even still alive.

"Wait!" Mikey hustled after me.

I swung around. "Why should I?"

"Because you can't expect us ordinary mortals to instantly accept that magic exists. It takes some adjustment. It would be like you discovering Santa Claus is real. Anyway, you know damned well you're not going to leave this alone."

"I'm not?"

"No, you're not." He didn't even try to argue he was right.

"Maybe, but what's to say I won't come back and figure this out by myself?"

"You can't do that."

I curled my lip. "Who's going to stop me?"

He tossed his hands in frustration. Or maybe it was an aborted attempt to strangle me. I was leaning toward strangulation.

"Listen, Beck, you need them. They have the badges. They have the resources of the department behind them, not to mention they know what the actual fuck they are doing when it comes to investigating crime."

"We don't need no stinkin' badges," I muttered. He was demonstrating a truly aggravating habit of being right. If he'd showed any sign of smugness, I'd give him an incurable case of crabs. Or maybe severe acne. Or both. Lucky for him, he simply looked earnest.

I made a growling sound and shoved past him, returning to the scene of the willful stupidity where Jeffers and Ballard spoke vehemently together.

"Okay," I said, moving aside to allow Mikey into the room. "This is how we're going to do this."

With no warning, I swept all three of them into the air. Jeffers squawked and Ballard swore—impressively—and Mikey let out a startled "Hey!"

"I am going to go look around the house and see where magic might have been used. Feel free to hang around."

I gave them all a Cheshire smile and headed for the stairs. They'd fucked around and found out and I wasn't one damned bit sorry about it.

CHAPTER SIX

A hallway led off the upstairs landing. It ran straight into a bathroom before turning and splitting. To the left was a round turret room that held an office. To the right, the hallway ran past two bedrooms on the left, the master suite on the right, and dead-ended into a wide family room that spread across the entire back of the house. It contained a TV and video games as well as over-stuffed chairs, a couch, a LEGO table, and a plethora of toys.

I searched each room, looking for signs of tell-tale pink. I ignored where it glimmered from the windows, since that was probably from the killer putting down magical locks. I found nothing in the office. In the two children's rooms, I found several pink-marked toys. I collected those, leaving them in a pile in the hallway before proceeding to the master suite.

Pink pulsed from the threshold. I squatted to get a closer look. Four glyphs had been etched into the wood. I stood and stepped inside, trusting that the magical shield I wore like a second skin would protect me. Inside, I found more glyphs on the footboard of the king-sized bed and the trim above the bathroom door. A dozen or more objects had been spelled as well. I added them to the pile I'd already collected.

The family room also contained a number of spelled objects. There didn't seem to be any particular pattern to them. I found a pen and a pad of paper and drew the various glyphs I'd seen so far, trying to memorize them as I wrote and snapping pictures with my phone. I didn't have much faith that they would survive long, given how Lindsey's spell had vanished from the walls and my phone. Magic didn't seem to like leaving evidence of itself. Then again…. I gave myself a mental note to try using my pink spell to resurrect Lindsey's.

I found a gym bag in the master suite and filled it with the things I'd collected and went back downstairs. I could hear arguing in the kitchen. I sighed and contemplated stealing the car and abandoning ship. I dismissed the idea because Ajax would be unhappy when I went to jail, and Stacey was going to need help, if only to escape her lovingly smothering family.

My three companions remained hanging where I'd left them, their argument cutting off when I returned. All three eyed me balefully.

"Get. Us. The fuck. Down," Jeffers demanded.

"Sure." I made a little gesture and they dropped to the floor. I landed Ballard more gently, given she wore heels.

Nobody spoke for a long moment.

"Well?" Ballard asked. "What did you find?"

My brows rose. Looked like my little education in magic's existence had worked. "The windows are all spelled, as I expected, and so were a number of toys and other objects. The weird ones were those on the threshold of the master suite, on the bed, and over the bathroom door."

"What were they for?" Mikey asked.

I shrugged. "No idea. I've never learned spell language. I collected up some of the spelled things to take to my Uncle Mason and my mother." That last word left a bad taste on my tongue. I didn't trust her. I barely trusted Mason, but he'd proven himself to me, and hadn't given me reasons to doubt him. Not yet, anyhow.

To be fair, my mother hadn't either. She just looked way too much like her sister—the woman who'd kidnapped and tortured me—for me to feel comfortable with her. Mostly I just wanted to keep my distance. Meanwhile she seemed on a quest to get acquainted, which made the whole distance thing difficult to maintain. I felt bad for her, given that all three of her children had been taken away at birth. I was one of triplets and the other two had gone to be raised by my asshole father, who I neither trusted nor liked. I will admit my mother seemed nice enough, and a little desperate and sad.

Jeffers grimaced, his lips working like he had to make himself form the words. "There are more of you...witches?" He looked like he had a mouthful of salt.

"Many more."

"Who?"

I was tempted to tell him where he could stick his interrogation, but it occurred to me he might suspect the girls. Stacey, Lorraine, and Jen needed that about as much as I needed a case of kidney stones.

I chose my words carefully. "Up until Aunty Mommy died, I thought she and I were the only ones, and I kept my abilities secret from everyone, especially her." Little did I know she had my pedigree and was well aware I was not only a witch, but that I'd been bred for power.

"So, you don't know of anybody who might have been responsible for all this?" Ballard gestured around us at the pink.

"No clue."

"It's not someone you're acquainted with?" Jeffers asked.

I shrugged. I doubted it was Mason or my mother. It definitely wasn't Damon or Ben Sharpentier, who was a young witch friend living in San Francisco and attending medical school. I could easily see my father doing it, but he had no reason and I'd have bet my life on him never doing his own dirty work. I'd met a few other witches, but I couldn't imagine a reason for any of them to come after this family.

That made me more nervous than I liked to admit. Damon, Mason, my mother, and Ben were constantly warning me that I had to watch my back. That many of the witch families wouldn't scruple to grab me and turn me into a broodmare for their family eugenics programs. After all, that seemed to be the whole purpose for their existence. The more magical power a family had at its disposal, the more value they had in society, to breed up the super-witches.

Getting me into the birthing room would be a major coup for most of the families, since my genes were that spectacular. Human puppy mill.

I shuddered at the thought.

What if this whole thing was actually some kind of trap for me? The concept seemed ridiculously far-fetched, since someone would have to know enough about me to stage the murder and kidnapping; get Mikey, Ballard, and

Jeffers on board; and know that they'd pull me in to the investigation. It wasn't just unlikely; it was absurdly improbable. It was also not impossible. Not with witchcraft in the mix.

I snorted to myself. In all honesty, I wouldn't know another witch from a hole in the ground, which meant that anybody could be a threat and just going to the grocery store could be a trap.

Good thing I wasn't prone to paranoia.

"Did you learn anything else?" Ballard asked.

I reluctantly shook my head. "I can tell magic was used, but I don't know what for."

"You can't, I don't know, find a way to show us what happened? Or do some kind of mojo to pinpoint the killer? Light them up pink?"

"Maybe my uncle or mother could. But...," I trailed off as realization set in.

"But?" Jeffers prompted.

"They might have to notify the witch police or whatever. They really don't like renegade witches, especially dangerous ones."

After Garret had kidnapped Mason and I and tried to kill Damon and the girls, the human cops had arrested him. A short time later, he'd 'escaped.' Damon assured me that he'd been taken into witch custody, as a human jail couldn't hold him, and he was being dealt with according to witch law.

He'd been reluctant to say more, but in the end he'd grimly explained that witch punishments had a lot more in common with the Spanish Inquisition than not, and were meant to set an example that nobody would ever want to follow. He'd turned a little green as he said it, then clammed up. Mason had been equally close-mouthed. My takeaway ended up being that witch justice was fucking scary and nothing I wanted to be involved in.

"Maybe that's what they ought to do," Jeffers said, glancing around at the pink of my spell.

"Maybe."

"You don't think that's a good idea?" Mikey asked.

"Might be a little like calling in a hurricane to solve a terrible drought. You're still going to end up with a lot of death, destruction, and disease, only it'll be a lot worse and no more in your control than your original problem."

"Anyway, it's *our* case," Ballard said with a glare at her partner. "It's going to stay that way." She looked back at me. "So all this pink tells you what?"

"Where a spell was active."

"What exactly does that mean? Why is there so much pink in here and not out there?" She gestured toward the combined dining and sitting rooms through the open doorway.

"The only magic worked out there was on the windows and it was small. The spells in here were much bigger workings. You had the magic preserving the body for sure. After that, I don't know what the other magic was doing. It encompassed the whole kitchen, though."

"And you're sure it was more than just the preservation?"

I nodded. The various opacities of the pink showed that.

"Doesn't give us anything to go on," Jeffers said. "We're back where we started."

Why he sounded so happy about that escaped me. My brows rose. "Are you? Shall we have cake and a party?"

"It's true," he shot back. "We've got nothing we can use. Magic? What are we supposed to do with that? We'd be laughed out of the department if we so much as mentioned the word. We needed something real."

"Magic *is* real."

"Maybe so, but we deal in evidence. The kind that holds up in court and leads us to our killer and victims. Magic is just a distraction and frankly a waste of our time."

He sent an accusing look at Mikey whose hackles had gone up. He looked ready to throw down.

A cock fight. Now *that* was a waste of time. Or maybe it wasn't wasted if I enjoyed the show. I would totally enjoy watching Mikey and Jeffers going at it.

But Stacey waited and so did the three victims of this crime. I had to get a move on.

"Fine then. Take me to my car and we'll pretend none of this happened." I grabbed the bag of bespelled goodies and marched to the door.

"Hold on," Ballard said, following.

I'd stopped on the porch to pet a worried Ajax. He'd stood up on his hind feet and put his paws on my shoulders and whuffled my face all over before snugging his nose around the back of my neck and mashing himself close in a doggy hug. I dropped the bag and hugged him back, scratching and petting all over. He whimpered, wagged, and wiggled like I'd been gone for a year. He hadn't been this happy when we picked him up. Odd.

"You're going to let us know what you find out on the stuff you're taking?" Ballard asked, though it sounded more like an order.

"I can call *you*." Emphasis on not calling Jeffers.

"Please do. Do you have suggestions on how we should handle a witch? Is there a way to neutralize their magic?"

Ajax had dropped back to all fours and I scratched my fingers through his scruff. "No clue. What I do know is that you're right to be cautious. Witches are dangerous and so far there seems to be a strong psychopathic streak running through the population. You don't want to face one down without magical defenses. Remember what happen to my shop? And my car?"

My vintage Thunderbird had been cleaved down the middle like someone chopped it apart with an elephant-sized axe. The rest of the place had been destroyed. Garret had been throwing a tantrum over me escaping his death curse. Or maybe me dating Damon. Or the murdering bastard had been hungry or constipated or had a ball rash.

Like I said: psychopath.

"Bullets still work on them, right?" Jeffers growled, clearly annoyed that he had to buy into the whole magic thing.

"By all means, try shooting them. Either it works, or you piss them off and they annihilate you." I gave him a shit-eating grin, still not feeling too forgiving of his attitude.

"What are you suggesting we do, then?" Ballard asked, shooting Jeffers a quelling look.

"Like I said, be careful." I shook my head and gave her an apologetic look. "I really don't know. I'll have to ask Damon and my uncle if they think it's wise to call the witch police. I'm just afraid their goal will be grabbing the witch and they won't care if the victims and half the city are collateral damage."

"Your boyfriend and uncle are witches, too?" Jeffers demanded. Or more accurately, accused. "Who else? Your girlfriends?"

I started to speak, but Mikey beat me to it.

"Just one you have to worry about: your killer."

CHAPTER SEVEN

I spent the trip to pick up my car fielding Jeffers's passive aggressive questions about magic and listening to him gripe about the impossibility of investigating a magical crime and that he didn't get paid enough for this kind of bullshit. I wondered what kind of bullshit he did get paid enough for.

I mostly chose to focus on Ajax who'd once again sprawled across my lap, across the seat, and up onto Mikey, and texted with Jen and Lorraine. Stacey's actual surgery had only just begun, hospitals moving at the speed of a snail in winter, it appeared. They said she wouldn't be out of surgery for another couple hours. After, she'd go to recovery and then to a room, after which she'd be inundated with family.

The poor nurses were going to have their hands full.

"You said there was a witch police force," Ballard said suddenly, interrupting Jeffers's grousing. "What makes you think they'll cause havoc?"

"It's not so much havoc, as collateral damage," I said.

"How so?"

"They really don't seem to like rogue witches, and they only care about cleaning up the threat without leaving witnesses behind. From what Damon said, that can get messy." Or painful. Or both.

Would they consider me a rogue witch now that so many non-witches knew about me? The girls, Mikey, and now Ballard and Jeffers. Did that make them targets for the witch police to clean up?

Fire burned in my stomach. Or maybe it was a new set of ulcers. My jaw hardened. Whichever, I was going to have to protect them, and I would, no matter what it took.

"How do we get in touch with them?" Ballard asked.

I blinked, pulling myself back to the conversation. "You want to get in touch with the witch police?" I scowled. "Didn't you hear me? They're scary dangerous. Why would you want to talk to them?"

"You said they deal in rogue witches. Apparently, we've got one," Jeffers said, looking like he'd swallowed an angry wasp. "Sounds like they're just what we need."

"What counts as a rogue witch?" Mikey chimed in.

I grimaced. Fuck all if I knew and that was the problem. "A murderer, maybe." Though I still wondered if they'd have bothered coming after Garret if his criminal habits had targeted humans instead of witches. Which brought the spotlight back to me.

From what Damon had told me, witch police weren't interested in justice the way I understood the concept. They also didn't go around handing out speeding tickets and pulling over drunk drivers. I didn't even know whether they'd have bothered to rescue me if Garret *had* succeeded in kidnapping me.

I didn't get the idea that the witchworld had many laws and I wasn't all that sure that killing each other counted. Breaking a birthing contract was probably a capital crime.

So, what did they do with all their time? I had a strong feeling I didn't want to know. I also had a strong feeling that one of these days I was going to find out. Hopefully not for a while. I had enough shit on my plate. I didn't need another helping.

WE ARRIVED AT THE PARKING LOT IN SPIRES STATE PARK WHERE I'd left my car before searching for Stacey.

"Thanks for the ride," I said, grabbing the door handle.

Not fast enough.

"When will we hear from you?" Ballard asked, eyeing me in the rearview.

"When I know something."

"Which will be?"

Cops were always so pushy. "I plan to talk to my uncle and mother after I go see how Stacey is."

"It's already after five," Ballard pointed out, glancing at her watch.

No wonder I was hungry.

"And the sky is blue and water's wet. What's your point?"

"The more time that passes, the more likely the kidnapper will kill his victims. We're already weeks in. We can't afford to waste any time."

What she was trying not to say was that the victims could already be dead. Part of me wanted to tell her it wasn't my problem. Except that actual people were missing and in danger, and I was the only one who might be able to find them. So, it totally *was* my problem and I needed get over myself and start acting like it.

"I don't know when I'll know anything," I said quietly. "I have a lot of questions and I won't know what I can do until I get the answers. I promise that I will do all I can as fast as I can."

Ballard glanced at Jeffers and then nodded. "You have our numbers. We'll be waiting. It doesn't matter what time of day or night."

Jeffers twisted to look at me, and for the first time he looked like his normal self instead of a skittish colt. "You're Matthew's, Melissa's, and Toby's best hope right now."

The 'don't fuck this up' was implied. No pressure at all.

I nodded. "You'll hear from me soon."

I got out and Ajax followed. I strode around my car and yanked open the door to let him in as the detectives drove off. Two of them anyway. My passenger door opened and Mikey slid inside. I glared. Ajax gave a woof. It was probably welcoming, but I preferred to believe it was his version of fuck off.

"I don't remember inviting you."

"My car's at the hospital."

I gave a little scoffing snort and buckled myself. "Don't think I believe for one second that you plan to leave me alone. You intend to stick to me like dogshit on the bottom of my shoe."

The corner of his mouth lifted and he shrugged. "Somebody has to have your back when you go off half-cocked. You're going to jump into this thing with both feet and you have no idea what you're doing."

I flipped him the bird but didn't argue. I didn't have a leg to stand on. Wait a second. Yes I did.

"So when a witch hits you with a blast of magic, what are you going to do about it, Superman?"

"I guess you'll have to have my back too."

"Oh."

"Oh? That's not comforting. Should I be worried?"

"Depends on how bad you piss me off when the bullets start flying." I grinned at him like I meant it.

"I'll be sure to update my will."

"You might want to stop at the pet store and pick up some toad food. Just in case someone turns you into one. Can't hurt to be prepared."

"I'll put it on my to-do list," he said drily, the corner of his mouth kicking up.

ON THE WAY TO THE HOSPITAL, I CALLED JEN. MY PHONE WAS paired to the radio, so Mikey couldn't ticket me for being on my cell while driving. Jen picked up on the second ring.

"About time. What happened? Those idiots didn't arrest you, did they? I swear I'll rip Mike's balls off if he's got you into trouble."

I smirked and lifted an eyebrow at Mikey. "He's sitting right here. I'm on speakerphone."

"Did he hear me?"

"I'm not deaf," he said.

"Good, then I don't have to repeat myself. Just so you know, Officer Douchecanoe, I do not make empty threats and I don't give a shit if you're armed or that you're a cop."

The corners of his mouth lifted in a smile. The man was clearly into masochism. "I'm aware."

"What's he got you into?" Jen asked, turning her attention back to me.

I'd tell her but first… "How's Stacey?"

"Still in surgery."

My stomach clenched. I tightened my hands on the wheel, my knuckles whitening. From the back, Ajax whined. That brilliant dog was my own personal mood detector.

"Still? What's wrong?"

"Nothing. Medicine moves at half the speed of snails. First they had to prep her, which took forever, and then just getting her into the operating room took another century, and she's been in less than an hour. Surgery should last another hour, and then she'll go to recovery, and then to her room. Her parents will be allowed to see her, and maybe some siblings, but they already said most of us won't get to see her until tomorrow. They said she probably won't be coherent until then anyhow. They plan to keep her doped up pretty good."

I made myself take a breath and relax, swallowing my residual fear. "What are you going to do?"

"Lorraine is heading back to the clinic to finish up some things. I'm waiting for you and holding Luke's hand when he isn't pacing around like a wounded lion. You going to tell me what's going on?"

"I'm on my way to the hospital. I'll fill you in there."

"I don't get a hint?"

"One person was murdered and his husband and two kids kidnapped. The perpetrator used magic."

"A murder?" Her voice rose into a squawk. "That motherfucker has got you involved in a murder?" She shouted the last bit. "What the hell was he thinking dragging you into something that dangerous?"

"I was thinking she could help us find the kidnap victims," Mike said evenly.

"That's *your* job and clearly you suck at it since you can't seem to solve a crime without her help. She's not a cop and you've no right to involve her. Are you trying to get her killed?"

I thought about pointing out how rude it was to talk about me while I was sitting right there, but as long as Jen was chewing out Mikey, I wasn't her target. I had a feeling I would be when I told her I was going to pursue the killer on my own. Well, hopefully with a little help from Mason and my mother.

"She's just helping figure out what happened. She's in no danger." He was beginning to sound pissed.

"Can you one hundred percent guarantee that?" Jen demanded.

"I'm sure she's not."

"Yeah, right. And you're never ever wrong, are you? I swear to all that's holy and not, if Beck even gets a scratch because you pulled her into this, I will make your life a living hell. I imagine Stacey will have something to say too. Your chances with her will go straight down the toilet."

"I'm not forcing Beck to do anything," he retorted, clearly stung by the last threat. "She can walk away free and clear."

Jen scoffed. "She won't, and you knew that going in. Beck hates bullies and she really hates when they fuck with innocent children and their families. She's going to get them back and get justice no matter what it takes. You know it, I know it, and she knows it. So shut your lying mouth. Beck, I'll see you when you get here."

The call cut off. Silence filled the car.

"She's right," Mikey said finally. "I don't think you're in

danger, but I can't guarantee it. And you do have a bad habit of putting yourself in the line of fire."

"I can handle myself."

"Stacey told me about how you fell in the river and got turned into hamburger."

I shrugged, wondering just how much she'd told him. I'd been cursed at the time and had gone into the river in a desperate attempt to save myself. It had worked. The curse hadn't killed me, but the cure nearly had. "Accidents happen."

"Was it an accident?"

"Far as you know."

"Ballard and Jeffers said you ended up in the hospital looking like you'd been burned alive not long after that. Didn't say how."

"I helped free some female gargoyles."

His head whipped around. "You what?"

I spoke more slowly. "I...helped...free—"

"I heard you. Now explain what you are talking about. Free gargoyles? From what? Wait, gargoyles are real?"

"Yes, they are real. Aunty Mommy imprisoned them. Me, Damon, my actual mother, my father, my uncle, and a couple others broke the spell. In the process, I got fried like a bug in a zapper."

His eyes narrowed. "You don't look like you've ever been burned. How is that?"

I rolled my eyes. "Magic. Duh. Do you even listen to yourself?"

He flushed, then annoyingly returned to his original point, which I had just helped prove.

"Like I said, you like putting yourself in the line of fire."

"I don't *like* it," I said, not yet ready to concede the point. "But if I'm the only one who can solve the problem, then that's what I'll do, which, by the way, is what you were counting on when you had Ballard and Jeffers hunt me down. Ironic, though, given you weren't at all interested helping when we went after Carson Flannery for abusing his wife. You didn't want anything to do with magic, then. Just when it's convenient for you."

"You were breaking the law. Probably a dozen or more of them. I'm a cop and a good one. I can't be a part of schemes like that."

"Then there's another reason for you to step off this train, because I will probably be breaking more laws. No, I'll *definitely* be breaking more laws."

I could actually hear him grit his teeth.

"I'll deal with that when the time comes," he said finally.

"Be still my heart," I said, pressing my hand dramatically to my chest. "What a resounding vote of confidence. Thank goodness I can rely on you. Maybe almost as much as I can rely on a ripped condom. I am so relieved. Whew!" I wiped pretend nervous sweat off my forehead using the back of my hand. "I'll rest easy now that I know you'll definitely think about not abandoning me in my hour of need. Thank you so much."

"I *won't* abandon you," he said, his eyes snapping with fury.

I snorted. "Right. You know leopards can't change their spots, right? You've got your priorities and the top one is the law. You're a straight arrow. I get it. Really. And I'm not arguing that you should be any different. But please stop trying to convince me you'll look the other way when I do some breaking and entering, or worse. You may think I'm stupid enough to fall for that bullshit, but I'm not. When push comes to shove, you'll yank away the football and I'll be flat on my ass, so I have no intention of counting on you or even telling you what I'm up to. I'm not letting you get in my way."

"My priority is to *protect* and serve the people of this city," he retorted. "That includes nutjobs like you. I told you I'd have your back and I meant it. *I don't lie.*" He spit the last three words like bullets.

"Watch what they do, not what they say," I muttered. He could shout his promises off the rooftops, but he'd bailed on me once. I had no reason to believe he wouldn't do it again.

"What'll it take for me to prove it?"

I shrugged. "Nothing I can think of."

"You can't do this alone. You're chasing down a killer and you don't have a clue what you're doing. You're not only going to get yourself killed, but the kidnap victims too."

I slid him a glance. He was a lot more right than wrong, but I wasn't as stupid or as arrogant as he thought I was. I also wasn't as alone as he thought I was.

"Challenge accepted."

CHAPTER EIGHT

Silence filled the car. A couple times Mikey started to say something, then clamped his mouth shut. Just as well. Neither one of us was going to change our minds. I turned my attention to the murder and kidnapping. Why kill one father and take the other and the children?

"No ransom demands?" I asked after awhile.

He considered me a moment, no doubt deciding whether he should tell me anything.

"None."

"Co-workers or neighbors have anything to say? Maybe there was an ex in the picture? Or a stalker? Or maybe husband number two killed husband number one in some kind of domestic dispute?"

He shook his head. "Nope. Not one person had anything really negative to say about either man. Arthur was a little fanatical about his lawn and hedges. No one saw them fighting beyond normal marital spats. Kids' school said they behaved normally, though the boy had some learning disabilities. The fathers volunteered, attended church, and generally were quiet and unassuming. Not a single person we interviewed thought it possible that Matthew Chapman could hurt a fly, much less kill his husband. They were shocked we even suggested it."

"You've been working the case too?" I asked, surprised. "I thought it was Ballard's and Jeffers's case."

"They're lead on the case, but that just means they organize and collate information and assign tasks. Most of the department is working on this, one way or another."

I digested that tidbit of information.

"They also don't have any enemies, no debts, no secret gambling addictions. They drink, but never to excess, and they don't do drugs, not even pot. No police records except for the occasional parking and speeding ticket. There is absolutely no reason we can see for anybody to want to harm either one of them."

He said the last in exasperation and dragged his fingers through his hair. "If we could find the motive, we could find the killer."

Just then I pulled into the hospital's Emergency Department parking lot. I drove slowly past the entrance. Jen jumped up from a bench and charged toward us. She looked like the Amazon warrior I always imagined her being. Her waist-length coffee hair hung over her shoulder in a thick braid and at six-feet-tall she was more than imposing. Give her a spear and some face paint and she'd totally look the part.

She reached us and yanked open the front passenger door. "Get out," she told Mikey.

He didn't move. She bent close.

"It wasn't a request. Get the fuck out of the car."

"I'm not going to let Beck go off half-cocked," he said, folding his arms.

"Unless you're arresting her, you don't get a say in what she does or doesn't do. Get out of the car before I help you out."

Jen's patience was fraying fast. I could have interfered, but watching was more fun.

"That would be assaulting a police officer."

"And you're not only trespassing, you're harassing an innocent civilian, and abusing your authority."

She looked at me. "Do you want him to stay?"

"Nope."

His head snapped around. "You need me."

"Like a case of crabs. You're no longer welcome. If I find out anything, I'll let you know. Probably."

"Goddamnit! You are the most batshit crazy and infuriating—" He broke off before he finished, leaving me to fill in the blank. Bitch? Asshole? Hard to say.

"Back atcha, Butch."

He leaned toward me, his gray gaze intense. "Do not try to take this killer on by yourself. Promise you will call me before you do anything stupid."

I gave him a pirate smile. "Sure. Before I do anything stupid. You've got it, Detective. Now go bye-bye. The womenfolk have important things to do."

He swore then, no doubt realizing that his definition of stupid wasn't the same as mine. His bar was a lot lower. Nevertheless, he unbuckled and got out. Jen jumped in and pulled the door shut before he could turn around. I didn't wait. My foot hit the gas and we squealed out of the parking lot, leaving him in our proverbial dust.

Jen buckled her seatbelt and then turned to face me. "All right. Tell me everything."

By the time we reached Aunty Mommy's mansion, I'd filled her in and she'd grabbed the bag from the backseat.

"This is all ordinary stuff," she said, rifling through it. Pink light poured from the interior. I hadn't removed my magic-revealing spell. "Toys, a shoe, a watch, toothbrushes, jewelry, ballcaps, a lunchbox, pens, a sock, coins…. Pretty random junk."

"I didn't even take it all. I'm hoping Mason and my mother can help me figure out what the spells are supposed to do and maybe, if I'm lucky, find some clue as to who cast them."

She closed the bag, effectively shutting off the lurid light. "What are the odds of a magical crime in Sweetwater having nothing to do with you? I mean, a couple of months ago you and your mom were the only witches in town, and now there's a random murder involving magic? I don't want to be paranoid, but what if your family or one of those other baby-breeding families are behind it? What if it's a trap for you?"

"I thought of that, but I can't live my life hiding from people who want to kidnap me. I just have to be careful is all. And mean. Make sure nobody wants to risk fucking with me."

"How?"

I grimaced and shook my head. "Fuck if I know, but I've got you, Lorraine, Stacey, Damon, Mason, and Ben to help me figure it out."

Jen tapped her fingers against her lips. "That's how the families do it, right? Kind of like the mafia. Be so strong nobody can take you out. Maybe that's what you've got to do."

I snickered. "Be a magical mafia kingpin?"

"They prefer to be called Don," Jen said with a prim sniff.

"As in the duck or don we now our gay apparel?" This was the silliest conversation I'd had all day.

She giggled, then changed the subject. "Have you talked to Damon yet? What does he say?"

"I plan to call him after I call Mason. Maybe I'll get a chance to talk to him for more than two minutes. Let's go inside and get something to eat and I'll make my calls."

We both got out of the car. Ajax didn't wait for me to open the back door for him but launched himself between the front bucket seats. He landed on the ground beside me and gave himself a shake before wandering over to a bush to pee.

"Wouldn't it be nice if we could just pee wherever we wanted to? Mark our territory the way dogs do?" Jen asked.

"That could get really disgusting, really fast. And Stacey would get pissed when Luke and Mikey started hosing her down."

"There is that," Jen conceded as we climbed up the steps to the front door. "I supposed it's not the best idea I've had."

"Not the worst either. Not even your top one hundred."

She sighed. "I can't argue that either."

I put my arm around her shoulder and squeezed. "On the other hand, you've had a lot of really, really marvelous bad ideas. Some of the best. It's really like science, when you think about it. You've got to try a lot of wrong solutions before you find the right one."

"You're saying I'm a scientist," she said in disbelief.

"Yep. A mad one. Like Dr. Frankenstein. Or Dr. Jekyll. Or Dr. Horrible."

"Dr. Horrible? That's not real."

"Of course he is. Captain Hammer and Dr. Horrible. Anyhow, you can be...Dr. Doom. Or Dr. Disaster."

"You're Dr. Disaster," she said. "A walking disaster. Everyday disaster. Disaster for breakfast, disaster for lunch, disaster for—"

"I think I take offense to that."

She grinned. "If the shoe fits. I mean, how many times have you been in the hospital lately?"

"Fine. I'm a complete and total disaster, but you're still Dr. Doom. We'll figure out who Stacey and Lorraine are later. Come on, I'm hungry and my bladder's about to explode."

She laughed and followed me inside.

It wasn't until we'd eaten that I remembered I'd been supposed to meet my mother for breakfast. After Stacey's call, I'd totally forgotten about it. I checked my phone, but she hadn't called. Probably either pissed or hurt that I hadn't shown up. Maybe both. Not that I really cared about her feeling one way or another—I barely knew the woman and Stacey was definitely the priority—but I hated being a flake. That was just rude.

"Ooops."

"What?" Jen asked.

I explained.

"No big deal. Tell her about Stacey. She'll understand."

I sighed. "She's been super eager to spend time with me and as awkward as it is, I feel bad blowing her off. Even for a good reason. Not to mention I've not had a lot of room in my schedule with getting the store rebuilt, bidding on estates, and trying to learn magic. Oh, yeah, and having a life."

"So long as Stacey, me, and Lorraine are your highest priority—aside from Ajax, of course—you're doing fine. Oh, and Damon can be up there, too, once he gets back. You really need to let him ring your bell."

I flushed and squirmed a little. I wasn't a virgin—quite —but my only experience had been a half-assed quickie in the back of a car when I was in high school, and once the boy had poked his dick into me and I'd discovered it hurt, I'd bailed. Which was pretty pathetic, given all that Aunty Mommy had put me through. By comparison, it hadn't hurt more than a little bug bite. The whole event had been utterly humiliating.

Now that I was older and supposedly wiser, I still had no idea what to do in bed, and every time I thought about it, I started to panic. I didn't want to disappoint Damon and couldn't imagine not doing so. It would be like him going to a five-star restaurant and expecting a world class chef and instead getting a fry cook from McDonald's.

Not that I didn't have time to figure it out. Read a couple books, maybe. Watch some porn. After all, I had no idea when he was coming back. Maybe I should buy some sex toys for practice. Or a box of cucumbers. Or maybe a chastity belt was the way to go. Then I wouldn't have to even worry about it.

I sighed. Like Jen said, I'm a disaster.

"I'd better call her and Mason. See if we can meet up

tonight so I can show them the bag of stuff and see what they think."

"Don't think for one second I'm not coming with you," Jen warned.

"Of course you are. Dr. Disaster would never leave Dr. Doom behind. It would be sacrilege. Betrayal of the highest order."

Deirdre, the housekeeper, came bustling out of the kitchen carrying a large bowl of chicken, rice, and vegetables. She set it on the floor on a mat just for that purpose. Ajax had already bounded over and sat down, tail wagging as his front feet danced. Deirdre smiled at him and patted his head.

"What a good boy you are, Mister Ajax. Don't wait. Dig in."

He didn't have to be asked twice and set about inhaling his food.

"Thank you," I said to her.

She smiled down at him. "Of course."

I might own the house, but Deirdre was the boss. Small and slender and of Indian descent, her rich brown skin was creamy smooth and sharp intelligence gleamed in her dark eyes. She wore her black hair in a thick plait down her back most of the time, and never had a hair out of place. A gold ring curled through her left nostril and berry lipstick stained her lips. She wore white palazzo pants and a sheer blue duster over a yellow blouse and Birkenstocks on her feet.

I couldn't help smiling. Deirdre had always been constrained and carefully correct in her behavior under Aunty Mommy. Ajax had definitely cracked that reserve. She always made sure Ajax got a hearty breakfast, lunch, and dinner of balanced nutrition and fiber. She'd even had

Lorraine discuss his dietary needs with all four chefs. I'd say he was spoiled, but he'd been tortured and abused before I got him, and no amount of spoiling would ever make up for that. Didn't stop me from trying, though. Most of the staff were on board too.

She raised her eyes to look at me. "Would you care for anything else, Miss Wyatt?"

I didn't remind her to call me Beck. It was never going to happen. "Not at the moment. Who's cooking tonight?"

"Felice."

"Please tell her thank you for me. Dinner was delicious."

She nodded. "I will do that and send Javi to clear your dishes." She withdrew.

"Let's go outside on the patio while I make those calls," I said to Jen. "Gargoyles should be waking up soon."

Aunty Mommy had kidnapped their female mates and forced the males to bind themselves to the house, guarding it from whoever or whatever might attack. I was still working on how to free them, but blood bonds were unbreakable according to everybody with any knowledge of the subject. I refused to buy that. Come hell or high water, I would find a way to set them free so they could go home to their families.

I called Mason first and explained the situation and he told me to come meet him at his lodgings. He actually said lodgings. Very old-money European. Next, I called my mother. I apologized for missing breakfast and explained what had happened to Stacey. After that, I told her about the murder and kidnapping and the involvement of magic and she agreed to meet us at Mason's in an hour.

"She seemed really happy I called her," I told Jen as I finished the called. "It's weird."

"Why? She's told you she wants a relationship."

"Because that's not how that whole world works. No witch raises their own kids and half the time, you never see them again if the contracted children go with the other parent's family. It's like livestock. Like what happened to slaves, except this is actually voluntary, which makes it even more bizarre."

"Sounds like your mom isn't a fan of the way things work, either. Anyway, I don't know how voluntary it is. Ben doesn't want to participate, but he says he'll have to," Jen replied.

I couldn't help smiling at Ben's name. He was a medical student in San Francisco with a sweet, caring personality. He'd been one of the first witches I'd met after Aunty Mommy died. He'd shown up in town eager to meet me and had ended up teaching me how to cast a basic shield spell.

He'd been fighting his family's pressure to come home and perform his spermy duties. Ben, on the other hand, wanted to have children with someone he cared about and then—*gasp*—actually be their father and raise them. His family was not impressed. Neither were they impressed by his becoming a doctor. Not when many witches, including Ben, had healing magic. The only point of becoming a doctor was to take care of ordinary humans, and why would anybody want to do that?

"Does he have to, though?" I wondered.

"He'd get cut out of his family and become fair game for kidnapping and breeding, just like you. His life would be hell."

"He could stay here."

"And do long-distance med school? His residency? And what about a job? He can't do any of that from here."

I shook my head. "I refuse to believe there isn't a way

around it somehow." Not only because of Ben. Damon was likely in the same boat. He was probably overdue for ejaculation duty. I couldn't help the snarl that curled my lips. Over my dead body. Aside from the fact that I was jealous as fuck, nobody was going to force him to do anything he didn't want to do.

"What?" Jen asked, noticing my expression.

"I was thinking that Damon's family probably has been lining up contracts for him."

"He'll never do it," Jen said instantly. "Not now that he has you."

"He doesn't know he has me," I said. "I haven't even had sex with him. Far as he knows, I still haven't made up my mind. Anyway, he might not be allowed to say no. Who knows what kind of leverage they have?"

Jen's brows rose, focusing on the first part of my statement. "First of all, sex is fun, but I don't think he'd walk if you chose never to screw him. That said, does this mean you've finally made up your mind to ride him hard and put him away wet? Not to mention drained?" She snickered.

I sighed. "Yes. No. Yes."

She laughed. "Which one?"

"Yes." I took a breath. Why was this so hard? I wasn't committing myself for the rest of my life. It just felt like it.

"As long as you're sure."

I flipped her off. "I've never been romantically involved before. It's hard. Sue me."

She slid an arm around me and squeezed. "You're right. I'm sorry. What's holding you back, really? You can't be scared of the sex. Bad sex is a little gross at worst, and I'm betting Damon is good."

"Excuse me, did you say gross?"

"You know, body fluids, body odor, hair in the wrong

places, bad breath, ugly feet...that sort of thing. Not that I think you'll have any issues with Damon. He's a good guy and understands hygiene. And he's not the type to get his rocks off and leave you hanging. I'm willing to bet he's the kind of guy who will worship your body and make you feel like you've gone to hell."

My brows rose. "Hell? As in fire, pain, and suffering?"

She shook her head and grinned. "Hell, as in sinfully good."

"I'm not sure that's how hell works."

"Whatever. The point is he'll take you to orgasm town and keep you there awhile. On top of that, he's a good guy. He makes you laugh, doesn't lie, cheat, or steal, and your friends like him. So fuck him already, would you?"

"Yes, ma'am." I gave a salute.

"Have you heard from him? When's he coming back?"

"A couple days ago and I don't know. He's been cagey about what's going on. I have no idea how long he'll be."

"Have you asked him?"

I hesitated before shaking my head. "I didn't want to be too pushy. Or clingy. Or demanding."

"Have you thought he might *want* you to be a little pushy, clingy, and demanding so he knows he's got a chance with you?"

I frowned. "No. That's a thing?"

"Try it. And by the way, just asking when he's going to be back isn't bad. It's called being interested. Telling him you miss him is also good. It's making him aware of what's going on in your head and heart. Given your habit of keeping everything inside, you should make more of an effort to at least hint that you care if he comes back or not."

"Of course I care," I said before I realized she was

needling me. "Now, shut up or your new doctor name will be Dr. Phyllis."

"That's just mean."

I just raised my brows, folding my arms and giving her the dead-eye stare. She caved.

"Fine. I'll shut up. For now. In the car you'd said you call him when you called Mason and your mother. Did you?"

I shook my head. "I want to see what we figure out first."

"Uh huh. You were a chicken."

I winced because she was right. "Call me Foghorn Leghorn."

"When are you going to call him?"

"I thought you said you'd shut up about him. That's not shutting up. That is, in fact, the exact opposite."

"Answer the question."

"Later tonight, I guess."

"You guess?"

"I will."

"Good. Tell him I said hello but tell him you want to lick his abs first."

I groaned. "That's the trouble. What if I'm a total failure at sex? I don't have a clue how to make a man get his rocks off. I was thinking I should watch some porn."

"You could, but most of it isn't all that interesting," Jen said.

"I take it you've watched a lot?"

"Enough to know it's repetitive and the stories are stupid."

"Word is you're not supposed to watch for the story but for the sex."

"Whatever. The thing you need to remember is men are easy. You don't have to do much of anything but show up and get naked, and honestly, getting naked isn't all that necessary. They come out of the box horny and a stiff breeze can make them blow their wad. You don't have to worry about making him feel good all. When in doubt, give him a blowjob. Yeah, I know you don't know how to do that either. Just treat his dick like a really good popsicle and you won't have to worry about a thing."

"I'll remember that," I said drily, my cheeks burning. I averted my gaze, searching for a new subject. I glanced up to the roofline where gargoyles perched every ten feet or so. They were a variety of shapes and each about the size of a gorilla. Each looked like a mythological mix of animal and human and every one was different from the other, and all of them were angry.

The sun hadn't yet dipped completely below the horizon, releasing them from their stone form. I didn't know if that was normal for them or if that was part of the spell imprisoning them.

"I'll have to check in with them later," I told Jen. "We'd better get going to Mason's."

We headed for the French doors leading back into the sunroom where we'd eaten our dinner. We'd gone about four steps when we heard a wuffling sound and the thud of hooves on stone. We turned. A buck stood on the steps. An enormous rack of antlers rose from his head, scraps of velvet peeling from it in tatters. He stood still, his gaze fixed on me.

"Holy shit," Jen murmured.

"Where did he come from?"

"More importantly, what does he want?" Jen asked. "I know nothing about deer, but walking up on someone's patio can't be normal, especially with people up here. Do you think he's rabid?"

"He's not drooling. All the same...." I pulled magic into my hand and pushed my shield out to surround Jen. "Back up slowly," I said, gripping her arm with my other hand and never taking my eyes off the stag.

As we did, he took another step and shook his antlers.

"He staring at you," Jen said.

Which wasn't super creepy at all. He made a gravelly huffing sound and lowered his head slightly like he was getting ready to charge. I shifted to get a little in front of Jen.

"What are you doing?" she demanded in a stage whisper.

"What does it look like?"

"Like you're doing stupid shit and trying to shield me."

"Then it sounds like you know exactly what I'm doing. Before you argue, I'll remind you I've got magic to defend us and you only have a wickedly sharp tongue. On top of that, it's undoubtedly here for me, and you don't need to get trampled while he'd trying to get to me."

"But you do?"

"Nobody needs to get trampled," I replied. "And I don't plan to."

"Tell that to Mister Pointy Head over there."

We'd edged back another few feet with the stag continuing to huff and shake its antlers. He pawed the flagstone and stared straight at me, which was unnerving as fuck.

Whatever was going on, it seemed personal. Had I offended him? How do you offend a buck, anyhow? Or maybe somebody had sent him. But why? To spy on me? Deliver a message? I didn't see anything that looked like a message holder. A little barrel under the jaw, maybe, like a St. Bernard on a rescue mission.

"Uh oh," Jen said softly.

The buck reared and lunged forward, stopping a few feet away to sniff at us before lowering his head as if to charge.

I thrust myself backward, taking Jen with me, even as I flung a bolt of magic at the beast. She shouted, "Hey!" at the same time my magic flared out in a cloud and sucked in around the stag. It would feel like a bunch of bee stings all at once. I meant it to distract. I really didn't want to hurt the poor beast. Whatever or whoever had sent him here, he was innocent.

My spell barely slowed him down. He paused to shake himself and make a low, angry sound and charged. Jen and I were backed up against the French doors. She fumbled with the door handles. I thickened my shield and braced for the impact. The antlers might not get through, but he could still send us tumbling like a ping pong ball, or in this case, through the glass doors.

A big, shadowy form dove from above. The stag hit my shield and was yanked up into the air. I caught sight of a leathery wing as I crashed back against Jen. Glass cracked but held.

I straightened. "Are you okay?" I asked, whirling to look at Jen.

She gasped for air and nodded, bending to brace her hands on her knees so she could breathe better, though that was made more difficult by the stream of curses reeling from her lips. Reassured, I turned to see what had happened.

Several gargoyles stood facing away in a protective half circle in front of me. I couldn't see much more than their wings and the silhouettes of their bodies. Overhead, others flew in a widening gyre.

I strode forward, but wings widened, keeping me behind the barrier of their bodies.

"Stay," one gravelly bass voice ordered.

"Let me through. What's going on?" I looked for an opening, but unless I crawled on my hands and knees or could vault a dozen feet in the air to get over them, I was out of luck.

"It's not safe," one told me, still not moving, not even to turn his head. "Be still."

"Better listen," Jen said, putting a hand on my arm.

"Who are you and what have you done with Jen?" I demanded. "The real Jen would be blowing a gasket trying to escape these..."

At that moment I realized I did not know how to safely insult a gargoyle without mortally offending them. Like you could call a guy a twatwaffle or a ball-less wonder, and that was no reason to go homicidal, but if you were to call a man a child-loving twatwaffle, that would be crossing the line. Almost nobody wanted to be called a pedophile.

I had no idea what insult constituted too far for gargoyles. Calling them brainless chunks of stone could send them into a rage. Or what if I called them cement? Or bricks? Or mud? I had no doubt they could hold a grudge so that when I finally broke this stupid binding that forced them to protect me and the property, they'd probably turn around and break my neck.

"These what?" Jen prompted, looking overly innocent.

She knew damned well what caused my hesitation. She also knew I didn't like using stupid or generic insults. Those were just lazy. I prided myself on targeting them according to the person requiring one. Unfortunately, my brain was sludge and I wasn't coming up with anything at this point.

"These behemoths."

"That's just sad," she said.

"You're ignoring the point. They aren't supposed to be guarding *me*. I didn't tell them to. I didn't ask for it, either!" My voice climbed as I spoke.

"Actually, you kinda did. Isn't that why you moved in here? You wanted all of us to move in after Lindsey wrote that spell on Luke's walls. You seemed to think the apocalypse was coming for you."

I hated when she was right. Still, I doubled down, rolling my eyes and snorting. "I doubt the spell was about a Bambi attack."

"And if it had picked you up on its antlers and tossed you through a window? Maybe stomped you like wine grapes? You'd have been dead. Sounds pretty dangerous to me."

"I was shielded."

"All the same. You should be saying thank you, not whining like someone stole your ice cream cone."

I sighed, annoyed that she wasn't wrong. Again. "Fine."

Her smile was smug. "You can tell me I'm right. I won't mind. Come on, you can do it."

"Bite me."

Just then the gargoyles leaped into the air. They made little sound but for the *whuff* of their wings as they flew upward. A couple seconds later, another glided down from above the trees. The leader of the group, Torastan, stood over eight feet tall, with bat wings, a long tail like a crocodile, a head like an Egyptian jackal with tall, pointed ears. His eyes were orange. His skin was dark gray like basalt.

Gargoyle expressions are tough to read. Maybe because they're living stone and don't have a lot of expressions. Pretty easy to tell when they're pissed because that's the default look. Or maybe that look means they are constipated. I wondered how turning into statues all day affected their digestive systems. Did they get hungry? Did rain bother them? Or heat? Did their intestines keep working and leave them needing to go to the bathroom without being able to do anything about it?

"Thanks for the help," I said. "I'm really sorry you were forced to, though."

"It is our privilege," Torastan said with a dip of his head.

"You don't have to do that," I said, irritated. "You're enslaved. You don't have a choice. There's no privilege in that."

He stared at me, long enough that I started to squirm.

"You freed our mates. You seek to free us. You have honor. You are worth serving."

I wanted to argue and tell him he didn't have to suck up, but no doubt he saw it differently. He was the one enslaved, after all.

"What happened to the deer?" Jen asked.

He twitched his ears and glanced at her. "Nothing." He shifted attention back to me. "I wish to know what you would like done with it."

I started to tell him to turn it loose, but then stopped. Could I figure out who put the spell on it? Probably not, but Mason or my mother might be able to. Presupposing one of them hadn't been responsible. I doubted Mason would do anything like that. He'd have no need. He'd given me Aunty Mommy's entire fortune, which was enough to run a small European country for several years. He wasn't looking for money, and if he'd wanted to kidnap me for breeding, he could have done that already.

My mother might want me dead, though there were easier ways to go about it than sending a killer deer. She might want revenge on my father for tricking her to carrying three children instead of the two he'd contracted for. It didn't seem likely, though, since she could have sent assassins without having to move here, and targeting him would be far more satisfying, I should think.

I couldn't think of any good reason either might want me dead. Though to be fair, I couldn't think of a good reason anybody *would* want me dead, except maybe Garrett, but he was out of the picture. But the real question was—who uses a deer for a murder weapon? That was bizarre, not to mention idiotic.

"Is there a place we can keep him for a little bit?" I asked. "A barn or a corral or something? We'll need to give him some food and water."

"It can be so."

"Let's do that, then."

He nodded.

"I should help you," I said, my dinner churning, acid burning up my throat. First because of the attack, and second because here I was giving the poor gargoyles orders and they couldn't even say no.

"There is no need. We can guard you better here."

"But we aren't staying here; we're going to Mason's," Jen said. "What if someone drops a tree or a boulder on the car while we're driving?"

Valid question, but I couldn't exactly hide under a rock. I said so.

"Some of us will go with you," Torastan said. "You will not be alone."

"I'm not making you chase me around," I said. "You are not coming with me. I am not your responsibility. You have your own lives—at least as much as that stupid binding allows you—and you deserve to enjoy that time as much as you can. Anyway, the argument is pointless. You can't even leave here, plus I'm perfectly capable of handling myself."

"It is painful, but we may leave for small periods of time, provided we are serving our oath, which is to protect and defend this household, and you are the head of the household. You have been attacked. We must protect you."

I gritted my teeth, my fists clenching. Stupid. Like I was going to hit him? He was made out of rock. Nor did I stamp my foot, even though it took a whole lot of willpower to stop myself. "No. I don't want to cause you more pain or force you to protect me when my aunt was the whole reason you're stuck here. It's wrong. It's evil and repulsive and disgusting. I don't want any part of it."

He looked down his snout at me, his eyes narrowing. "It is not your choice." His tone had gone from merely stony to arctic.

I tossed up my hands in exasperation. "Why the fuck not? You don't want to be my bodyguard and I'm telling you that you don't have to be."

"Even if our oaths did not compel us, we would guard you until the last one of us fell. You seek to free us. If you die, all hope is lost."

His stark words slammed me. He might as well have punched me in the chest. I couldn't catch my breath. I grabbed the back of a patio chair, swallowing down the boulder-sized knot of both anger and sadness that wanted to choke me. I felt two inches tall. I was a total dick.

I straightened, meeting his gaze. "I promise you that if I die, other people will still work to free you. The entire witching world is furious on your behalf. Someone will figure it out, even if I'm not in the picture."

"How about you call Mason and your mother and have them come here?" Jen suggested. "They can look at the deer and the stuff from that house. Kills two birds with one stone. Three if you count the fact that you'll be safe here."

"Yeah. Yeah, that's a good idea." I spun around and walked back into the house, my face flaming with embarrassment and guilt.

I called and both Mason and my mother agreed to meet at the mansion. When they asked why, I said we had a witchy kidnapping and murder, and a homicidal deer problem. That neither seemed inclined to ask more questions I found both odd and informative. What did it say about them that neither problem inspired curiosity?

Shaking my head, I went to tell Deirdre we were having guests. After that I retreated to the bathroom and scrubbed my face with cold water. I still felt slimy. I doubted a wire brush could scrape away my self-disgust.

I hated Aunty Mommy for all the things she'd done to me, but I hated her more for the harm she'd caused others. Especially the gargoyles. They'd been separated from their families for years, their mates imprisoned. They'd been humiliated and tormented. Now that the females were free, the males still couldn't go home. Who knew when they'd have the opportunity or if their mates would wait? And on top of that shit sundae, they still had to protect me and the house. In their shoes, I'd want to see me dead and the house razed to the ground.

"If I could, I'd kill you again, you fucked-up batshit-crazy bitch," I muttered. "You deserved so much worse than you got."

I found Jen waiting in the sunroom. She was practically dancing. When she saw me, she squealed and threw her arms around me.

"I got a text from Luke! Stacey's in her room. Surgery

went well. They'll keep her there for a day or so and then she should be good to go home. She'll be on crutches."

Staggering relief poured through me. The sudden shift from coiled tension made me feel giddy. I hugged her back.

"That deserves a celebration. Margaritas or sugar? I'm sure we can find some ice cream in the kitchen, if nothing else." Mostly because I bought some salted caramel ice cream once and ever since, it had become a stock item in the fridge, along with peanut butter and chocolate ice cream, and caramel macchiato.

"Why not both?"

"Let's go see what we can find." I looked through the bank of windows overlooking the broad patio. Torastan stood conferencing with several others. "Actually, go ahead and see what you can find. I'll catch up with you."

I went back outside and approached the group, setting a tentative hand on Torastan's arm. That's when I realized he was covered in a very fine fur, so velvety I'd thought it was skin. I'd never touched him before and wasn't sure whether doing so now was a horrible insult. Hopefully not. Even so, I drew my hand back quickly.

"I want to thank you and tell you how sorry I am that my aunt did this to you. Is there anything I can do that might make your predicament better? Anything at all?"

He seemed to think about it, then gave the tiniest shake of his head. "It cannot be done."

Not exactly a firm no. "What can't be done?"

"We would see our mates and our cubs. But our warren is far from here, and they would not come here where they were imprisoned."

"But.... haven't they've visited you? Since they got free?" To say I was appalled, horrified, and heartbroken for them would be an understatement.

"A few have brought news, but they do not stay."

He didn't have to say the separation was agonizing. His expression, stoic as it was, gave away his pain. He might be made of stone, but he felt the loss of his family deeply.

"I'm sorry." Least helpful thing possible to say, except maybe for: it is what it is. "If you think of anything I can do, please tell me."

I left him there and went back inside, my brain tumbling. I'd have to figure out a way to convince the females to visit. I promised myself I'd put that at the top of my to-do list after finding the kidnapped father and daugh-ter, and maybe figure out who'd attacked me.

Easy as making a pie without butter, flour, sugar, or an oven.

CHAPTER NINE

"You need to name this mausoleum," Jen said, spooning ice cream straight out of the gallon carton.

We sat on the front steps after the chef banished us from the kitchen. To be fair, he'd made us a pitcher of margaritas first. I was going to need his recipe. It tasted citrusy with the smoothest tequila I'd ever had. Ajax lay behind me, his head between our thighs.

"What brought that on?"

"You can't call it your home. It's anything but that. You can't call it the house—it's a mansion and a half plus and a ton of land. You could call it an estate, but that's pretentious as fuck. You need to be able to call it something, so give it a name. Like they do with English cottages or castles."

"How about Hellhouse? Devil's Crossing? Oh! Witch's Lair!"

"Aren't you going to turn it into a sanctuary? Those names don't match the concept. Might put people off, and you're going to want support, especially from the community."

I sipped my drink, thinking. Mason had suggested turning it into some kind of sanctuary. I liked the idea. A lot. I'd been talking to Lorraine about moving her vet practice over here and expanding so that we could create a refuge for all kinds of homeless animals, small and large, domestic and wild. It would protect the gargoyles, too, since if I did it right, it would be self-sufficient and completely independent so nobody could ever shut it down.

Having community support would help smooth the way with all the necessary permits and permissions, and Lorraine had already indicated she'd want to be more than a sanctuary. She wanted it to be a learning center and resource for other sanctuaries around the world. She was even talking about creating internships for vet students, animal conservationists, and generally for people who wanted to help animals.

I had more than enough money to fund everything she wanted. According to Damon and Mason, I had enough money to buy a small country. I'd also been thinking of buying up some of the land surrounding the place. The place. She was right. It needed a name.

"I could call it Home on the Range," I suggested to Jen. It was lame, but I was apparently sitting on my creative braincells.

She made a face and eyed me like I'd mixed mustard into my margarita. "Uh, no, you couldn't. I have sworn on all that's holy not to let you commit asinine idiocy while I'm alive."

I chuckled. "What would you suggest?"

"I don't know. Something with a little flair. Magic Kingdom, maybe."

"Disney would definitely object to that."

"Okay, what about No Paws Left Behind? Animal Empire? Furry Freedom? Bountiful Beasts? Oh, no! I've got it. S.O.S—Save Our Skins."

"Isn't that from *101 Dalmations*?"

"Hell if I know, but it's perfect and you know it."

I laughed. "Fine. It's perfect. You're a genius."

She preened. "Good of you to notice." She sipped her margarita and scooped up another spoonful of ice cream.

"Who do you think sent that deer after you?"

The question had been gnawing at me, but I didn't have any answers. "Too many possibilities to make a serious guess. I know my father is still after me. I get calls from him every other day. I'm running out of new ways to tell him to fuck off. And if Damon and everybody else is right, most of the witching world wants a go at my uterus. And that's a sentence I'd never thought I'd say."

Jen chuckled but kept her nose to the trail. "Who else?"

"Whoever can ensorcel a deer. Far as I know, that's only witches, but who knows what else is out there? Maybe there are other beings that can do it too. Maybe Voldemort is out to get me."

She shook her head with heavy solemnity. "Afraid he's out. He's into snakes."

"Okay, what about Sabrina? Or the creepy triplets from *Hocus Pocus*? Or Endora from *Bewitched*?"

"I'll check their alibis, thought to be fair, Endora was damned cool and Samantha was an idiot," Jen declared. "Now can you think of any other non-fictional people who might be out to get you *and* able put a spell on a deer? And are still alive," she tacked on after a moment.

"No, and that's the problem, isn't it? I never saw Garret coming. I had no idea who or what he was until he drugged me and tossed me into his car. We'd been friends for years. I am not the best judge of people. Anybody could be an enemy."

"You can't blame yourself. Sociopaths are chameleons," Jen said with a dismissive wave of her hand. "You had no idea that world existed or people like him. Now you do. You won't fall for that crap again."

"I hope not." If I was honest, wondering if I could be deceived like that again kept me up some nights. What if someone came for me and I couldn't protect the people I love? Or the people I'm responsible for? Or innocent bystanders?

One night I woke from a nightmare and put safety wards in the kitchen and on every water tap in and around the house. Just in case someone decided to use them to drug or poison me and everybody else.

I was starting to get paranoid and I didn't like it. I didn't want to live my life always looking over my shoulder or wondering where the next trap was. I didn't want to worry about the girls every time they were out of my sight. A tiny voice had been wondering all day if one of my enemies had attacked Stacey. Maybe the same one who sent the deer. Was I a danger to my best friends? My sisters of the heart?

The possibility crushed me. It also pissed me off. No way was I going to let someone come after them. That meant I was going to have to hunt my hunter and deal with them once and for all. I also needed to make sure the entire witching world knew better than to fuck with me and mine. What that would take, I had no idea, but it would have to be huge. Nuclear even.

"Looks like one of our guests has arrived," Jen said as

headlights turned into the drive. They paused at the gate-house before driving in. "Mason or your mom, do you think?"

"Depends on whether karma is for or against me." I glanced upward, sensing more than hearing a gargoyle coast through the air. I could barely see him.

"If she's for you?" Jen asked, following my gaze.

"Then Mason shows first."

"Looks like karma does not have your back," she said as my mother's gold Porsche convertible crunched across the gravel and parked.

"I figured that out when the deer tried to skewer me on its antlers."

I scooped up a spoonful of ice cream to fortify myself. Everything with my mother was awkward. I didn't trust her and I didn't know if I ever would. Nothing that had happened to me was her fault, but she looked so much like Aunty Mommy that I had a hard time separating the two. All the same, I needed to be polite.

She opened the door and got out. She moved like water, all grace and silk. Everything about her was elegant, from the top of her honey-blonde head to the white peeping-toe pumps she wore on her feet. Her flawless skin was tanned, her clothes so designer that they put Vogue to shame, and her jewelry was understated while screaming money.

Upon seeing us, her brows rose slightly. She put on a careful smile and walked over to join us. I should have stood up to greet her. Instead I scooted over to make room beside me. Ajax made a huffing sound and stretched out behind us. I scratched his neck apologetically.

"How is Stacey?" she asked before I could speak.

I was a little surprised she remembered Stacey's name. "She's out of surgery and should be fine once she heals up."

"If you like, I can help her."

I'll admit the offer surprised me and warmed my heart. I knew my mother had healing skills, but I hadn't expected her to offer them up for Stacey. I hadn't gotten around yet to the idea of asking her.

"Thank you. I'll see what she says."

The unfortunate part about magical healing was the doctors getting a hard-on wondering how it happened. On the other hand, it would put Stacey's bones back together good as new.

"Have a seat. We're still waiting on Mason." I didn't think she would. Not with those white pants.

She surprised me by settling into the space I'd made. Then again, she could magic dirt off her clothing, so not exactly an inconvenience. Imagine all the businesses witches could power with magic. A dry cleaner's, for instance. Set up some spells and instant cleaning. Or a cleaning service where a little wiggle of the nose cleans all the dirt out of a house. The possibilities were endless. Of course, that would put a whole lot of people out of work. Maintaining the spells could be exhausting too. Maybe to the point of depleting a witch entirely.

And then there were all the bad witch services that would likely crop up. Revenge on your boss services. Revenge on your cheating spouse. Criminal stuff. Terrorist stuff. War.

Plus, there'd be all kinds of dissatisfaction and depression when people didn't have a purpose. They'd probably start doing a lot of stupid shit like vandalism and self-harm. Better to do acts of kindness behind the scenes. Create something like the sanctuary we were planning and use the normal means of doing things most of the time, and magic for what we couldn't.

"Would you like a margarita?" I asked.

"Please. That sounds delicious."

"I'll get another glass," Jen offered and flitted away before I could grab hold of her.

"Mason should be here anytime now," I said pointlessly. She already knew that.

She nodded. "The gargoyles are keeping watch over you?"

I sighed. "I wish they wouldn't. It makes me feel like a slave master. It's gross."

I was pretty sure she wouldn't understand. Not given who she was and where she came from. Mason didn't even seem to think it was that big of a deal. He totally agreed that Aunty Mommy kidnapping their mates and blackmailing them to make the blood bond was pure evil, but when it came to them having to guard me, he said they might as well while they were forced to be here anyhow.

My mother didn't respond right away. Her brow furrowed and she chewed her bottom lip. It wasn't until Jen came back outside with two clean glasses that she responded.

"Your feelings are understandable and honestly I'm relieved that you do feel that way."

Say what now? I gave her a sharp look as Jen passed her a filled glass. My mother took it and swirled it a little.

"I know you don't trust me and I understand why," she said in a careful voice. "You've made a lot of assumptions based on what you know of witch politics and our approach to families and children. Understandable assumptions." She gave a humorless smile. "What you don't know is that I never wanted to be part of the contract system. I tried to run away, but my family forced me back. With the help of my elders in the family, Ethan raped me and got me pregnant."

She grimaced at my gasp and Jen's "Jesus fucking Christ."

"It was painless. I didn't even know it was happening at the time, so it wasn't a real rape."

Jen scoffed. "You can't believe that."

"It doesn't matter if it hurt or not. You didn't want it and they forced it on you. That's rape," I declared, fury knotting in my stomach. What sort of psychos did that to anyone, much less family? "Was Ethan aware you were unwilling?"

She shrugged. "I think it unlikely that he didn't know."

"Asshole," I muttered.

"He really had no more choice than I did. Anyway, if he didn't do it, someone else would have. Witch culture punishes those who don't participate in contract breeding." She paused. "Please don't tell Mason. He doesn't know how it happened, and as long as he doesn't, I can still imagine that he would have thought it wrong and defended me."

Hearing that was heartbreaking and honestly, my heart hurt for her. Here I'd been judging her, deciding that since she looked like Aunty Mommy, she must be just as cruel and vindictive, when. in reality, she'd been through hell, too. Though what it all had to do with how I felt about the gargoyle situation, I had no clue.

She drank from her margarita before continuing. "After you and your siblings were born, I was to be given a year to heal and then be forced into a new contract. The thought enraged me. I knew I had to pull myself out of the breeding pool, somehow. Running away hadn't worked."

She slid me a sideways glance. "Sooner or later they rope you in, willing or not."

I nodded. Warning received.

"What did you do?" Jen asked.

A sly smile. "I cursed myself."

"You did what?" Jen said.

I have to admit I had the same question. Plus, curses could be broken, so how had she avoided that? Her entire family would have been trying to break it.

"I went on a retreat to recover from the whole ordeal. I figured I could run away well before my new contract time and nobody would look for me until the year was up. By the time I had a plan and knew what to do, I had only four months left. I just had to escape my companion. They hadn't allowed me to leave alone. They pretended she wasn't a prison guard and said I needed her so I wouldn't get lonely." Air quotes around *lonely*.

"They decided to send a cousin. She was in her thirties and had fulfilled all her requisite contracts. And she was ready to have *fun*. We went to Las Vegas, Monte Carlo, the Riviera, the Mediterranean, Tahiti, New Zealand, Australia, the Bahamas. Everywhere we could play. My cousin—Juliana—couldn't get enough. Men and women fawned over her. We had no limits to what we could do. Drugs, alcohol, sex, gambling...anything and everything. We're witches, after all, and illness can be cured, and addiction can be eradicated. We would never run out of money, and unwanted pregnancies can evaporate just like that—" She snapped her fingers.

"After a while she met a wealthy Greek couple with an enormous yacht. They invited her to sail with them to Belize. She wanted me to come, but I told her I wanted to visit a man I'd recently met. He had a ranch in Canada. For weeks I had pretended to be head over heels for him. I told her that I had only a little over a month left before my next contract and I wanted to spend it with Justin. She agreed, believing I was committed to my fate and she wanted me to have that happiness before I went back. Little did she know."

She took another drink.

"What then?" I asked. "What about the curse?"

"The thing about magic is that it has rules and limits. It can cure a great many injuries and illnesses, but it cannot replace what is gone. I couldn't get pregnant if I didn't have a uterus. I had decided to get rid of mine."

"A hysterectomy," I said, nodding. "How does the curse come in?"

"Again, magic has its limits, and sometimes a witch has no skill for what she wants to do. It's difficult to influence a person's mind, and even more difficult to maintain it for any length of time. Few have the talent, knowledge, and training for it, so, I couldn't influence doctors to operate on me. They don't want to take out a healthy uterus because I might want to use it someday. Condescending, self-righteous bastards."

"You go, girl!" Jen said with a giggle.

I laughed, too. It was unexpected and fun to hear her my mother get angry and swear. I didn't know she had it in her.

"The only chance I had was to make them have to take it out. So, I cursed my uterus. Cut off the flow of blood to it and gangrene quickly set in. I turned septic. I was taken to the hospital and my uterus removed. I then was given massive hits of antibiotics. I almost died from it."

"That was fucking risky," I said because I'm the queen of obvious.

"I was ready to die," she confessed. "I refused to be used as an incubator ever again. The family never had any idea I brought it on myself and no one would ever think I'd put myself through that hell voluntarily. The sepsis ravaged my body. I was kept on a respirator for weeks. They induced a coma. By the time I was brought out of it, I could barely walk, my kidneys were failing, and my heart, lungs, and brain were damaged. I called my family and they took me home and I was healed. And I was utterly useless as a baby factory."

"Wow," Jen said, blowing out a long breath. "You're one badass bitch."

"Thank you. I consider that a compliment."

"Good, because it was," Jen said. She looked at me. "I see where you get your stubborn streak and death-before-submission attitude."

I did too. It was actually kind of nice learning more about my mother and seeing myself in her. I wondered what I got from my father. Hopefully not much. He was a complete and utter prick.

My mother gave me a cautious look. "I know what it's like to be used against your will. To be desperate for your freedom. It wasn't nearly as bad for me as you, but I do have some small idea of your suffering. I also know how much you hate the idea of being used for your body and treated like a broodmare. I will *not* let that happen to you."

Her lip curled and her eyes turned cold and she looked so much like her sister that I got chills. It was suicidal zealotry. Only for once it wasn't directed at me. It was to protect me, which I had to admit kind of short-circuited my brain. She was waiting for a response, though. I scraped together a few of my fractured wits, which lead me to another question.

"If it was so easy to track you down, why didn't somebody find me and your torture-loving sister?"

"Two reasons. The first is that she was better about hiding her tracks and becoming someone else. She cut every tie to every person, place, or thing that she cared about."

"And the second reason?"

"If nobody could find her, then Ethan couldn't take you and benefit from his manipulations and lies. Nobody wanted that. So, our family didn't really look."

Made sense. Except.... "He had every reason to come hunting us. He's supposed to come from one of the most powerful families and yet he didn't find us. So, either he wasn't trying all that hard, or—"

"Or my family and our allies worked to cover any tracks Adriane might have left," she said softly. "That's exactly what they did. They protected her, and you, or so they thought. None of us imagined how evil and dangerous she'd become."

"They didn't bother to find out either," Jen said. "You can't tell me there wasn't something wrong with her before she went on the run. Somebody had to have noticed her cutting up animals or enjoying other people's pain."

"She was older than I by a number of years and we were not raised together," my mother replied. "I did not know her very well. She watched over me during the pregnancy, but we didn't really talk much. I had horrible morning sickness and Ethan was always there comforting me. I thought he was nice. I imagined we were both in the same boat and he was as sorry as me to be trapped into contract breeding. Adriane was cold and I was grateful for his kindness."

"Except it was an act. He was just covering up what he was doing," I said. "Keeping me a secret from you and everybody else."

She flushed and stared intently into her drink. "I was a fool."

"You were desperate for some human kindness. None of this is on you."

Ethan had shown her care and kindness, things Elena had clearly not experienced. She'd been lonely and hurt and he'd made her feel better. Maybe even loved. She'd fallen for him. and he'd been manipulating her the entire time.

"I'm surprised you don't hate me," I said.

"You were his victim, too, and a victim of my sister's hatred. What you went through—"

Her hands tightened and I wondered if she was going to break the glass.

She took a breath and made herself relax. "I never imagined Adriane could be so ghastly, so.... Evil. She was truly evil. I should have tried to find you, but at the time, just thinking about you was a rusty knife in my soul." She sighed.

"I was so very angry and hurt at how Ethan had used me. I couldn't think about anything else. I hated myself for being so naïve and trusting him. I wanted to kill him and I wanted to kill myself. It wasn't long until they told me I had to do it all over again in a year and I stopped thinking about anything but escaping my fate. I wish I could have been stronger."

Jen snorted. "That's bull crap. You *were* strong. With all that they did, neither your family nor Ethan broke you, and then after that hellish experience, you found a way to get away. It took a lot of guts to put yourself through the kind of suffering you went through. You have every reason to be proud of yourself."

She shook her head. "It was selfish. I should have found Beck and saved her from my sister." She gave me a haunted look. "Even if Ethan had found us and taken you, you'd have been better off."

That gave me pause. Would I really have been better off? Maybe I wouldn't have been tortured, but I also wouldn't have known Jen, Lorraine, and Stacey. I would have had to be a baby factory. I wouldn't have become as independent and strong. I wouldn't have learned to stand up to bullies.

"I disagree," I said. "I may have hated Aunty Mommy and all that she did to me, but I wouldn't change things. I like who I am and I like my life. Given the same choices, I'd go through it again."

My mother stared at me in disbelief. "I can't believe that."

"Given a choice, would you curse yourself again? Or would you succumb to a breeding contract?"

Her forehead puckered. "It's not the same. You suffered *years*."

"Yeah but look what I have now. Three sisters of my heart. Damon. Ajax. Freedom. Mental and physical strength. A life I like. I wouldn't have had any of that without Aunty Mommy."

"It's too high a price to pay," she said. "Mason has told me about that torture room and the cage. I saw that wall. It's far too high a price."

"I can't argue that, but I'd rather pay it than lose what came from it."

"Since this argument is entirely academic, not to mention pointless, can we move on?" Jen asked. "Mason's here."

Headlights had appeared at the guard house and now moved up the driveway. I stood and stretched.

"Why don't you two go inside and I'll wait for Mason?"

Not terribly subtle, but I wanted a couple minutes alone with my uncle. Jen and my mother gathered up the glasses and pitcher and went inside. Ajax leaned against my leg.

Mason pulled up in a Cadillac Escalade. It still struck me as odd that he didn't have a chauffeur. Not because he needed one, but because he exuded old-world nobility, one that would never drive himself, never cook for himself, never do his own laundry, and quite possibly never hold his own dick to pee or wipe his own ass.

He was pretty well-put-together for his age. He stood around six foot two with a lanky build. His brown salt-and-pepper hair was combed straight back, revealing a receding hairline with a widow's peak and a largely unlined face with chiseled features. He was dressed in a finely woven tan wool shirt and Italian flannel pants.

He smiled when I approached, reaching out to give me an affectionate hug. "How is Stacey?"

I returned the gesture, though it still felt weird to hug anyone outside the girls, Damon, and Ajax. It felt weird to let my emotions hang out for anybody to see. Aunty Mommy liked to take advantage of that kind of weakness.

"She's out of surgery and her parents are with her." And her former and current stepparents, not to mention the huge array of siblings and cousins. The hospital wasn't prepared for her clan. Military bases weren't prepared for her clan. NATO wasn't prepared for them.

He stepped back and looked at me. "What's wrong?"

"You're here because of a witch-related murder and kidnapping and a murder deer. Aren't those enough?"

He shook his head, his frown deepening. "That's not it, though, is it? It's not Stacey either." He glanced at my mother's car. "Did something happen with Elena?"

I don't know if it annoyed me that he knew me well

enough to see my distress, or if I was pleased to have some family out there who cared enough to notice.

"She told me some things I didn't know."

"Like what?"

I gave a little shrug. "She told me about Ethan and that she didn't want the contract but couldn't say no."

He nodded. "The contract system doesn't care what anybody wants or doesn't want."

I crossed my arms, tapping my fingers on my bicep. "You know that this system is just people forcing other people to participate, right?"

I didn't wait for an answer, instead going straight to the heart of what I wanted to know. "How can you keep supporting such a crap system?"

"I don't."

"Do you speak out against it? Help the victims?"

He scratched his chin as he considered his response. If he had to think about it, then the answer was 'no.' I wasn't surprised, but something inside me wilted in disappointment. I chastised myself. Mason had been nothing but supportive since finding me. He might not have challenged the contract system, but he'd backed me up when I made it clear to the witching world that I wasn't going to be an incubator for anyone. That counted for a lot.

I was about to tell him never mind and get inside when he finally responded.

"I'm gay."

I blinked, my mouth dropping open. It took a moment for me to scrape together my wits. "You are? Does anybody know?"

He nodded. "I've never tried to hide it, but it became public knowledge when I started seeing another man. I'd just turned eighteen. Shortly after that, I participated in my first contract." He grimaced. "The pregnancy was a product of good old-fashioned conception."

"Fucking."

"Fucking," he agreed.

"Even though you were gay."

"Even though."

"Sounds like a nightmare."

He sighed. "It wasn't pleasant, but don't feel sorry for me. It's far more traumatic for women. They not only must be violated, but they must bear children they will never be able to care for and possibly won't see again."

"To answer your question, I have tried many times to move the mountain over the years with little success. The fear of the Siddiqui prophecy overwhelms any sense of personal rights."

"Bullshit," I said. "That's just an excuse to pursue power at all costs. Even if that prophecy comes true, so what? Ben told me that the threat is that the witches that got cursed will rise up and bring pain and destruction."

"In a nutshell, that is the case," Mason agreed.

"Well, the whole breeding program is dripping with pain and torture for most involved, plus it destroys their mental health. My actual mother came close to suiciding rather than being forced to go through it again. Anyway, it's just as likely that the whole breeding program is going to cause the fuckery that the prophecy predicts. Just because you're breeding super-witches doesn't mean that you'll escape it or win. The real purpose of this whole eugenics thing is power and it's fucked up."

Mason sighed, nodding. "I agree. We had an organization whose sole purpose was to hunt the cursed witches. After the prophecy, our people weren't content to let the curse kill them off naturally. The Cascadors were fanatical about their hunt.

It was—" He made a face. "Distasteful. I would compare them to the Spanish Inquisitors. They were very effective and left no stones unturned. I cannot imagine how anybody could escape them, and yet the Cehata—our ruling body—refused to concede that fact and promoted the contract program."

I chewed my lips. "I guess they could be right. If Aunty Mommy could hide, stands to reason others could, too."

"For a while, perhaps. Remember that Garret Hornsby eventually found her and killed her. Nobody can hide forever."

Unless they could. I didn't say it. I didn't want to be right on the subject since it would make the whole shit breeding project sound reasonable. "When did the Cascadors disband?"

"They never did, actually. They were absorbed by our Hedlue, which is the policing branch of our Gawarcheidad."

I blinked. "I'm sorry, your Gawarcheidad?"

He smiled. "Think of it as our version of Homeland security. It has a variety of sub-organizations that focus on specific areas of safety. For instance, the Hedlue pursues rogue witches. The Ement monitors magical objects and makes sure they don't fall into the wrong hands, the Saobra monitors trafficking in both humans and non-humans, including their physical parts. There are a few other agencies under the Gawarcheidad umbrella, as well."

"So, what you're saying is this group of Inquisitor types —the Cascadors—are probably somewhere deep inside a government basement sacrificing small animals and chanting around a cauldron of blood while wearing black hooded robes just waiting for the day they can pop out and burn these supposedly evil witches at the stake." I put *bad* in air-quotes.

"A bit melodramatic."

"You say that now, but wait until I tell you about the murder and kidnapping, not to mention the murder deer. Some witch or other magical entity is up to no good, and for all you know, it's one of those witches coming back from the dead."

"I rather doubt it," he said with a smile.

"Yeah? It wouldn't surprise me one bit. In fact, the way things have been going for me the last few months, I wouldn't be surprised if Jesus showed up in rhinestones and pink drag drinking a mai tai and riding a dinosaur after having converted to Hinduism."

"I'd enjoy seeing that."

"Not if he had the four horsemen with him," I said.

"Will they be in drag too?"

I glared at him. "I think you're missing the point."

His brows rose, clearly enjoying our conversation. If it could be called that. More like a rant-ersation.

"Which is?"

That I needed another margarita or ten and probably a bottle of Xanax.

"I don't trust your Gawarcheidad, I don't trust your Cascadors, and I sure as hell don't trust that prophecy. I'm not saying that witch was wrong about what she foresaw, but I'm pretty sure the bastards in power twisted everything to suit their own best interests and the rest of everybody didn't matter and still don't."

"You shouldn't trust them."

"Is that supposed to be a warning or are you kissing ass?"

"Neither. I'm just making an observation."

"Here's an observation for you. I don't trust them and I

hope I never have to meet them. Now let's go inside and figure out our current, actual problem."

"By all means. Let's do that before you develop another."

I snickered. "Now you've got the idea. Still thinking it's a good idea to hang around me?"

"I've never had a better one."

"Then you must have a shit IQ."

"On the contrary, I'm considered quite brilliant."

I snorted. "Then you might have a mental condition. No, you definitely have one."

"No, my dear. I have a most fascinating niece. I wouldn't turn my back on you for the world."

I didn't say anything, but I got a case of the warm fuzzies, and even a little misty-eyed. Maybe having family wasn't such a curse as I'd thought.

CHAPTER TEN

I led the way up the steps, Ajax trotting along beside me. I tangled my fingers in his ruff. Linus opened the door, looking so crisp in his uniform you'd never know he'd been on the job since early in the morning. I'd tried to tell him to stick to an eight-hour day, but he had selective hearing, just like Deirdre and the rest of the staff. I might be paying them, but I was certainly not the boss. They ran the place as they saw fit, occasionally making small concessions so that I would think I had some say in the household.

They'd accommodate anything I asked, so long as they approved, and they approved of taking care of me in the way they felt I required, which is to say I wasn't allowed to lift a finger on my own behalf. If they had their way, they'd probably wipe my ass, brush my teeth, and dress me.

I had declared my personal suite of rooms off-limits except for cleaning and enforced it with wards, though I couldn't bring myself to complain about the pot of coffee Deirdre sent up to me when I got up. I have no idea how she knew when I was out of bed, but she always did. Within minutes I would have a silver pot of piping hot coffee, plus fruit and pastries. When I came downstairs, breakfast would be waiting. Did I mention they also seemed to want to fatten me up like a harvest pig?

The truth was I did like the pampering, but I hated having servants. It felt pretentious and lazy. Not that I was against laziness as a rule, but people shouldn't have to pick up after me or feed me or do my laundry or scrub the soap scum out of my shower. Turns out I didn't have a choice. I could probably fire them all and they'd ignore me. That really should have made me feel better about them having to clean up my messes, but nope.

I was going to get the last laugh, though. They would all be getting giant raises and I intended to send the entire staff—both inside and out—and their families on an all-expenses-paid vacation. I planned to rent a small cruise ship and send them all around the Mediterranean, around Spain and up to France. I'd fire anybody who tried to say no. Of course, it wouldn't take, but I'd still do it.

We found my mother and Jen in one of the small salons. The same one where Garret had held me and Mason prisoner while he lay in wait to kill Ethan and my mother. Unfortunately for him, Damon and the girls showed up first and he decided they had to die, too. That's when I killed him, with a fair bit of damage to myself. I thought of Mikey and him commenting on me being danger prone. Damage prone. Suicidal even. Asswipe.

Jen had set the bag of stuff I'd brought from the house on the coffee table. She'd sat in an armchair. My mother perched on the couch. I took a spot at the other end and Ajax jumped up and curled up between us. Mason settled opposite on the loveseat.

Mason had lost his smile and now eyed me with a kind

of militant expectation. Like he was a general and I was a reporting corporal. "Please fill us in on your situation."

I decided not to salute or snap my heels together, and instead calmly recounted meeting Ballard and Jeffers at the hospital and Mikey's suggestion that they contact me. I then went over what I'd discovered.

"That's the stuff there," I said, gesturing toward the bag.

Mason opened it up, revealing the odd collection of items, still glowing pink from my spell. He eyed them but didn't touch.

"Can you get any information from them? Maybe figure out who's behind it?"

"Remove your spell," he said, before sitting back and crossing his legs. His brow creased and he tapped his fingers thoughtfully on his knee. "For future reference, it's good practice never to leave a spell active if it's not necessary, particularly if you haven't used a protective circle for casting. Any witch can use it to reach out to you in a variety of unpleasant ways."

Oops. I hadn't considered that. Not that I really knew much about how magic worked or what witches could or couldn't do with it. I filed the information away and did as told. I'd have to go back to the house and take it off there. The neon pink faded, leaving the room feeling dim despite the more than adequate lighting.

"Maybe that's why murder deer came looking for you," Jen suggested.

I cast her a quelling look. Not that she was wrong, but my stupidity really wasn't in question and I really didn't need her to underline it with a neon highlighter. She grinned and waved at me. I flipped her off and grinned back.

"Now what?" I asked Mason.

My mother answered. "Discovering a spell's caster isn't easy and often doesn't work. Because you layered over it with your discovery spell, it likely isn't possible."

"We'll try," Mason said. "But Elena is correct. Don't get your hopes up." He glanced at his sister. "I think an overlay is the best method, don't you?"

"Interwoven would work better."

His eyes widened. "You're willing to do that?"

She gave a barely perceptible shrug. "The cause is good."

"Care to give the Wikipedia version of this conversation for the cheap seats?" Jen asked.

"I second that motion," I said.

"Interwoven spells are cooperative," my mother explained. "Overlay are not."

"Which means?" Jen prompted when nothing else was forthcoming.

Mason took the reins. "When interweaving spells, you leave yourself vulnerable to your partner. He could do great damage to you, steal some or all of your essence, and even enslave you. At the very least you end up crippled in unimaginable ways."

"Scary." I looked at my mother. "Does that mean you trust Mason?"

She swallowed and I could tell that she didn't really. After all she'd been through at the hands of her family, I couldn't blame her. Hell, I'm not sure I'd be willing to take that big of a risk on him.

"You can't defend yourself while doing this inter-weaving thing?" Jen asked, giving my mother a chance to collect herself.

"You can," Mason replied. "But if you do, your spell will

be no more effective than had you chosen to go the overlay route. Interwoven spells require trust and vulnerability to your partner. You shouldn't do it if you have any doubts of your safety."

"Go big or go home," I murmured. I looked at my mother. "Why would you risk it? You don't know the victims. They're complete strangers to you."

"You don't know them either," she said. "But you will help them anyway."

"*I'm* not risking my soul for them," I countered.

"But you totally would," Jen pointed out.

I glared.

"What? You can bullshit them, but you can't bullshit me. There's nothing you wouldn't risk and you know it. You have no sense of self- preservation when innocent lives are on the line, especially animals and children. And women," she tacked on.

"We'll have to agree to disagree," I said loftily.

"As long as we agree I'm right."

I flipped her off again and she laughed.

"I haven't trusted anyone in a very long time," my mother said suddenly. "I have lived isolated and alone and I'd like to change that. I trust you," she said to me.

I drew back. "Why would you do that? You barely know me."

"Because you nearly killed yourself to save the female gargoyles and took nothing in return. Because you have good friends who would protect you from witches knowing they could not win. Because you don't suffer idiots and you don't want anything from any of us. Because you won't sell your soul, but you'll give it away for those in need."

"Oh, please. You'd better get your head checked. I'm told it was very stupid to rescue the female gargoyles the way that I did. Likewise, I have idiotic friends who don't have the brains to get a better class of friend. Idiots deserve whatever they get so long as it's a kick in the ass, and what do any of you people have that I could possibly want?"

"Power."

"Yeah, the power to scare the piss out of people. No thanks."

She smiled satisfaction. "You see?"

I made a face. "You know there's a good mental hospital here. I'm sure you could get admitted tonight."

Jen threw a pillow at me. "Shut up, Beck. Take the compliment already. You know she's not wrong or crazy. You're about as dependable as the sun coming up every day."

"Agreed," Mason said. "Looks like you're outvoted."

He turned to my mother. "Are you certain you want to do this?"

"Do I strike you as a simpleton who doesn't know her own mind?"

"Ouch," Jen said. "I didn't even see her slip the knife in. Do you need a doctor, Mason? How bad are you bleeding?"

"I'm not sure I've ever heard simpleton used in a sentence before," I mused. "It really should be used more."

"Focus, Beck," Jen said, snapping her fingers.

"What do you need for your spells? How can I help?"

"First we need to figure out a plan of attack," Mason said, and then proceeded to do just that.

I understood about a quarter of what they talked about. There was a whole other language for witch symbols, kind of like kanji or hieroglyphs, and a whole other one for how to build spells and what each bit did. It reminded me of building a car. You've got to attach the piston to the cam shaft and that turns and moves the ankle bone and that connects to a set of pulleys, which integrate with a toilet brush, which ties into the motherboard and sends electrical pulses through the magnetic field causing a collision between the Romulans and a swarm of wasps, which in turn releases graham cracker particles that accelerate and cause a switch to flip on Mars and that drops the basket over the mouse.

Easy peasy. I was really going to have to work harder to learn some of this. Damon was supposed to teach me, but with him out of town, maybe I could have my mother or Mason start with some basics.

Amazingly, that sentence didn't freak me out as much as it would have an hour ago. Listening to my mother's story plus her rationale for participating in doing the spell this way gave me a lot more confidence in her motivations. That and I understood longing for family and friends you could trust and who would have your back rather than stab you in it.

She and I were more alike than I'd thought. Or had wanted to think.

"What do we do while they do—" Jen circled her hand at Mason and my mother who didn't look up. "Talk about the latest fashions?"

"Who do you suppose would want to kill one husband and kidnap the other and the daughter?"

"Jealous lover?" Jen suggested.

"Ballard and Jeffers didn't seem to think so."

Jen shrugged. "They could be wrong. Maybe the guy is good at covering up for himself."

I eyed her. "Could be a woman."

"True, but she'd have had to wrestle with a grown man and two children."

I scoffed. "She's a witch, so that wouldn't have slowed her down one bit."

"Fair enough. So okay, a lover of any gender is one option. Who else?"

I pondered. "Maybe one of them fucked somebody over and this is about revenge. But then why go through with the kidnapping? Why not just kill the loved ones and make their enemy watch and then maybe kill him too? Can't be ransom. The kidnapper killed the person who might've paid out."

"Maybe they were taken because the kidnapper wanted them for something."

"Okay, but for what?"

"No clue, but you know better than I do that there are psycho-freaks in the world who enjoy hurting others. Maybe it's another one of those. Plus the witching world seems to have more than their fair share, if Aunty Mommy, your sperm donor, and Garrett are anything to go by."

I scratched Ajax's ruff and then his stomach when he rolled onto his back. "I can't argue that."

"Whatever reason the fucker took them, I hope he hasn't killed them," she said.

"Or worse," I said. I had a lot of experience with "or worse" and the only reason I hadn't committed suicide was a really nasty case of pigheaded defiance.

"Or worse," Jen agreed and we both fell silent.

CHAPTER ELEVEN

It took Mason and my mother about two hours to prepare. They'd asked for plain white paper and had cut it carefully into strips, then written pieces of the spells onto each. It was like reading really complicated math equations with extra swirls and flourishes. They tried to explain some of it, but mostly it went right over my head.

"How many symbols in spellcraft are there?" I asked.

"Impossible to say." Mason carefully touched up some of the figures he'd drawn. "Many of these I'm using are specific to our family. Over the years combinations get tried and new symbols are created. Each family has a library of spells and symbols and studies of magic to record success and failures. They're as closely guarded as nuclear launch codes."

"You won't get access to ours unless you officially accept your role in the family," my mother said, her lip curling at the idea. "Since that is as likely to happen as Ethan giving up on claiming you, Mason and I will teach you all we can," she said, directing a meaningful look at Mason. "You're *our* family after all."

"I'm sure Damon will teach you what he knows as well," Mason added. He glanced up at me. "There will be many who will not be happy for you to be taught these. It'll put a target on your back. Damon's too."

"What's one more?" I asked, rolling my eyes.

"Maybe you should start writing your own stuff down," Jen suggested. "At least the basics. Start writing your own books."

"There are many books covering the basics of witchcraft and spells," my mother said. "Even a couple of websites, though they can be fiddly. Magic—even if it's just being written about—doesn't always play well with electronics." She'd finished checking her work and stretched. "It's the more advanced magical knowledge that is controlled. And you're right. We should start writing them down."

She'd written her spells in red ink and Mason had used blue. She shoved the strips of hers over to him to examine while she looked over his. When both were satisfied, they started layering the strips in a complex pattern, weaving them together and holding them in place with tape. The last bit surprised me since they'd been careful to use paper with no other marks.

"The tape won't interfere?"

Mason shook his head. "Not as long as we're careful how we place it."

By the time they were done, it looked like a craft project created by a dozen blind and hyperactive fifth graders. It had a glorious nonsense and energy to it that reminded me of a Salvador Dalí painting.

"What now?" I asked.

"We each invest it with energy," my mother said.

"Meaning you flip the on switch," Jen said.

Mason smiled. "That too."

"Then what happens? Now that the spell is created, could anybody use it?"

My mother shook her head. "Some spells maybe, but not this one."

"Why not?"

"We didn't want any intrusions or interference, especially given how vulnerable we will be in the casting. We essentially locked it to our own magical DNA. For anybody else, the spell might as well be a rock."

"Okay, so what exactly is it going to do?"

It was Mason's turn to answer. "We'll be basically attempting to triangulate, focusing on where the spells were cast. You need to manage your expectations, however. It's possible the person cast the spells near to the house or even inside, in which case, we won't be able to track them beyond that. Additionally, if the spell residue is too old or made to quickly disperse, there may be little left to follow. And of course, your own magic casting may interfere. It's quite possible we may get nothing useful from our efforts."

I chewed my lower lip. "Hardly seems worth it."

"It will be if we get a hint of the kidnapper's whereabouts," Mason assured me. "I wouldn't try if we didn't have some hope of success. Now you, Jen, and Ajax should stand back. We'll establish a ward circle to contain any problems that might arise."

He shooed us back toward the door and went to work.

"What kind of problems do you think he's talking about?" Jen asked, propping her shoulder against the wall as she watched the two witches work. "An outbreak of giant earthworms? A sharknado? Quicksand?"

I shrugged. "Giant earwigs, would be my guess. With rabid koala bears riding on their backs bleeding from their eyes."

"I'll be seeing that in my nightmares tonight."

"Glad I could help."

"Don't be smug. I can give you nightmares too."

That deserved the eye roll I gave it. "Sure you can."

Her eyes narrowed and a smile that should have worried me curved her lips. "Is that a challenge? Okay, let's see here. Picture this...Aunty Mommy's dildo drawer—"

Ew! I should have known she would go there. I held up my hands. "Okay, you can stop. I surrender."

"Oh, come on. You've got a stronger stomach than that."

"No, I don't. You've scarred me for life with four little words and I will not forgive you."

"I didn't even get to the part about the tampons, the pineapple, the oil, and the pony."

"That's it. I'm cursing you. You're going to have horrible body odor."

She snorted. "You, Stacey, and Lorraine will love that when we're taking a road trip."

I wrinkled my nose. "Good point. I don't want you giving us crabs or lice, so that rules those out. How about a never-ending yeast infection?"

"You're being a sore loser. You're the one who threw down the challenge. You should be cursing your own sugar box."

"Sugar box?" I echoed incredulously.

"I could have said pussy, but we're in polite company."

I snickered "Yet you said it anyway."

"We're ready," Mason said, ending our very important conversation.

"And not all *that* polite," my mother added.

"That's good," Jen said. "I'd hate to be responsible for corrupting you."

"Far too late for that, I'm afraid."

"All right then," Mason said, rubbing his hands together. "Let's get started. Beck, Jen, both of you need to stay outside the wards and make sure nobody crosses. While active, they'll kill anybody who tries."

"A little extreme, isn't it?" I asked.

"Not really. We will be incredibly vulnerable both physically and magically. These wards will guarantee our safety, even if the attack comes from afar. It will also protect you if anything goes awry."

"I'd like to know how to do a protective circle like that. It could come in handy," I said.

"Any time you want, I'll teach you," he said.

"I'm better at them," my mother said. "If you want to learn from the best."

"I hate to say it, but it's true," Mason conceded. "But I know a hell of a lot more."

My mother's brows arched. "Is that what you think?"

"I know it."

"I bet you knew Santa Claus existed too," I said. "Right up until you didn't."

"What are you talking about? Of course he exists."

The look he turned on me was both shocked and utterly serious. Doubt stirred.

I looked at my mother. "Please tell me he's joking."

Her mouth quirked. "Oh, no. He's perfectly serious. He named his favorite goat Santa Claus when he was a child and has continued the habit until now. His current Santa Claus is six years old, I think."

I blinked, trying to wrap my brain around this news. "Mason has goats."

"I breed the finest cashmere goats in the world," he clarified. "I also have dairy goats and meat goats."

My mother snorted. "That's true, but what's also true is that Santa has the run of your house. He's a not a dairy goat, a meat goat, or a wool goat. He's a pet and as spoiled as they come."

I looked at Jen. "Mason has a pet goat. Does that make it a lap goat? Does he sleep with Santa? Take him for walks? Let him up on all the furniture? I have so many questions."

"They can keep," Mason said. "Right now, we have work to do." He looked at my mother. "Are you ready?"

"Of course."

He held out his hand and took hers. "Let's begin."

CHAPTER TWELVE

I pushed Ajax out of the room. Jen and I stood in front of the door to keep him from sneaking in. I doubted he'd go jumping into the warded circle, but I wasn't taking any chances.

Mason and my mother knelt on opposite sides of the coffee table with the taped-together spell on top of the pile of stuff I'd taken from the murder house. Mason placed his hands on either side, palms down, and my mother followed suit, placing hers on top of his.

Magic burgeoned in the room. It stayed inside the wards, but I could feel its increasing intensity. A greenish-brown light sheathed their hands. It intensified, then spilled over onto the pile of stuff, then spread over the spell. The light chased along the strips and the whole thing rose off the table. It expanded and lengthened into something resembling a mobile some sixth grader made in art class.

The magic split apart into streams of red and green. Both shot outward through the ceiling. That was pretty much the whole thing. The paper spell remained frozen in air and the only way we knew Mason and my mother were still alive was that they didn't stop breathing. Other than that, they stared glassy-eyed at one another.

"Exciting," Jen said. "Even better than picking lint off my clothes."

"I told you to get a better hobby, but no. You had to go for the lint-picking world cup. Disappointing you didn't make the finals."

"And now I've aged out. No lint-picking trophies for me."

"You'll have to find a new hobby then. Maybe competitive pig wrestling."

"I was thinking goat yoga. Think your uncle will let me borrow a few?"

"Doubt it. He sounded pretty possessive. Anyway, where would keep them?"

"I've got an extra bedroom."

"That's your lair. I don't think it's safe for them. They might trip one of your booby traps."

"Goats are smart. Anyway, they wouldn't do it more than once." Jen slid a glance at me. "Then we could have a barbecue."

I made a face. "Mason might turn you into a goat to replace it."

"Fair." Jen was silent a moment. "You ever wonder what it would be like to change your shape?"

"Like turn into a werewolf or something?"

She lifted a shoulder. "Or something."

"What would want to turn into? Not a goat."

"An eagle maybe," she said after a moment. "Be cool to fly."

"What about a dragon? Or a pegasus? They fly."

"They don't even exist."

"Neither do were-beasts or shapeshifters. We're talking

impossibilities here, so why not go for the big fairy tale?" A totally reasonable point, I thought.

"How do you know?" Jen asked, tipping her head to the side as she looked at me.

"How do I know what?"

"That were-beasts and shapeshifters don't exist? Witches and gargoyles do. Is it such a leap to think other magical beings do? Legends and stories have to come from somewhere."

"Well if they do, then why not choose a dragon or a pegasus?" I was nothing if not tenacious.

"Too dangerous. Nobody thinks eagles are unusual, but someone sees a dragon and they're calling in the fighter jets and RPGs. I'd like to enjoy my flights in peace and quiet, thank you very much."

"You could be a buzzard."

"I don't look good bald, and anyway, I hate raw intestines. Especially when it's been sitting out in the sun too long."

I tapped my lips with a finger, pretending to ponder. "What's too long for carrion? Before maggots? After?"

"Good question. You can ask the next were-buzzard you meet. Careful not to get too close, though. They'll probably have shit breath, not to mention serious body odor if they forgot to clean up after having their head in a dead deer's gut."

"He could be a billionaire bad boy, though, with eight-pack abs and an ass that would make gods weep, if any of the romance novels are correct, so that might make it all worth it," I suggested.

"We'll introduce him to Luke. *He* doesn't care what his lovers smell like as long as they're pretty and give good head."

Jen had a good point, but... "What if he sucks at blow jobs? Pun intended."

"Luke will give him lessons, even if it means billionaire-buzzard-boy has to suck him hundreds of times to get it right."

"Hope billionaire-buzzard boy is a quick learner, or his knees are going to hurt. And Luke... I wonder if chapped dick is a thing?"

I didn't get an answer. The paper spell burst into flame, ashes floating through the air. Both Mason and my mother sat back on their heels. Something shuddered through the air.

"It's safe. The wards are down," my mother said.

"Did you get anything useful?" he asked her.

"We'll have to see." My mother looked at me. "Do you have a map handy?"

Since I doubted Google Maps was what she had in mind, I went to ask Deirdre. She found a handful of city, county, and state maps and I returned with them. By this time, the ashes had been cleared. I handed my mother the maps.

She spread one on the coffee table. The items from the house had been returned to their bag. The map proved too big for the table, so we moved it aside so she could spread it flat on the floor. She unfolded the others and looked each over before folding them back up.

The one she'd selected was of the city and its surroundings. "I'll start with this one."

"What are you going to do?" I asked.

"Try to pinpoint where the magic came from."

I frowned. "Isn't that what that last spell was about?"

Mason replied this time. "We need to refine the information if we're to get any use from it."

When he realized I hadn't comprehended the answer, he humored me with a more detailed explanation.

"Elena and I followed the trail back to the house. That was simple enough. That gave us a second triangulation point, with this house being the first. After that, things get a lot fuzzier. I provided an anchor while Elena sought the source of the magic."

"Unfortunately, it's not a straightforward process," my mother said. "The witch didn't attempt to cover their tracks, which certainly helps, but boiled down, I can't tell if I was able to trace the magic back to where it the spells were cast. Mason and I will need to do a little more work. It's going to take a while." She scowled at the map.

"What's wrong?"

"Nothing. Not yet anyway. Just—"

"Just?" Mason prompted.

She shook her head. "It's nothing. I'm probably just tired."

"What's nothing?" Mason demanded.

"It's just a feeling like something's off."

I frowned. "How off? I don't want you two risking yourselves."

She smiled and waved away my concern. "The risky part is done. This part is a little time- consuming, but easy. Don't pay any attention to me. I just have one of those itchy feelings something's not the way it should be, but it's probably a case of witch paranoia. That's a natural side-effect of growing up in our world, I'm afraid. You learn to be suspicious of everybody and everything."

"That sucks," Jen said. "Hell of a way to live."

"I can't argue." She hesitated. "I hope that can change for me."

"Sounds like you need your own family—mafia style."

She swiped a finger along her nose. "Make sure everybody knows those who fuck with you and yours end up dead or worse."

My mother considered. An unpleasant smile curved her lips and her eyes hardened. Not going to lie, the expression looked so much like Aunty Mommy I recoiled and took a step back.

"You might be on to something," she said to Jen and then looked at me.

"You never have to be afraid of me," she said. "I will always be in your corner. I know you don't believe it, but I will show you. Now, Mason, let's get to work and see what we can see."

As the two pored over the maps, Jen leaned against me, putting her head on my shoulder. "You've got your mother, Damon, Mason, and you. I bet Ben would come into your family fold too. You really could create a group—like a mafia family—that would be strong enough to protect every member who no longer wanted to be part of the business as usual of the witching world. I'm sure there are other unhappy witches who don't want to be part of the breeding economy."

I didn't answer, but the wheels had begun to turn.

CHAPTER THIRTEEN

Around one in the morning I sat in the middle of my bed with Ajax. Mason and my mother had worked late, narrowing down the location of the killer kidnapper to a small section of town full of ordinary houses built in the eighties. They couldn't narrow it down farther, probably because the place was warded and/or had deflector spells cast over it.

They'd gone home, planning to have a look at the buck the next day. Jen's sister had come and picked her up. She had a deadline tomorrow on a project and then she planned to see Stacey.

That left me alone on my bed staring at my phone. I wanted to call Damon but had bats careening through my stomach. *There's nothing different about this call*, I told myself. *So get your shit together, girl.*

I had no idea why I was so nervous. Maybe because I was getting really close to the *l*-word and that scared the piss out of me. Maybe because I wasn't convinced that after going back to his life, he'd want to return here to me. Especially since I had been dithering and he might have got tired of it and figured he had pretty good life back home.

Home.

Fuck, but I wanted him to call this town home. So maybe you should tell him. Stop worrying about being embarrassed or blowing it and just pick up the damned phone already.

I blew out a breath and hit the speed dial for him. It rang several times before he picked up.

"Pronto, Testarda."

I shivered at the rich rolling consonants and the warmth of his voice.

"Hi. What's that mean?" I repeated what Damon said, and by repeated I mean I butchered it like taking a chainsaw to a roasted chicken.

He laughed and said it again slower. *"Pronto* is the Italian version of hello, and *Testarda* means stubborn."

"You're calling me stubborn? Is that supposed to be a term of endearment? 'Cuz if it is, you've got an odd idea of romance."

He laughed again. "I miss you more every time I talk to you."

"Can't say I'm sorry to hear that." I really sucked at flirting. I probably should have said something like 'I'm counting the days until you come back,' or at least 'I miss you, too'."

"How are you?" I asked. "What time is it there?"

"Ten in the morning. I'm on my way out. Is everything all right? It's very late there." He sounded concerned.

I gave him the rundown of the day's and evening's events. "Tomorrow morning I plan to go see Stacey and then go back to the house to take off my spell. After that, I've got a couple of potential clients to meet and then I'll go out to that neighborhood where the spells came from and see if I can pinpoint the house."

"Not alone. Take Mason or your mother with you."

That comment both annoyed me and made me gooey inside. Damon had a protective streak and nobody in my life had ever wanted to keep me safe like he did. On the other hand, I could take care of myself just fine. I said so and added, "I'm not going to confront the kidnapper; I'm just going to figure out where he is and then we'll come up with a game plan for taking him out without risking his victims. If they're still alive."

He made a growling sound. "I'll remind you your so-called kidnapper is a murderer and a witch. Don't do anything without backup. Remember Garret and the mesmer dust he used to incapacitate you. This witch could spring a booby trap on you and nobody would know where you were. Promise me you won't go alone. Ajax doesn't count. Neither does anybody who's not a witch. *Capisce*?

"You sound like you stepped off the set of the Godfather," I said.

"It's the language I grew up with. It leaks through sometimes, especially when I'm back here in Italy." He sounded a little apologetic.

"I'm not complaining. Well, maybe I'd like you to find a better pet name for me."

"You're changing the subject. Are you going to promise me? This situation is dangerous. You need to be very careful."

I gave a one-shoulder shrug that he couldn't see. "I'll be fine.

He swore. "Beck—"

"How much longer are you staying there?" I hesitated,

then pushed the next words off my tongue. They shot out like they'd been launched. "I miss you."

When he replied, I could hear his wry amusement. "How much did it hurt to say that?"

"Maybe I shouldn't have if you're not going to appreciate it."

"I want to kiss you," he said, his voice husky.

"I don't think your tongue stretches that far." It occurred to me at that moment that maybe he was going for some encouragement rather than snark. "You haven't said when you're coming back." Not home. I still wasn't ready to quite believe that wherever I was was his home. I held my breath.

"I'm...not sure," he said slowly. "Things here are complicated."

That sounded a whole lot like a brush-off. Felt like it too. I was getting really tired of feeling that way. "Yeah, you keep saying that. Listen, I'd better get to bed. I've got to get up early. Good talking to you. Good night."

I hit the off button on my phone before my voice could crack. I blinked hard, trying to keep myself from crying. I looked up at the ceiling like I could keep them from overflowing that way. Swallowing was hard around the knot in my throat. I had to be getting close to my period to be this weepy. Whenever it showed up, I could count on going through a half dozen tissues while watching a Humane Society ad. Then I'd call and throw money at them.

My cell rang, starling me out of my misery. I stared at. Should I answer? Did I want to? Why couldn't I be calm and cool like Damon was? My bitch of an inner voice answered that. *Because you're more emotionally invested than him.* I sniffed, my brows furrowing. Did that mean I loved him?

My inner bitch cackled and pointed a finger at me like I

was an idiot. I squinched my eyes shut, like if I couldn't see anything, I wouldn't have to admit I'd fallen for Damon. *Yeah, 'cuz reality works that way.* Truth was I was fucked because now I was stuck with feelings that I didn't know what to do with. Mostly I wanted to run away and leave them far behind. My chest felt bruised.

This was why relationships sucked. Too much of feeling like you were having a heart attack or losing your mind.

My cell stopped ringing. And started again.

He wasn't going to stop. I needed to either put my phone on silent or act like a grown-ass adult and answer. I definitely didn't want to have a feelings conversation at the moment. I felt too exposed and embarrassed and hurt. I told him everything and he told me nothing at all. Things were complicated. What the fuck did that mean?

Flames of anger flickered to life inside me. I embraced it. This kind of emotion I knew what to do with.

I picked up my phone. "Hey." I made an audible yawn. "I've really got to hit the hay. It's been a long day." I patted myself on the proverbial back. I didn't sound remotely upset. I sounded perfectly calm and controlled. Go me.

"Don't do that," Damon said.

"Sleep?"

"Shut the door on me."

"What door?" He was the one shutting all the fucking doors.

He blew out an annoyed breath. "You know what I'm talking about. Don't go cold and distant."

"Is that what I'm doing? I can't see any reason I'd do that. Do you?"

I winced. Now I was getting into petty territory. I could feel myself withdrawing behind my protective walls and I wasn't sure I wanted to stop myself. I felt out of control, like

I was running on instinct without any interference from my brain. It was one thing when Aunty Mommy was torturing me. At least I knew myself and could focus on my hate for her. But this? I was in the deep end kicking and floundering like a blind cow having a seizure.

And Damon was calling me out on it.

"Games, Beck? I thought you were more honest than that."

Oh, now *that* pissed me off. I didn't even care if he was right. Or maybe that made it worse. Once again he knew more about me than I did about him, and he wondered why I wanted to slam a few doors.

"What do you want, Damon? I told you about my day and how things were going. I asked you about yours and you say 'it's complicated,' which even *I* know is code for 'none of your damned business.' But I'm the one playing games?"

He didn't immediately respond. I heard a woman's voice in the background. Probably a cousin twelve times removed. Or maybe one of a fifty sisters. Who knew? I sure didn't. Course that was the point.

"Dammit, Beck, I really can't get into it right now."

That's it? All he could come up with? How underwhelming. "Then I guess that brings me back to saying good night."

"Please don't."

I sighed. "I'm tired and starting to get a headache."

"Just—"

"Just what?"

"Be patient with me. Please."

I could hear the strain in his voice. Because of me? Or because of whatever he was dealing with half a world away? Fuck if I knew and that was the problem.

I considered, watching my fingers tapping on my knee. How long was I supposed to be patient for?

"I'm not known for my patience," I finally replied, trying to be understanding. Fake it 'til you make it, right?

He barked a humorless laugh. "Tell me something I don't know."

Okay, I deserved that. "You sound stressed."

"Yeah, well, this conversation isn't helping any."

I flinched. "Wow. I'm sorry. Didn't mean to burden you. I've got an idea. How about we just table all this until you come back? Then you don't have to even think about me and you can be all Zen."

He went quiet, and when he spoke, his voice was rusty steel. "Table all this? What the fuck does that mean?"

I lay back on the bed, knees bent, bare feet flat on the bed, my eyes fixed on the ceiling. I should keep my mouth shut. I was going to say something I'd regret and I just needed to swallow it down until we finished talking.

Except I'm really not good a shutting up and worse at self-preservation. I was on a runaway train with no brakes and no way off. This wasn't going to end well. "It means you've got a lot going on and I'm just causing you aggravation."

"So, what else is new?"

Yo, Ref! Call the foul! Unnecessary roughness!

Now I was mad. Frost crystalized on my words. "So, we table whatever this is we've got going and pick it up again when you've got less going on."

"Seriously? *That's* your solution? Jesus Christ, Beck! I'm so fucking tired of you pushing me away and blaming me for it," he snapped.

"Yeah? Well, *I'm* so fucking tired of you treating me like I'm a dimwit you barely know. You pat me on the head and say 'nothing to worry about' and 'it's complicated,' and I'm supposed to just eat that with a spoon and pretend I like it. The worst part was I *knew* falling in love with you was going to bite me in the ass and I was totally right. I'm going to bed. You go do whatever it is you do. I don't want to keep you. Good night."

I stabbed the off button, flicked the quiet button on the side and tossed the phone on my nightstand. Ajax wriggled up beside me and laid his head on my stomach, making a little whimpering sound as he nosed my hand. I stroked his head and scratched behind his ears, trying to figure out what had just happened. The only thing I knew for sure was things had gone badly and it was my fault. Damon probably had great reasons for keeping me in the dark. He'd also had my back through some dire situations. A reasonable woman would just trust him.

I groaned. "I'm such an idiot. An idiot on steroids, actually. I think Damon and I just broke up." I rolled my eyes at myself. We had to be together to break up and we hadn't gotten that far.

I sighed. "This romance crap is hard. I need an instruction book. Or a lobotomy. That might be better. Then I wouldn't feel like this. It *hurts*."

Ajax inched up closer. I flicked a string of magic and shut off the lights. I'd figure it out tomorrow. I really did have a headache now, like a bunch of tap dancers clacked in my skull. I turned on my side and snuggled Ajax. I totally wasn't thinking about Damon. Neither did I cry. I just had some eye sweat.

CHAPTER FOURTEEN

I woke up in the morning with a nose full of fluffy tail hair. Ajax lay sprawled, tail flopped across my mouth. I pushed it away and scrubbed my hands over my face to get rid of the tickle-itches his fur had left behind.

My head felt like sludge and my nose was stuffy. A dust bunny had died in my mouth. I'd slept fitfully, trying my best to not thinking of how I'd blown things up with Damon. Why couldn't I have kept my mouth shut? Why couldn't I just be patient for once?

I groaned and pushed myself out of bed. I found my phone and checked it. No missed calls.

My lungs collapsed and my stomach lurched. Bile burned up my throat and spilled onto my tongue. I swallowed it down. I typed a text. My finger hovered over the *Send* button. I deleted it. A text wasn't going to fix this, if it could be fixed. I needed to talk to the girls. They'd have some good ideas—right after they kicked my ass. Stacey would beat me with her IV pole.

I got dressed and headed downstairs. I stopped to let Ajax out. Or rather Linus put him out. I thanked him and headed toward the kitchen. I heard voices and walked in on Ballard, Jeffers, and Mikey having breakfast. Make yourself at home, why don't you?

Deirdre walked out carrying a pot of coffee.

"Don't you ever sleep? Or go home?"

She gave me an admonishing look. "Someone woke up on the wrong side of the bed. Sit and have some coffee before you stab someone."

"Are there knives on the table?"

"Butter knives. Do I need to remove them?"

"That would be rude to our uninvited guests," I said, casting a scathing look at the three invaders. "Anyway, there are lots of other implements of destruction."

"I'd tell you to be nice, but I'm well aware that cannot happen before coffee. Do try not to kill them, won't you?" Deirdre gave me one of her unreadable smiles, and retreated to the kitchen, undoubtedly to fix Ajax's breakfast.

I sat and poured coffee, doctoring it with cream and sugar, and ignored my unwelcome visitors. I grabbed the plate of bacon and dumped half of it on my plate, along with some eggs, potatoes, and fruit. I had a feeling I wasn't going to get a lunch.

Jeffers cleared his throat. "Uh, we wanted to check in with you about the case," he said.

"You could have called. Why is Sergeant Jizzwizard here?" I pointed my fork at Mikey who winced and gave me an impatient look.

"He knows more about...magic...than we do," Ballard said, obviously forcing the word out, her voice dropping low on the word.

"Next time dump him off a tall bridge before you get here, will you?"

"We'll take your request under advisement," she said dryly. "Have you learned anything since yesterday?"

"My mother and uncle managed to narrow down the kidnapper's location. It's across the river on the southeast side. They're sure the spells were cast from there but couldn't pinpoint an actual location."

"We'll push some patrols into the area and start doing a house to house," Ballard said, shoving back her plate. "Pull traffic cams and set up check points. Get drones going."

"And look for a house with a big red X on it?"

"Can't hurt to have eyes in the air," she said, dismissing me. "Anything else?"

I considered having them arrest Killer Bambi, but handcuffing the buck would be awkward, plus he wouldn't fit in their back seat. Anyhow Mason and my mother planned on returning later today to see if they could figure out who sent it. If only the woodwork wasn't crawling with my enemies. Cockroaches, every one.

Ballard pushed her plate away and stood. Jeffers followed suit, leaning in to gulp down his coffee and grab a fruit danish for the road.

"Let us know if you come up with anything else," Ballard said.

"What are you going to do when you find the kidnapper?" I asked. "I mean, you'll be taking a banana to a gunfight."

"What do you suggest?"

"You should take me with you. Or you could take my uncle or my mother. One of them might be better. They've got more skills than I do."

"Rather have you," Jeffers mumbled through his danish.

If I'd been more awake, I'd have been shocked. As it was, I was mildly startled. "Why?"

He swallowed and sucked his teeth before taking a mouthful of coffee. "You won't quit on us."

"Neither would they."

He shrugged. "Maybe, maybe not. But you? I've seen you. You could have been a helluva Marine."

"That's high praise," Ballard said. "Consider it a compliment."

"I do." I looked at him. "Thanks."

"Don't let it go to your head," he growled. "You're still a boil on my ass. And you can keep that magic crap away from me."

"That'll make it hard to keep you from getting fried or turned into toad."

He blanched. "That's impossible. Isn't it?"

I shrugged. "If you say so."

"Not reassuring."

"You're the one who told me to keep the magic crap away from you. Better hope your murderer is on the same page."

At that point Ajax trotted into kitchen. He stopped and looked at the rest of us and then at the kitchen doors. One opened and Deirdre let him inside where he would get a breakfast fit for a king and without annoying guests. Lucky dog. He'd probably get a massage along with it.

"We'll call you when we need you," Ballard said. "We'll get some eyes in that area and start canvassing."

"Try to pay attention for places where you decide not to go, for whatever reason," I said.

"What?" She looked confused, her eyes narrowing at me.

"I'm sure they'll have warded their location and maybe have turn-away types of spells to keep people out."

"How would that work?"

I shrugged. "Depends on the witch. You might suddenly be super scared and have to leave. You might suddenly need to pee really bad and have to go find a bathroom. Maybe you'll get hungry or thirsty or get a craving for deep dish pizza. Something in the spell will make you disinclined to return. If I were you, I'd split up on opposites sides of the street so only one of you gets caught in the trap and hopefully the other will notice what happened."

"How are we going to tell the patrol officers to keep track of shit like that? I fucking hate magic," Jeffers declared, folding his arms across his chest.

"I imagine that's what they said when they burned witches at the stake," Ballard said dryly. "Anything else we need to watch out for? Meteors? Dinosaurs? Flying monkeys?"

I pictured shock-stick-wielding flying monkeys chasing Jeffers and suddenly my mood lightened. "It takes concentration to make magic work for you. If you get too up close and personal, try to break the witch's focus, but I wouldn't count on being able to do it. Better if you can avoid a confrontation altogether." *Congratulations, Beck! You win the award for the ultimate obviousness.*

"Maybe we *should* take you with us," Ballard said.

"Can't. I've got a couple of meetings and I'm going by the hospital to see Stacey."

Something had started itching in my brain like I'd forgotten something. Did I have another appointment? I checked my phone calendar. Nothing. I'd put on underwear, so I hadn't forgotten that. Did I need to get something from the store? Call someone? Nothing clicked.

Annoyingly, the gnawing itch refused to let up. It was going to bug me all day, worse than getting ear-wormed with the Piña Colada song. I yanked my thoughts away.

Why why why did I think that? Just thinking the name could allow it to set its hooks and then I'd be suffering for days, maybe weeks. I shuddered. Talk about a nightmare.

I slurped more coffee because I obviously wasn't thinking clearly and needed more caffeine. I did not need a scalded tongue and throat. I refused to let anybody see my pain, so I swallowed slowly and reached for some ice water and sipped slowly, even though I wanted to pour the whole glass down my throat.

"You coming, Crowe?" Jeffers asked Mikey who hadn't yet got up from the table.

He tipped his head at me, then shook it and pushed himself up. "Yeah, I'm coming."

Ballard and Jeffers headed out.

Mikey paused to look at me. "Don't go looking for trouble on your own," he warned.

"Or what? You'll arrest me? Put me in handcuffs? Fair warning: that's not my kind of kink. I'm not into the whole bondage scene."

He flushed red. He's such a boy scout.

"Just try to be smart for once? So you'll still be around when Stacey gets out of the hospital." He walked out without giving me a chance to reply. I flipped him off anyhow. He was the dickwad who got me involved in this mess in the first place.

I finished breakfast, thanked the staff, collected my things and Ajax, and left. It wasn't until I got out on the road that I finally realized what had been itching at my brain.

I'd told Damon I was in love with him just before I hung up on him.

Fuck me.

It was all I could do not to bang my head on the headrest. Maybe it wasn't true. Maybe it was just one of those things that you say when you're pissed off. Except I was pretty sure I was in love with him. I had to be, because he hadn't called me back after my confession and now I just wanted to bury my head under my pillow and bawl my eyes out.

My chest clenched like a fist and I had to blink fast to keep the tears back. I did not need my mascara running down my face and turning me into a female version of Alice Cooper. I also didn't need to crash. I pulled over on the shoulder and rested my forehead on the wheel.

I'd told him I loved him and he hadn't cared. Or maybe he hadn't noticed. Maybe he hadn't actually heard me. Right. He'd heard every other word I said but conveniently missed those. Entirely believable. Likely, even.

I groaned.

Not a snowball's chance in hell he hadn't heard. So what? It didn't have to mean anything that he hadn't called me back. He could have had a sudden emergency. He could have gotten distracted by a hundred different things.

Maybe he just didn't care. Maybe I wasn't worth the angst.

Self-pity is not a good look. I told myself to pull up my big girl panties and quit whining. I had things to do and I'd figure out the situation later. Maybe the girls would have some good ideas.

I pulled back onto the road and headed toward town. Ajax stepped up onto the center console, his back feet on the back seat, and pawed my arm. I petted him and he licked my cheek before resting his head on my shoulder.

"It's a good thing you don't care how moody and bitchy I get," I told him "You love me no matter what."

He gave a little whuffle.

Since I had a little time, I decided to drive the river road into town. It isn't much farther, but it was windier and therefore a slower drive. The marine layer hung low but promised to burn off quickly. The day would be sunny and beautiful.

I'd just crested a hill and begun down the other side when an older model Camaro passed me. I admired it its sleek lines as it went by. It had just come out from a bend ahead when it lost control. It fishtailed and then spun around. Smoke came off the tires and the vehicle skidded off the side of the road and slammed into a tree. The passenger side caved in and I could hear the crunch of it through my rolled-down windows. Steam erupted from the hood and dust swirled up to block my view.

I slowed and pulled over, hitting my hazard lights before jumping out and running over to check the driver.

The car was too old for a shoulder-strap seatbelt or an air bag. The engine continued to run surprisingly smoothly. The passenger seat was twisted inward from the force of the impact, but it wasn't near as bad as it could have been. That Camaro was made of sterner stuff than newer cars.

The driver's window was rolled most of the way up. A woman sat dazed in the front seat. She appeared to be in her thirties. Blood dripped from her nose and one eye was already swelling, as was her lip. She must have hit her head on the window or steering wheel. Not surprising, given how close she sat to it.

"Are you okay?"

She didn't seem to hear me. I tried her door. Locked. My arm wouldn't fit through the window opening. I used a tendril of magic to pull up the lock and yanked the door open.

"Hey, are you okay? Can you hear me?" I touched her shoulder.

She started and turned to look at me, but her eyes didn't seem to focus. I waved a hand in front of her. "Hello? You've had a car accident. Are you okay? I'm going to switch the car off, okay?" I reached across her and twisted the key to off. The impact had already popped the shift into neutral territory.

Her eyes managed to focus. "I.... What happened?" She touched her fingers to her nose and lips and looked at her fingertips. "I'm bleeding."

"You had an accident. Your car went off the road."

"My head hurts."

"It looks like you banged it on the steering wheel. Come on. Let's get you out."

I unclipped her lap belt and helped her turn in her seat. Her breath caught and she moaned.

"Easy, now. Go slowly. I'm Beck. What's your name?"

"Angie. Angie Patterson."

"Okay, Angie. You're going to be okay. Can you stand?"

"I think so."

She leaned on me as she stood and then staggered and yelped as her ankle turned. She wore a mid-sized heel with jeans and a blue silk blouse, blood spotting down her breasts. Her glossy brown hair was caught up in an elegant chignon and she wore a two-carat solitaire diamond wedding ring.

I caught her. "Can you stand okay?"

She drew a breath in and let it out. "I think so. Yes. Thank you."

I let go of her and she remained upright. I glanced past her at the car. "You got lucky. What happened?"

Angie grimaced. "A deer jumped out in the road and I

swerved and lost control." She looked at her car. "I guess it could have been worse."

Another car slowed down and stopped. The window rolled down and the guy driving leaned over the seat to look out at us. "Is everything okay? Do you need help?"

"She seems to be fine," I said to him and then looked back at her. "I can take you to the hospital and call a tow truck if you like."

"Here's some tissue for your nose," the guy said, opening his glove box and extending a small box.

"Thanks." I pulled several out and handed them to her and she wiped at the blood on her face and pressed the tissue against her nose.

"I don't think I need a hospital," she said, sounding like she had a bad cold. "I just want to go home and wash up and put some ice on my face."

"I don't know. You might want to get an x-ray and make sure you didn't break any bones."

She shook her head and winced. "I'll go home and make an appointment with my doctor." She turned and looked at the wreck. She wilted visibly. "What do I do?"

The guy in the other car pulled up in front of the wreck and got out. He was in his forties with silvering hair, cargo shorts, and a navy button up shirt, and wearing flip-flops. He walked back and gave a low whistle.

"You wrapped that tree pretty good." He eyed Angie. "That eye looks bad."

She touched her fingertips to the swelling. "It's getting worse."

"You sure you don't want to go the hospital? I'm happy to take you," I said. "It's no problem."

"I don't want to spend hours in Emergency. I just want to go home and lie down." Tears welled and rolled down her cheeks, making trails through the blood. She sniffed and dabbed at them with her bloody tissue. "I'm so sorry. I never cry. I don't know what's the matter with me."

"You were in an accident," I told her. "Of course you're upset. It would be strange if you weren't."

She gave me a watery smile. "Thank you. I feel so stupid for crashing. I'm normally a good driver. I saw the deer and I reacted. I didn't even think."

"Should we call the cops?" the man asked. "Your insurance company might need the police report.

She sighed. "You're probably right."

"I can do that for you," he said, digging out his cell. "You want I should call you a tow truck, too?"

"If you don't mind."

He turned and walked back toward his car as he dialed.

"I know you're probably on your way somewhere," Angie said, giving me a diffident look. "And I know that this is going to sound strange, but would you mind staying with me until the police come?"

I hadn't planned on leaving, anyhow. The police would probably want to get my statement, and anyway, Angie looked scared and alone.

"No problem," I said. "Do you want to come sit in my car? I have a dog, but he's friendly."

She flicked a look at my car and gave a small shake of her head. "I'm okay."

She wasn't. She'd started to shake, no doubt a delayed reaction as her adrenaline subsided. She wrapped her arms around her stomach, balling her hands into fists. Her chin had begun to quiver.

"Come on," I said, leading her to the back of my car and popping up the hatch. Inside, Ajax hung his head over the seat, giving us a soulful look. Angie saw him and startled backward.

"Is that a wolf?" she whispered.

"He's a dog," I said, even though he probably was mostly wolf. "He won't hurt you. Here, put this around your shoulders. You're shivering."

I grabbed a folded bath towel off the stack I kept in the back. I used them to clean up Ajax when I took him to the river. I shook it out and wrapped it over her shoulders like a shawl. She clutched the ends, pulling the cloth tight around herself.

"Thank you."

"Have a seat," I said. "I think I have some water. Maybe we can clean your face up a little."

"That would be nice. I really can't thank you enough for your help—"

"Not a problem," I said, cutting her off. She didn't need to thank me for being a decent human being. "Is there anybody you need to call?"

She hesitated before shaking her head. "I don't want to worry my family. I'd rather go home and clean up first so they won't worry as much."

I nodded and grabbed a bottle of water out of the tote I kept in the back, along with a microfiber cloth. I dampened the cloth and offered it to Angie.

"Would you mind doing it for me?" she asked. "I can't see."

"Sure. Tell me if I hurt you."

I dabbed gently at the blood, trying to be careful around her swollen lip. Somehow some blood had managed to creep up around her eyes and forehead. She was shivering when I stepped back to check my handiwork.

"Thank you. You've been so kind to me."

"It's no problem. I'm just glad you weren't hurt worse."

The man from the other car approached. "Police are on their way and the wrecker said he'd be here within the hour."

After a little while, the man left as he was late for a meeting. I texted my first appointment and let them know what happened and asked to reschedule for the next day. Unless the police report and picking up the car took forever, I should easily make my second meeting.

The police showed up about twenty minutes later, took pictures and measurements, and interviewed me and Angie. A flatbed tow truck showed up soon after and as soon as the cops gave the okay, the driver —Brian— loaded the car onto the truck and chained it down. It didn't go willingly. One of the wheels had twisted and the vehicle no longer wanted to roll forward. His winch handled it pretty easily. When he was done, he handed both Angie and me a card.

"Pretty good bet your insurance company will total it out," he said. "I'll take it back to the yard. Have your insurance agent contact me."

"I will," Angie said. She'd gained back some color, though she held the towel tight around herself.

He gave a little salute and hopped back in his truck and drove off. A couple of minutes later, one of the cops came over with an e-tablet in her hand.

"We're finished here," she said. "Give me your email and I'll send you a copy of the report once it's finished."

Angie recited it. The officer typed it in.

"You sure you don't want to go to the hospital? You should get checked out. You never know about head injuries."

"I'm fine. I'll check in with my doctor tomorrow."

"Do you live alone? You'll want someone who can help you if you need it."

"I have a family," she said. "They'll take good care of me."

"Alright then. We'll be on our way. Here's my card if you need anything. I should be finished with my report by the day after tomorrow."

"Thank you. I'll keep an eye out for it."

"Sorry about your car. I'll send a copy to your insurance company, too. Give them a call as soon as you can."

"I will."

The cops took off, leaving Angie and me.

"If you're absolutely sure you don't want to go to the hospital—"

"I don't," she said quickly.

"Then I'll take you home."

I felt bad for her. She looked droopy, like she was on her last legs. She almost couldn't see past the swelling in her eye, and her lips had grown fatter. She looked like she'd taken a couple of hard punches to the face. I wouldn't be surprised if she'd broken her nose. All the same, I wouldn't have been in a hurry to get to the hospital, either.

She gave a nod and then winced. "Yes, please."

We loaded up in the car and started off.

"Tell me about your family," I said when the silence felt too thick. Small talk wasn't one of my skills. "Are you married? Have kids?"

"I'm engaged," she said and held out her hand so I could see the ring.

A large marquis-cut diamond sat in the middle surrounded by a starburst of baguette diamonds.

"Pretty. Do you have a date set?"

She pulled her hand back and admired her ring. "We're

thinking a December wedding. I'd go to the courthouse and get married tomorrow if I could. He wants a real wedding, though. He eloped for his first marriage and doesn't want to do that again. Plus my daughter wants to be a bridesmaid or flower girl. She's looking forward to picking out dresses and helping with all the rest. My son isn't as excited, but he wouldn't change clothes for a week if I let him. He thinks a suit will kill him." She started to chuckle and made whimpering sound and stopped. "Anyway, I don't want to disappoint my fiancé or daughter, so I am doing my best to be patient and wait for December."

She touched her swollen eye. "Just as well now that I look like a prizefighter. I wonder how long it will take for it all to heal?"

"I'm sure you'll look like yourself by your wedding day," I said. "Sadly it probably won't last long enough for you to dress up for Halloween."

Angie chuckled. "I don't know if I could pull off dressing up as Rocky."

"You are a little big for the role," I deadpanned.

She laughed. "Oh, ow! Don't make me laugh. My whole face shakes and aches."

"So, you're saying laughter isn't actually the best medicine?"

She pressed her hand to her mouth to keep the laughter in. "It appears not."

"A lot of people get that wrong, I guess."

"We'll have to notify the press. Get the word out."

I chuckled. Now that Angie had begun to get past the shock and fear of her accident, she was proving to be fun.

"What do you do for work?"

"I used to be a teacher, but...." She shrugged.

"But what?"

"Overworked and underpaid and a distinct lack of respect all the way around. I felt like I'd get punished for actually helping a student and punished for following the rules. There were never enough books or supplies and the classes kept getting bigger and bigger. It just poisoned the experience you know? I couldn't win for losing, so I quit."

I nodded. "I've heard that before. What do you do now?"

"I'm taking some classes and working freelancing. I write curriculum and do a little tutoring."

"What are you taking classes for?"

"Making jewelry. And computer stuff and accounting classes. I'd really like to make a business of making jewelry, but it's a long shot. I'll probably go back to teaching at some point, or I don't know, get my real estate license."

"Let me know when you have pieces to sell. I have an estate-sales business and a shop. I'm remodeling and putting in an area to feature local artists. I've got high-end clientele. Could help you develop some customers."

"You'd do that for me?" She asked, clearly startled.

"Sure, why not?"

She shook her head and looked out her window. "You're really nice."

I snorted. "Not really."

"You stopped to help a total stranger, stayed with me, and are giving me a ride home, and now you offer to showcase my jewelry. That's pretty much the definition of nice."

"Or stupid. What if you were a serial killer?"

"Because serial killers arrange accidents to lure their victims to their homes? I mean, I'm not that smart, but even if I were, crashing a car seems both expensive and risky. I'd think there would be better ways to get hold of a victim. What if I'd ended up in the hospital? Was I going to hunt you down in a backless gown? Getting the police there was part of my diabolical plan. I suppose this is where I should give a malevolent cartoon laugh, but I don't think my face can handle it."

"I'll pretend you did if it makes you feel better."

"Please do."

We chatted the rest of the way, me telling her about my estate sales business and about Stacey's accident. She told me she had three brothers. Her parents had divorced and her mother had moved to Gig Harbor and now lived with her girlfriend. Her father had a rotating cast of girlfriends and Angie couldn't keep up. Her brothers were older than she and none married, though the middle one had a boyfriend.

"I love them all," she said, "but I'm kind of the oddball. They live fast-paced glamorous lives and I'm just average."

"Except for the serial killer hobby," I said with a grin. "Or do you come from a family of killers?"

She snorted and pressed her hand to her cheek. "None of my brothers like the sight of blood, my father is too exhausted after all his sexcapades, and my mother cries at Hallmark commercials." She pondered, tapping a light finger against her chin. "Now my grandfather might be a closet serial killer. Probably retired, though. He's seventy-two."

"You never know. Some people love their jobs and work until they drop."

"He uses a cane."

"Probably has a sword hidden inside," I suggested.

Angie was silent a moment and then nodded. "Knowing my grandfather, that's a fair point."

"He sounds like an interesting man."

"He is. Probably more like the curse, though."

"You don't like him?"

She shrugged. "He's just got old-fashioned ideas about life and disapproves of mine."

"Why? Wait, are we back to you being a serial killer?" I grinned at her.

"He'd probably approve of me being a murderer," she said. "I'm too plain vanilla, I think."

"I've never heard of getting disapproval for being too ordinary," I mused.

"My grandfather is nothing if not surprising," she said dryly.

I got the impression she didn't want to talk about him anymore, so I dropped the subject. We were close to her home anyway, and our conversation shifted to instructions on where to go. She lived across the river and down in one of the older neighborhoods. Her house sat on a large lot surrounded by trees. It was an older house with a steeply pitched roof, a stone front sidewalk, and a froth of flowers running along the small front porch.

I pulled into the narrow driveway. It went past the house and stopped at what had probably once been a carriage house. It looked like it had been rebuilt to hold a modern car.

I shut the car off and rolled down the windows for Ajax. "Let me help you in."

"Oh, you don't have to do that," she said, but I could hear the pain in her voice.

Her head had to be pounding.

"I know I don't, but I'm doing it anyhow."

I went around to the passenger side and helped her out. She swayed and grasped my arm for balance.

"Why do I feel drunk?"

"Because you've been in a car accident, and I'm willing to bet you're hungry, too."

I held on to her as we walked across the thick grass to the cobblestone sidewalk. She struggled in her heels. She was a little more steady on the path, but the cobblestones were old and uneven.

"Will Ajax be all right?"

"The windows are down and he's in the shade. He'll be fine for a little bit. I won't be long. Is your fiancé home? And kids?"

"Kids are at school and my fiancé is at work. I'll get cleaned up before they get home."

The house was blue-gray with white trim. The front stairs and railing also gleamed white. The door was light blue with an ornate black screen door. Two enormous hanging baskets trailed flowers and vines to the porch. Pots of flowers added to the cacophony of color. A bistro table with a couple chairs sat in a little nook, and two scarlet Adirondack chairs sat on the opposite end of the porch.

"This is beautiful," I said. "It's so lush and welcoming. Makes me think of a fairytale."

"There you go being nice again," she said, but clearly was pleased at the compliment.

Angie fished out her keys and opened the screen door, which was really a steel security door, and then opened the front door.

"Please come in. You can use the restroom and I'll make you some coffee. I have blackberry pie, too. Picked them myself."

I did have to pee and the mention of it made the problem instantly acute. I went down the short hallway past the kitchen where Angie said the bathroom was the second door on the left. It was surprisingly modern with a freestanding tub set in a glass enclosure with marble countertops. It overlooked a patch of vigorous grape vines.

I did my business and washed up, before hunting Angie down in the kitchen. She'd cleaned the blood off her face, started a pot of coffee, and now held a bag of frozen peas wrapped in cheesecloth and against her face while rummaging one-handed for plates and forks.

"I really should go," I said, checking the time. "I have a meeting in an hour."

"Oh, please stay a few minutes. I want to do something to thank you for all your help. It would mean so much to me if you'd accept."

She was so earnest and hopeful that I caved like wet cardboard. "I guess I can stay a few minutes," I agreed after taking a few moments to think. "Can I help with anything?"

"Grab a couple of plates from that cupboard there and a couple forks. Put them on the table." She rummaged one-handed in the freezer and brought out a carton of French vanilla ice cream. She set it and the pie on the table. The latter was covered in plastic wrap with about a quarter of it missing. She grabbed a spatula and ice cream scooper. The coffee finished, but before she could grab the pot, I brought it to the table. She took two cups out of the cupboard.

A few minutes later I was eating some of the best pie I'd ever had the pleasure of introducing to my tongue, along with coffee. I'd dropped a spoonful of ice cream into the hot drink to give it a rich, creamy flavor.

"Good idea," Angie said, smiling as she followed suit.

I ate faster than she did. She took tiny bites and the entire process didn't seem to be particularly pleasant give her facial injuries.

She wrinkled her nose. "I think I have a loose tooth."

"Better than a broken face."

She sighed. "Too true." She sat back and watched me, once again applying the frozen peas to her face.

I finished and did not lick the plate, but it was a close thing. Angie was a really good baker.

"I'd better get going."

"You haven't finished your coffee." She looked down at her barely-touched slice of pie and pushed it away. "It hurts too much to eat."

"Do you want me to put it away for you?" I was starting to get itchy to leave and the coffee wasn't helping to perk up my drooping eyelids. The sugar from the pie hadn't kicked in yet either. I'd have to make a pitstop for a gallon of espresso on the way to my meeting. I'd have to hurry if I wanted to make it on time.

"Oh no, that's not necessary," Angie said as I reached for her plate. "I'll take care of it."

"Are you sure? Well, then I really should go."

"Of course. And thank you again for all your help. I can't tell you how grateful I am." Her brows winged down. "And how sorry."

"Sorry? I told you I'm happy to be able to help you. You don't have to be sorry."

"No, I'm not sorry about you helping me. You're really nice. Nicer than I'd thought you be."

I was really starting to have trouble keeping my eyes open. My head felt like it was stuffed full of sawdust and I was having a hard time focusing on her words.

"Nicer than...thought...?" I repeated, trying to piece together what she was telling me. My hands slipped from the table and my arms dangled at my sides. My head lolled and I could barely focus my eyes.

"I honestly never really thought you'd stop for me and

then you were so kind. I really do feel bad I have to repay you this way."

"What...?"

My eyes wouldn't open anymore and shadows blurred the edges of my mind. I was floating in a rolling sea of cotton candy. My stomach lurched. Bile coated my tongue. I couldn't organize my thoughts. They felt like the loose pieces of a puzzle.

I felt myself slewing to the side, then suddenly I was caught by a thick band. It fastened me to the back of the kitchen chair, pulling me upright. Unsupported, my head fell backward, leaving my mouth gaping.

"You see," Angie said, and I could hear her clearing the table. The sound came through a thick wall of gelatin, and it was hard to make my mind follow the words.

"I really didn't have any time to plan. Before yesterday, I had no idea you even existed. I panicked when you left that spell at Matthew's house. It was strong and I knew it wouldn't be long before you found us, so I had to find you first, which you made easy by leaving the spell active. Thanks for that.

"Anyhow, I managed to get close enough to your place and then connected with a buck and mind-rode him in to check you out. I'm good at using animals to explore. Color me surprised to find that you're guarded by gargoyles. I knew that even if I got through your wards, they'd protect you, or at least avenge you. Either way I wouldn't get out alive."

I was starting to hear colors. I fought the drugging effect of her spell. What she was saying was important. Why couldn't I move? Why wasn't I panicking?

Angie kept talking, but the words stretched and twisted like taffy. I was entranced by the sounds. I could see them floating in the skyscape of my mind. Pink bleeding into orange, yellow, purple, blue. Spinning. Collisions. Shapes. Whirling and dancing and a vibration deep into my bones.

I forgot who I was. I forgot *that* I was. I became nothing. Everything. Shiver on stone. Moss on light. Heat on song. Scrape on breath. Glitter shimmer wobble scream giggle flitter wallow fire. Shards and confetti swirling, fitting together, exploding apart, tumbling in a river of wild currents.

Pieces of me floated near one another and underneath the torrent of wildly gyrating thoughts, memories, and nonsense gathered a vast waiting stillness, seething in silence, dangerous and malevolent. A burst of me, like fireworks, like starlings in flight, swooping, rising, escaping. Sticky threads anchored all the sparks, unreeling like fishing line, never setting the hook, but never letting me go. It felt...not right, but...normal.

And then...nothing.

CHAPTER FIFTEEN

I had no idea how much time had passed since I'd scooted off into Hallucination Land. Coherence slowly coalesced, leaving me exhausted with a pounding headache. My head felt like it had taken a couple hits from a sledgehammer. Sound was muffled, like my entire skull was wrapped in a wet wool blanket. Too bad it wasn't wrapped around the rest of me. Shivers wracked me and my teeth chattered. I could feel the goosebumps prickling all over my skin, even in places I didn't know goosebumps could form. I mean, pubic goosebumps? How is that a thing? I think I had them inside my nose and armpits, too.

Noise filtered through, sounding more like the teacher in a Charlie Brown movie than actual speech. I concentrated but couldn't make out anything over the sound of my teeth clacking together.

I summoned my magic to warm myself and panic stampeded through me.

It was gone.

Gone.

Panic rolled through me and I screamed. Or tried.

Mostly I made a sound like a dying bat. I struggled to clear the fog from my brain. What had happened?

Angie.

She'd drugged me. And then....*took* my magic? Was that possible?

Duh. Mine had vanished and logic said the Easter Bunny hadn't hopped in and taken it. Angie was the only explanation.

Panic engulfed me again and I prayed to whatever gods might be listening that my atomizing trick would kick in and I'd be able to just turn into smoke and blow off to freedom. I held my breath, waiting for the moment when I'd suddenly make the shift. I'd never done it on purpose before, only when I was desperate or really pissed off. Since I was feeling both at the moment, I should have been able to do it.

Nothing happened. Zilch. Nada.

Terror turned electric, zapping through my brain like a lightning storm. I fought to squelch it. Fear only made me stupid. I needed to think. *Think, dammit!* There was a way out of this. A way to get my magic back. I just had to find it.

I snatched onto that idea, ignoring my inner toddler who was screaming that I was stuck forever. I also tried not to think about the fact that whatever shitstorm I was in the middle of, getting my magic back might be the least of my worries.

Angie really set up her accident just to kidnap me. My own damned fault, too, for leaving my spell active so she could find me. The only thing I could have done worse was leave my address and a note saying 'Dear Murderer, come kill me.' If and when I got out of this mess, Jen, Stacey, and Lorraine were going to be seriously pissed at me for being so careless. Not to mention Mason. And my mother. Ben, too. Probably Ballard and Jeffers and even Detective Scrotum. Damon, too, if he ever decided to talk to me again.

My heart pinched. When had I acquired so many people who cared about me? Up until a few months ago, all I'd had were the girls, and now I had actual family, other friends, and a boyfriend. And a dog.

Fuck! Where was Ajax?

My panic ratcheted up exponentially and I thought my heart might explode out of my chest. I almost couldn't believe that the power of my emotions didn't make me rocket straight through the roof, yet all I did was lie there like a discarded rag doll. My breathing didn't even speed up or grow uneven.

A couple tears managed to squeeze free of my eyes and I sent another prayer wafting away into the ether along with a curse if anything should happen to Ajax. I'd make someone pay if he got hurt...or worse. If only I could communicate with the gargoyles somehow. But if that was a thing, I didn't know how, and I even if I could, their binding would likely keep them from leaving the property.

I tried to focus on the positive. With any luck, Angie had forgotten about Ajax and left him in the car. *Oh shit. How long had I been conked out? How long had he been locked in the car?* I'd parked in the shade with the windows down, but the temperature was supposed to get above a hundred.

It's okay, I reassured myself. The windows were completely down and he could jump out at any time. Maybe he'd gone for help. *And not come in search of me.*

The possibility that he might have triggered more panic, but I forced it down. Fear couldn't help me. I needed to think. The only person who could rescue me was me.

I tried to remember what Angie had told me before I passed out. The only thing I knew for sure was she'd set up the accident to kidnap me. If she'd told me what she wanted, I didn't remember. I'd have guessed she wanted to find out what I knew and who I'd told. I was probably in for an interrogation, and after that, well, it couldn't be good for me.

Whatever her plans, I doubted I had much time before she inflicted them on me. I had to get on with escaping.

I struggled to open my eyes. My eyelids felt like cement. Finally, I managed to crack them. It took a minute for the blurriness to clear. I was sprawled stomach down on a floral couch, my head twisted to the side. My nose was about four inches from the back pillow. It smelled new.

I was still shivering like I was inside a freezer. Though urgency beat me with heavy chains, it took me another minute or two to lift myself enough to turn my head the other direction. I now faced a coffee table. Beyond that loomed a rock fireplace bracketed by bookshelves.

Two wingback chairs sat on either side. In one sat a girl with red-blonde hair. She was probably around ten. She had her legs curled up underneath her as she watched me. She held her arms tightly crossed. Shadows circled her eyes like she hadn't been sleeping all that well.

I stared back at her. Not that I had much choice. My mouth still wasn't answering my commands. If I could speak, maybe I could convince her to call the cops. Or an Uber. Hell, at this point I'd take Hannibal Lector.

The voices in the other room grew louder as if the speakers—Angie and a man by the sounds of it—were arguing.

The girl rolled her eyes and muttered something, then spoke more loudly. "I'll tell them you're awake."

With that, she unfolded herself from the chair and disappeared somewhere to the left. I didn't get to wonder who she was for very long. She said something to the others and a moment later all three trooped back in. The girl came back into view first and plopped back down in the chair. I noticed then that she'd chewed her nails to the quick. Her clothes looked oversized and too old for her, like maybe they belonged to somebody else.

A blanket cascaded over me, soft, thick, and heavy. It smelled like lemons and fabric softener.

"That should help you warm up."

My ungrateful-as-fuck kidnapper squatted in front of me so she could meet my gaze. The bruises and swelling from the accident had vanished. Either Angie had healed herself or all that had been fake. So much for doing good deeds. Next time someone crashed in front of me, I'd let them bleed to death.

She patted my shoulder.

"You'll warm up soon. The cold is a side effect of the charm I used on you. It makes you need my permission to do most anything beyond your autonomic nervous system. You know, heart, lungs, blinking...." She sighed. "Honestly it's really inconvenient to have to give you instructions, but it'll keep you alive and me safe, so I guess it's worth it."

I blinked at her. Inconvenient? *Inconvenient*? She turns me into her robot-slave and it's an inconvenience?

I snarled. "Fuck off, bitch." Finally, I could talk!

She sighed. "I suppose I deserve that."

"You deserve a fuck-ton more than that. I *helped* you." I struggled to get up in her face, but I'd used up all my strength.

She sighed unhappily. "I know, and I'm honestly sorry to have trapped you, but you really gave me no choice." Her voice turned brisk. "Anyway, you should be grateful. I haven't killed you, and with any luck, I won't have to."

"Careful, your inner psychopathic serial killer is showing."

"That's rude. I'm trying to be nice."

"Yeah, right. You put the ice in nice. *Nice* people like you are the same kind who tie kittens in bags and drop them into rivers."

She flinched and thrust to her feet. She drew a breath and let it out slowly. "Here's what you need to know: if you don't want to end up in agony, don't try to escape, call for help, or try to hurt me."

She held up a hand when I started to tell her to fuck off again. "Please trust me on this. I really don't want to see you suffer."

I snorted inwardly. She was in for a shock if she thought pain would stop me from picking my nose, much less escaping. I'd learned to handle pain from the best. Angie couldn't come up with anything worse to do to me than Aunty Mommy had already done.

Probably. Anyhow, if it came down to it, I was willing to risk it. Unfortunately, I knew pain could knock me cold and drop me like a sack of mud, which meant if I decided to attempt the pain route, it had to work or Angie would incapacitate me totally, and I doubted she'd go for tying me up. Maybe I should make that my last resort. Definitely should make that the last resort.

I took a breath and focused. "Why can't I move?"

"The combo of the drug I gave you and the charm. You should get your strength back soon now that you've woken up."

"And then what?"

She gave a little shrug and glanced toward the man she'd been arguing with. "We'll see."

Not comforting. Since my body wasn't working at the

moment, the best thing for me to do was to get all the information I could get.

"Who's the girl?"

"That's my daughter, Melissa."

Wait, what the fuck? Melissa? Like one of the missing twins from the murder? And Angie thought she was her daughter? Holy crap on a cracker. I was in more trouble than I thought. Here I'd been thinking the woman was a little unhinged, not a psychopath with a screw loose. Turns out she wasn't just batshit crazy, she had coked-up brain weasels chewing up her wires and running laps inside her skull.

"Your daughter," I repeated slowly.

"Yes. I also have a son, Toby. They are twins."

"I must have been out of it awhile for you to be *that* drunk."

She scowled. "What do you mean?"

She stamped her foot. Seriously. Stamped it.

"I mean, you killed their father and kidnapped them. That doesn't make you their mom."

"I *am* their mother."

"Saying it doesn't make it true." I really shouldn't be poking pins into her, but my mouth was on autopilot, as usual.

"Giving birth to them certainly does," she snapped back.

At my obvious shock, she knotted her fists on her hips and sneered.

"Didn't expect that, did you? Well, it's true. They *are* my biological kids."

"And after giving them away, ten years later you want them back?" I winced. *Do not poke pins into the unhinged psychopath, Beck.* Good advice. Too damned late.

Angie's face flushed and I think her eyes bulged. Her mouth twitched like she was looking for words. She must've found them. She pointed a finger at me, her hand shaking with fury.

"I thought you were nice and kind, but you're not. Maybe I'll be giving you what you deserve after all!"

A flash of phosphorescent light, a wallop like I'd been hit with a fifty-pound sack of sand, and that was all I knew.

CHAPTER SIXTEEN

When I woke up again, I was lying on my back and staring up at the ceiling. My head throbbed and so did the rest of me, down to my little toes. I think my toenails hurt. I groaned and rubbed my eyes. At least my arms were working again.

"Do you want some water? She said you might be thirsty."

I turned my head to look at the boy sitting at a card table that hadn't been there before. He'd begun putting together a jigsaw puzzle. He looked so much like Melissa that I figured he had to be Toby. Now that I knew he was Angie's biological kid, I could see the resemblance. His sister had vanished along with Angie and the man. Matthew Chapman, I presumed, though whether he was there of his own free will or not, I had no idea. Angie could easily have spelled him not to leave the same as she'd done to me.

"I would love water." I pushed myself up and turned to sit properly. My head whirled and I felt drunk. I closed my eyes and waited to settle before opening them again. "Are you Toby?"

The kid's eyes widened and he nodded. He grabbed a metal water bottle from a table at the end of the couch and passed it to me.

"Thanks." I unscrewed the cap and hesitated. "It's not drugged is it?"

He shrugged. "She didn't say it was." Then, "You made her mad."

"I noticed. Not unusual for me."

The water in the bottle was cold. I was too thirsty to care what might be in it and chugged it dry.

"Want more?"

I did, but then Angie might find out I was awake. First, I wanted information.

"Angie's your mom?"

Toby, who had tousled, auburn hair, wrinkled his nose and returned to his seat at the table. He started pushing around puzzle pieces.

"I guess."

"How long have you known?"

"Since..." He lifted his shoulders in a speaking shrug.

I wondered if he knew about his other dad being dead. What did he think he was doing here?

"Since?" I prompted, deciding not to mention the murder if he didn't.

"Coming here."

Gotta love kids. They have knack for not telling adults what we want to know.

"You like it here?"

Another shrug. I couldn't help snickering. Toby glanced at me.

"What?"

I shrugged and his eyes narrowed.

"You like Angie?"

"She's cool, I guess."

Not a ringing endorsement, but also not what you'd expect of a kidnapped child to say of their kidnapper.

"What happened?"

He lifted his gaze and gave me a measuring look. I recognized it. It was the kind that evaluated the risk of speaking up. What punishment might follow? It hit me then. Toby had been abused. I knew it down to the bottom of my throbbing feet.

My fingers tightened on the water bottle, but I kept my expression bland, waiting for him to decide if he wanted to tell me. Maybe I lifted an eyebrow just slightly in a silent dare. It worked.

"Dad was freaking out again. Melissa and me forgot to take the garbage can to the curb, and dinner burned when he was yelling. It was worser than normal."

He paused as if waiting for me to correct his grammar. Maybe it was a test. I didn't fall for it.

"Then what happened?"

"My other dad wasn't home yet. Dad started...doing his thing."

"Hitting you?" I guessed, deciding not to play coy. "That sucks."

A smile flickered across his lips. "Yeah. Melissa always tries to distract him. He hates me more."

My heart ached at the matter-of-factness of that statement. "Did it work?"

He shook his head. "He got mad about the sauce burning, so he threw the pot, but then the spaghetti water spilled and burned him. He really freaked out then."

"Nothing like a grown man throwing a temper tantrum over his own stupidity," I said, sympathetically.

Toby smirked and then turned somber again. "He... He started in some more." He probably didn't even know he held his arm against his chest and rubbed it, no doubt where it had been hurt. He scowled. "It seemed different this time. Dad wouldn't stop. He just kept—"

Toby bit his lips and looked down, clearly trying not cry.

"My mom was like that."

His head jerked up. "What did you do?"

I snorted. Bled. Screamed. Broke. Cried. "Survived. Same as you. It's all any of us can do. Can you tell me the rest of what happened?"

"My other dad got home and started yelling at him to get away from us. Melissa and I hid upstairs. They fought."

"Fought physically?"

Toby nodded. "It was loud."

"Did that happen a lot?"

Another shrug. "They would both fight, but my dad—Arthur—is a lot bigger and meaner. He'd drink and sometimes other stuff, then go crazy when any of us would do something wrong. He doesn't mean to hurt us. He's just got a bad temper. He's always sorry."

"He *did* mean to hurt us," Melissa said, sounding more like a jaded woman than a ten-year-old. She walked in and perched on the arm of a wingback chair. "He *liked* to hurt us. It made him feel big and powerful."

"Now he can't anymore," I murmured. By the sound of it, Arthur Chapman had deserved to die.

"No, he can't," Melissa said defiantly.

"Good thing."

"It is." Her chin jutted.

"Now the question is, what to do with you?" Angie asked as she entered, followed by Matthew Chapman, who looked haggard.

He had dark hair and a pleasant face, but shadows circled his eyes and his cheeks looked sunken like he hadn't been eating. The comfort cook in me wanted to go make a big plate of linguini for him.

Toby jumped up and flung his arms around his father's waist, knocking a handful of puzzle pieces onto the floor as he did. Melissa sighed and picked them up.

"Why don't the two of you go play in the basement," Angie suggested to the kids.

"Are you going to kill her, too?" Toby asked without letting go of his father.

"Hey," Matthew said, squatting down on eye-level with his son. "It was an accident. Your other dad was drunk and he took a swing at me and fell. He hit his head on the corner of the counter and died. An accident. It was nobody's fault. Angie wasn't even there. If anybody is to blame, it's me."

"Yeah, but Angie drugged the lady, and she's a *witch*." Toby's voice dropped on the last word and he cast a fearful glance at Angie.

I wondered if Toby and Melissa were also witches and didn't know it yet.

"I won't hurt you," Angie said, hands twisting together. "I won't let anybody hurt you again."

Her vehemence didn't reassure Toby who thrust his face into his dad's chest, wrapping his neck in a death-grip.

"Let it be," Matthew told her, standing up with Toby tight in his arms. "They've been through a lot. I'll take them downstairs." He reached a hand out to Melissa who took it. They started for the door and he paused to look back at me and then Angie. "Don't forget your promise," he said and then left.

"What promise?" I asked.

She dropped into one of the wingback chairs, propping her elbows on her knees and rubbing her forehead with the tips of her fingers.

"How did this turn into such a mess?"

"Maybe killing their father?"

She sighed and flung herself back against the chair. "I didn't. If what Matthew says is true, it was an accident, but even if it wasn't, Arthur was a monster who needed to die."

Her face twisted with a fury so pure it took me aback, almost like she'd suffered the bastard's blows. Maybe she had. Maybe she'd been somebody's punching bag. I could actually sympathize.

"You weren't there when it happened? Why did you show up?"

Angie stared up at the ceiling. "I was supposed to tutor Toby that night. I've been tutoring him twice a week. I got to the house and Nathan was a complete mess. He was covered in blood and desperately trying to wake Arthur up. I calmed him down and cleaned everything up, then brought them here. Told them who I really was, that I'd gotten pregnant young and had to give up my babies. When I was able to, I started looking for them."

"How'd they take it?" I was actually curious.

"Better than I thought. At least they don't hate me. They are starting to get their powers. My family tends to bloom late. They like the idea of having magic." She sighed. "Anyhow, the business with Arthur made my news a lot less interesting by comparison."

"And Nathan? What does he think about you being in their lives?"

She shrugged. "He'll have to deal with it, because I'm not going anywhere."

"Is he the fiancé you were talking about in the car?"

She looked at me. "That was just part of the fairy tale."

To fool me? Or was she the fool? I had a feeling that Angie cared a lot more for Nathan than she was willing to admit. Sad, since he wasn't into women. Or maybe he was bi. Not impossible, but I wouldn't be holding my breath if I were Angie. My gaze dropped to her hand. The diamond ring had vanished.

"So now what? What are you planning to do with me?"

She considered me, catching her lower lip in her teeth. "Why were you at Matthew's house? Why were you working magic there?"

The command in her voice hit me like a kick to the stomach. I fought the power dragging through me, but there was nothing I could do. Whatever spell she'd laid on me took control. "The police suspected magic had been used and asked me to look at the scene."

Angie's mouth dropped open. She sat straight. "They know you're a witch? How?"

Again, I couldn't stay silent and vomited out the information. "One knows—knew," I corrected. "He told the lead detectives, and they took me to the scene since they had no other leads."

"Why did he think magic was involved?"

"The symbol on the door, and the fact that that the key wouldn't work and then later it did. The symbols on the windows. And the way the body suddenly went from fresh corpse to a couple weeks old."

I tentatively reached for my magic again and again I found emptiness. Panic clawed its way up inside me. I clamped it down and refused to let it show. *Not today, Satan.*

I was in deep shit and couldn't afford to show vulnerability to this woman. My only shot was to learn something about her and use it to get away somehow. I was sure she'd told me not to leave the house without her permission. She clearly wasn't stupid.

"Do they know about me?"

"No. Just that magic was done."

Did Ballard and Jeffers even know Toby had had a tutor? Had Angie cast spells to keep anybody from noticing? Or to keep them from sharing that information? I'd have thought that at least his teachers would have wanted to know why his schoolwork was improving, and if she was going to the house twice a week, surely the neighbors would have taken note?

Then again, she was a witch and she'd made me unable to use my magic. That, or she'd stolen it from me. If she could do that, why couldn't she make people forget about her or not see her?

Angie didn't immediately answer the question. She stared a long moment and I could see her thoughts flicker through her eyes along with chill calculation. I swallowed. She might not have killed Arthur Chapman, but that didn't mean she wasn't dangerous. She had a lot to protect and I didn't think murder was an uncrossable line. She was like a stick of unstable dynamite. The slightest wrong move could set her off. I needed to get her to relax and see if I could talk her out of whatever she was thinking to do to me. Best way to do that was with food.

"Look. Things are clearly a little unsettled right now. Even though you wrecked your car on purpose, it had to freak you out a little. Plus with all the murdering and kidnapping, you're stressing out. What if I rummaged in your kitchen and made lunch? I'm hungry. I'm sure Matthew, Toby, and Melissa are hungry. Aren't you? You didn't even eat your pie."

I was surprised to realize I was starving. How long had I been out? Minutes? Hours? *Days*? What the fuck day was it?

Her brows drew together. "What are you up to?"

"Honestly? Calming everybody the fuck down, including me. I'm hangry and you're wound up tighter than a gnat's ass. I'll fix us all something to eat and then maybe we can all figure this out."

She eyed me askance. "Figure what out?"

"How we all get out of this alive and happy."

An expression of regret slid across her face and she gave a little shake of her head. "That isn't possible."

The flat certainty in her voice made my stomach twist. "It's worth trying to figure it out, isn't it? Plus I'm a really great cook."

She sighed. "Okay. Make some food if you want. It's not going to change anything, but I suppose it couldn't hurt."

I'd been putting off asking about Ajax, but it was past time. "How long have I been here? My dog...?"

"Four or five hours," she said. "I put Ajax in the garage with some water. He's fine."

I gripped hard on the sudden surge of protectiveness and fury flaring through my body. I didn't have to ask to know she'd used magic to get Ajax in there. He wouldn't have gone otherwise. He ought to be howling his fool head off and trying to rip apart the garage door to get out. I bit the inside of my cheek to keep myself from raking her over the coals. Instead, I arched brows in obvious distrust of her assurance.

Like most people, she couldn't stand yawning silence

and quickly sought to fill it. "I wouldn't hurt him," she declared. Her lip curled. "People who hurt animals and children deserve to burn forever in hell!"

"At least we agree on that."

"I can let him in if you want."

I stared. "You don't need another hostage. Besides, you can already make me do what you want me to do." I didn't mean to let my bitterness show, but I wasn't a particularly good actress.

"I don't hurt animals." She folded her arms over her chest and glared. "Don't push me too far. You won't like what you get."

"Why? Do you turn into the Hulk?"

Her forehead wrinkled. "What are you talking about?"

"You know, the Hulk. Giant green guy? His shrimpy human self tells people—'don't make me angry; you wouldn't like me when I'm angry' because when he gets pissed he morphs into a giant green man."

"I know who the Hulk is," she said, then shook her head. "This is so stupid. What's your point?"

Remembering that I did not want to piss her off any more than she already was, I chose discretion. I got up and headed into the kitchen, my wobbly legs firming as I went. Once there, I started rummaging through the refrigerator and pantry.

I found the makings for lasagna, or at least most of them, plus some Italian sausage in the freezer. I started by making the noodles. Angie wandered in and sat down to watch me.

As I kneaded the dough, I wondered if the spell she'd laid on me required verbal commands, or if she could just think them at me. I was leaning toward actual speech since I had yet to hear about any telekinetic spells.

I scoffed at myself. Like I had enough experience in magic to make an educated guess. I didn't know you could take somebody's magic or cut them off from it. Whichever it was she'd done to me. It was better for me if she had to speak, since gagging her would stop any orders she might give. Otherwise, I needed to knock her out—a temporary fix —or kill her. I doubted I could commit murder. At least hers. I could probably kill my father, and if she were still alive, I could definitely kill Aunty Mommy, but not Angie. She was just trying to protect her family and that didn't rate a death sentence.

"Tell me what you're thinking," Angie said suddenly.

I felt the compulsion take hold and spilled out all that I'd been pondering.

"I have to use words," she said when I'd finished vomiting up all my thoughts. "But you can't hurt me or restrain me in any fashion, so you can forget about that."

"Good to know." I'd found a rolling pin and began rolling out the dough.

"I have spaghetti in the cupboard."

"And it will be there next time you want some."

"Easier than lasagna from scratch. Nobody makes their own noodles."

"You're wrong about that because I do and fresh noodles are much better than the boxed stuff."

She fell silent and continued to watch me work, her fingers tapping slowly on the quartz countertop.

"What do you mean by Aunty Mommy?" She asked finally. "Did your mother marry her brother or something?"

"Incest would be a hundred percent better than reality," I murmured, taking a knife and cutting the dough in to strips.

"Sounds like an interesting story."

I glanced at her and then back down at my dough. "More like a painful one. Basically my aunt kidnapped me when I was born and pretended she was my mother. She hated me and spent a lot of time showing me how much. Somebody killed her not so long ago and that's when I found out she wasn't my actual birth mom. That's also when I found out she and I weren't the only witches in the world."

She didn't speak for a long minute, then stood up. "I'm going to make some coffee."

Taking a pod out of a drawer, she pressed it into the coffee maker and put a cup beneath it. A few seconds later the glorious scent of coffee wafted through the kitchen. When it was done, she fixed another one and handed it to me before returning to her seat.

I doctored my cup with some cream and sugar and took a sip, reveling in the sweet bitterness running over my tongue.

"You said you had three brothers and your parents actually got married. That's unusual. How did they manage that?" The witch breeding program revolved around arranged pregnancies. From what I could tell, most parents didn't raise their own children, and usually what children belonged to them either had multiple fathers or multiple mothers, depending. "Are your brothers whole or half?"

She frowned. "That's a weird question. We all have the same parents, if that's what you're asking."

"Well, you know how it is." That brought up another question. "How come you gave up Toby and Melissa to a non-magical couple? I wouldn't have thought that was allowed."

Not that I knew how the witch world worked, really. I didn't know if there was some kind of president and congress or a monarch or flying spaghetti monster in charge. Oh, wait. There was the Gawarcheidad Mason had talked about. But they had to be under the direction of some kind of government.

"I didn't tell anybody. Their father isn't magical and didn't know he got me pregnant. Not that he'd have cared."

I waited for her to say more, but she remained silent. I had so many questions. I'd have thought non-magical parents would have called for instant abortions, given the insane obsession of magic in bloodlines. "Do you see your family much?" I asked finally, deciding to see if subtlety would get her to spill information.

She shrugged. "Not really."

"Why not?"

"I'm not so good at following their rules."

"Well, we have that much in common, anyway," I said as I began to brown the sausage. "Any in particular you were allergic to?"

"All the ones telling me who I should be."

"Who did they think you should be?" I more than half expected her to say she didn't want to be part of the breeding program, but was surprised. Or maybe confused was more like it.

She sighed. "I'm an Adept, but in my family that's not good enough. They wanted me to be an Arbiter or at least a Warden. When I wouldn't, they agreed with each other that I could be a Keeper or a Sentinel, but they didn't bother asking me. I'm not interested in politics or hyping up the family status. I just wanted to find the twins and be normal."

I frowned at her. "What are all those?"

"What?"

"Adept, Warden, the others."

Her head cocked as she scrutinized me. Then she paled. "Oh, no. Oh damn! You're one of *them*, aren't you?"

"One of who?"

Her eyes went wide and she swiped a shaky hand over her mouth. Her head swiveled back and forth in denial. "This is bad. Really, really bad."

She lunged to her feet and started pacing. "I'm such a fucking idiot. Why didn't I think? Why didn't I realize? This is so bad. I'm in so much trouble. What the fuck am I going to do?"

Angie sounded like she was beginning to hyperventilate. So much for calming her down and figuring a way out of this mess. She wasn't an unstable stick of dynamite anymore. She'd morphed into a ticking bomb and her countdown clock had gone haywire. She was about to blow.

CHAPTER SEVENTEEN

"Why don't you have a glass of wine and tell me what's going on," I suggested. "Maybe I can help."

She faced me, her hands clenching into fists, her entire body shaking. "What's going on? What's going on?" Her voice rose to a shout. "I've opened up Pandora's Box and I don't know how to close it. What are you even doing here in Sweetwater?" Her pupils had enlarged so her eyes looked black.

"I live here, same as you."

"No. Your kind doesn't just live in a place like this. Tell me about yourself," she ordered. "I want to know who you are, how many other witches are here, whether any of them know about the murder and that magic was involved, and how close they are to finding me."

The compulsion in her words rose up and took control of my lips, tongue, and jaw. I felt like a puppet as I vomited out the information she wanted. Ironically, every word I spoke made me more and more nauseous. Maybe I could spew my stomach contents all over her, too.

She interrupted me several times to ask questions. She focused on Mason, Damon, my mother, and the witch world. She had no questions about me once I'd explained about Aunty Mommy and my upbringing and told her I'd never been trained as a witch. I wasn't a real threat, apparently. Of course that perspective was reinforced by the fact that she had me totally under her control.

I fought the coercion, but it was like trying to climb out of a hole in a lake of ice. I just couldn't get a grip anywhere. Again and again I reached for my magic, but the well was empty. I wrestled with my frustration and anger. Even when Aunty Mommy had me trapped or dangling on a hook, I never felt this out of control or this helpless. At least then I could fight, even if it meant she hurt me worse. But this—being a prisoner inside my own body—this was a living nightmare I couldn't wake up from.

You still have a brain, I told myself. *Use the fucking thing before she gives you a frontal lobotomy.* Metaphorically speaking. Could she tell me to simply forget everything I know? Or tell me to have the mind of a baby again?

I'll try Things I Don't Want to Find Out, Alex.

"You said you were helping the cops to find me. Explain how."

I reported on the previous night's activities and the conclusion that Angie lived in the southeastern quadrant of town, which turned out to be entirely accurate and that the cops were already searching the area. Not that they'd find her. The house was totally innocuous and so was she.

"Once my uncle and mother know I'm missing, they'll come looking, too." I added, thanks to the compulsion. That news could easily send her straight into a psychotic break. Not that she had to go. She was sitting on the top of the slide and just needed a tiny little ass-scootch to go screaming down to the bottom. Helter Skelter.

I winced. Helter Skelter was Charles Manson territory and nowhere I wanted to be.

Her phone rang at that moment. It played the theme song to the movie, *Halloween*. Angie jumped out of her skin like she'd been hit with a taser gun.

She glanced at the screen, her eyes bugging. "How does he know?" She whispered, dread shaping the words.

"Who?"

She set the phone on the island like it was a live grenade. "My grandfather."

The phone stopped ringing and she closed her eyes in relief. Short-lived relief, because it immediately started playing the ominous ringtone again. Angie wrapped her arms around herself and watched it.

"You aren't going to answer?"

She shook her head.

"Why not?"

The look she gave me was incredulous.

"He'll tell me to turn myself over to the Wardens. They'll vanish Matthew and take my kids. I'll be locked down and I'll never see them again."

Deciding that I didn't really want to know what 'vanish' meant, I focused on the rest. "So just tell him to fuck off. You're a grown-ass woman."

She snorted. "It doesn't work that way. He's a Senior Magister. I have to do what he says."

"What happens if you don't?"

"Bad things."

"Worse than what you said these Wardens would do to you?"

"Yes. No. I don't know. Nobody says no to a Magister, especially not a Senior."

The phone stopped ringing and immediately started again. It was getting on my last nerve. I reached out to pick it up.

"Don't!"

Immediately I stopped, my hand caught by her invisible order.

"What do you think you're doing?"

"Someone has to answer."

"No. Just cook."

Without a conscious thought, I returned to stirring the ground sausage. My fury had been burbling along at a steady simmer, but it turns out telling me to just cook was my last straw. I was tired of being at Angie's mercy, and whatever was going to happen, I didn't want to just be along for the ride. If I was going to go off a cliff, I wanted to be behind the wheel.

I let go of the spatula I was using. Or rather, I *told* myself to let go of it. My fingers twitched a little and pinpricks of discomfort ran along every square inch of my nerves. At first it made me shudder, but as I continued to force my hand to let go of the damned spatula, the pain increased from level one to five to ten to straight up off the chart.

It hurt so much I thought I might piss myself. For a moment, the lights flickered as agony overwhelmed me. My knees sagged and I grabbed the counter with *both hands* as the spatula clattered to the floor.

I squeaked my triumph and then snatched the phone. I held it tight, making myself breathe as power and pain battered at me with dozens of invisible clubs. The pounding increased in fury and intensity. I felt the blood vessels in my eyes blow and my vision turned pink. Bloody tears dripped onto the white quartz countertop.

I sucked in a breath. Ordinarily I'd push back with magic, but that well remained dry. I lifted the phone and touched the green answer icon. As I did, a new level of pain zinged through me. It felt like someone was peeling me with a vegetable peeler. I gasped, vaguely hearing a man speaking.

"Hello? Hello? Angie? Are you there? Answer me."

The command in his voice poured through the phone and I could see it hit Angie, who instantly opened her mouth to speak.

Oh, fuck no. This was not going to be Grandpa's shit-show. It was all mine.

I grabbed for my magic again, and something *snapped*. The shock ricocheted through me and power flooded back inside. Finally.

I whipped a lash of power at Angie, wrapping it around her head to keep her mouth closed. Her eyes widened and she started to raise her hands, but I shook my head and wrapped more magic around her so she couldn't move. I didn't know if that was enough to keep her still, but I couldn't take the time to find out. I had to deal with her grandfather. Looking at her, I rested a hush finger over my lips and I lifted her phone to my ear.

"Angie's phone. How can I help you?"

"Where's Angie? Put her on."

"Angie's unavailable at the moment. Would you like to leave a message?"

"Put my granddaughter on the phone."

Power swelled and flowed through the phone. It wrapped around me with that same demanding compulsion that earlier had forced me to answer Angie's questions, only stronger. Much stronger. Difference was, last time she'd managed to drug and disarm me beforehand. I had my power back now, and I was eager to get on with using it.

I let the compulsion's pressure build like steam in a kettle, this time from the outside. I wanted to make Grandpa Bossypants wait. I was willing to bet he wasn't used to it. After a good minute had ticked by, I swiped away the compulsion with a sizzling snap of my own power.

I stretched out my hand and pretended to examine my fingernails and switched over to my best snotty teenager voice. "Sorry, she said tell you she's in the bathtub and she'll call you back at a quarter to never."

Silence. "Who are you?"

I glanced at Angie who looked absolutely horrified, the color entirely drained from her face. She'd even forgotten to fight my restraining spell.

"Angie invited me over for a visit."

"That doesn't answer the question."

I could feel magic worming out of the phone. It felt sticky and oozed around me in groping tentacles. I made a face. Disgusting. Once again I zapped it off me.

"Angie said you were senile, but you're right on top of things, aren't you, old man? You knew right away I hadn't answered, almost like you'd been listening."

I wasn't just being rude for the fun of it, though it was fun. I wanted to gauge Grandpa's temper and how likely he was to fly off the handle. I had no idea someone could send magic through a cell phone. Or maybe Angie's was special. Maybe he'd turned it into a conduit. Would be handy if she were in trouble. He could give her immediate aid. Or spank her ass fast for crossing boundaries.

"Who are you?"

"Name's Beck."

"Beck what?"

"Beck None-of-Your-Business."

"You're a witch."

"You're a genius. How did you figure it out? It's like you're psychic or something."

He didn't take the bait. "Are you threatening my granddaughter?"

"Yes. Absolutely. I'm cooking her lasagna and if she doesn't eat it, I'm going to have to tickle her until she pisses her pants."

That one caught him off guard. I could hear him processing.

"If you aren't threatening her, why is she suddenly so scared she's practically having a heart attack?"

My brows rose. I was just about to ask how he knew she was scared when I managed to bite back the question. Duh. Magic. Anyway, it didn't matter how he knew.

"Would you believe a giant spider just crawled under her shirt and into her bra?"

A dry, almost imperceptible, laugh. "No."

"Maybe a snake came up out of the toilet?"

"Terrifying, but no."

"Then I can't say what's got into her panties, but I'm sure we can handle it."

"We?" He asked at the same time Angie squeaked in surprise, her eyes growing into saucers.

Before I could answer, someone pounded on the front door. Not just the door. I felt magic smashing against the house's protective wards. Angie's expression turned from startled to flat out terrified. Much worse than when her phone had rung.

"Uh oh," I said. "Looks like we've got company. Wonder who it is?"

"Listen to me, carefully," Gramps said, his voice turning clipped and hard. "Do not challenge them. Do whatever they say and don't resist. Whatever you do, *do not* antagonize them. I'm on my way."

The phone cut off. I lowered it.

"When you see your Grandpa, let him know I don't take orders and I certainly don't take shit lying down. I was also voted Most Likely To Antagonize Satan in my high school. So buckle up. This is about to get interesting."

CHAPTER EIGHTEEN

The pounding came again and Ajax howled in response. His eerie song rose like a declaration of war. I took the moment to release Angie from her restraints.

"Who's at the door and what do they want?"

She shook her head. "I don't know."

"Yes, you do. Or you think you do. What kind of trouble are we in?"

She gawked. "We?"

"We. As in, you got me into this mess and I have no intention of letting anybody do anything to me I don't want, and from the sounds of it, that's exactly what is on the agenda. Now tell me what's going on. The short version."

"I'm a black sheep. I'm supposed to stay under the radar. I'm usually careful and cleaning up Arthur's death didn't ping any alerts, but maybe spying on you or bringing you here could have."

I had no idea what black sheep actually meant, or what

staying under the radar entailed, but it was clear her visitors were unwelcome and unfriendly.

"They'll take my kids," Angie said woodenly. Tears rolled down her cheeks.

"You going to just let them?"

She shook her head and shrugged. "I'm strong but I can't take on the whole system. Anyway, I could fight off these guys, but they'll send more. An army. I can't win. If I throw myself on their mercy, maybe..."

Her maybe wasn't particularly hopeful.

The pounding came again and this time the protective wards crumbled to dust. Angie went white. We hurried to the foyer. The door rattled as someone tested the lock and then suddenly it flung open and bounced off the wall. Two people stepped inside.

Both were women. The plump one stood a little over five feet tall, with straight mousey brown hair, gold-wire glasses, and dressed in jeans and a paint-covered tee shirt. She wore Chucks on her feet. I guessed her to be around forty-five or fifty years old.

The second one wasn't much taller, with a muscular and slender body, tight red-brown curls, and wore black pants and a white shirt like she was getting ready for her shift at Red Robin. She had cat-eye makeup with electric blue lipstick, a bunch of piercings in both ears and another in her septum. She looked to be about the same age as the other one.

Both wore chokers with a pendant. It appeared to be an upside-down tree. Its roots glistened with tiny rubies and its limbs gleamed green with emeralds. In the center of the trunk was an amber stone.

Magic crackled around them. These two were loaded for

bear. The first one honed in on Angie while the other watched me.

"Angie Patterson? You are hereby accused of breaking the Covenant laws," Eyeglasses said more loudly than necessary, and with an air of great importance. Or pompousness. "You will allow us to bind your magic and come quietly, or we will take the necessary steps to neutralize you. Neutralization has grave risks and could leave you seriously damaged or dead. Will you comply?"

"Don't think so," I said before Angie could agree, which she clearly planned to do, if her panicked look meant anything.

"And you are?"

The punk waitress lifted her brows and looked down her nose at me. Given that she had to look up at me to even see me, the effect was more fighting-mad wet hen than powerful wizard. Or maybe she was going for the wet hen vibe.

"Annoyed," I told her, "since you're asking."

"Your name," Eyeglasses demanded.

"Is none of your business. You should leave."

There's no real good reason for witches to gesture in order to work magic. You should be able to focus your intent and push your magic out to do it. Gesturing just helps the brain focus more strongly, or at least that's my theory. Anyhow, the trouble is that the gesture signals intent. So when Punk Waitress lifted her hand, her fingers curled loosely together, I figured she was about to send a spell my way.

I could have poured power into my shield, but instead I went on offense. I whipped out thick strands of power and cocooned her in it, sealing off any air she might have wanted to breathe. She'd break through fairly quickly, but for the moment, I only had one opponent to worry about.

Without skipping a beat, I wrapped Eyeglasses's legs in magic and yanked. She dropped like a sack of wet cement and her head bounced on the tile. I wrapped her in an oxygen deprivation spell like the other.

"What are you doing?" Angie asked, horrified.

"It's called defending myself," I said. "Are you going to help?"

"I can't. They'll destroy me. They'll take Toby and Melissa."

The words slipped out before I thought about them. "I'm not going to let that happen. I'll protect you all."

"You can't do that. Nobody can."

"Maybe, maybe not. If you want to let them take you without defending yourself, that's fine, but there's not a snowball's chance in hell that I'm going to let them take *me*. That might mean I have to do some serious damage."

Hopefully not kill them, but I wasn't going to sacrifice my own life so they could have theirs, either. I'd never killed anybody, and it would probably scar me for life, but I'd do it if I had to.

"Why would you help me after what I did to you?"

"I like your kids and I don't know what these assholes will do to them, but I doubt it will be in their best interests."

"But you're one of *them*. They hate us. They've been trying to wipe us out for centuries."

Punk Waitress was starting to figure her way out of her bindings. I added some puzzling loops to the spell to delay her. Glasses was slower. It must have been the whack on her head when she fell.

"What the fuck are you talking about? One of them?"

"Stop it! Why do you keep pretending? Your people decided that stupid prophecy meant you needed to kill off half the witch population and you annihilated us. Or you tried. We've been thriving under the Covenant Laws, which have kept us secret and safe. Until you," she said bitterly. "If I help you, then your people find out we exist and come after us again. It'll be war. I should be helping them to kill you. I've made such a mess!" Her voice rose in a wail.

It took me a couple seconds to make sense of her words. The breath went out of me.

Holy shit. I'd been teasing Mason about the other witches surviving, and it turned out I was right. Holy fucking shit. They hadn't just survived, they'd thrived. At least enough to have some kind of law enforcement and what did Angie call them? Warders, Adepts, Sentinels, and Keepers? They had a whole social and governmental structure.

A jagged-edged sound caught in my throat, half laugh, half sob. The irony was epic. Not only was there one witch society I'd only recently learned about, but there was a whole second one, too. And apparently the one I came from had no clue about the second one and if they found out, they'd be trying to slaughter them. Again.

I tried to imagine Damon or Mason or Ben or even my mother out committing genocide on the basis of some prophecy, but couldn't make that work in my head. Still, the fact was their ancestors had hunted down other witches, and that had given rise to the ridiculous breeding program. Because the bad witches were supposed to rise up again.

Was I the trigger in this stupid prophecy? Was I about to start a witch war?

Fuck that noise. On the other hand, I might not have a

choice. War wasn't my primary problem at the moment. I had to save Angie's ass along with mine, not to mention her kids and Matthew. After that, I could worry about Witch War 2. One thing was for certain, though. I wasn't going to go kill people on the basis of some woo-woo prophecy. For now, though, any killing I was going to have to do was going to be to save my myself and Angie and her family.

Time to kick some ass.

CHAPTER NINETEEN

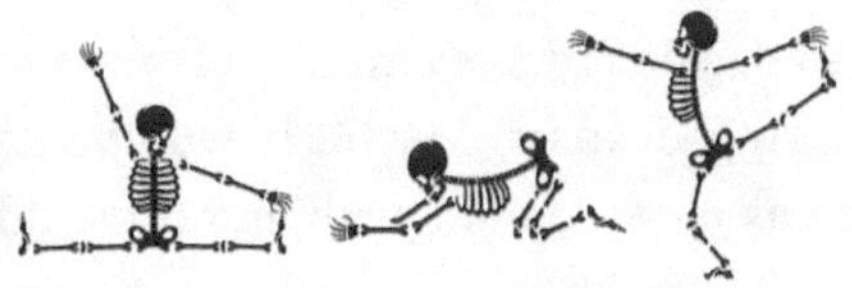

Glasses and Punk Waitress burst out of their bonds at nearly the same time. I'm not sure what they did next, except suddenly I was encased in a big ball of sticky magic. I could hardly move. I flicked out a tendril of magic to swipe it away, but it stuck like a fly in glue. I tried it again, this time using heat. Same result. I tried three more ways, and each ended in the same result.

Meanwhile, my two attackers ignored me and put cuffs on Angie's wrists and ankles. No chains, just three-inch-wide bands inscribed with spells. As the last one clicked shut, all four flared bright red, then dimmed to a pale glow. Angie stood passively while they imprisoned her. I rolled my eyes. Maybe she deserved whatever she got if she wasn't willing to fight.

As soon as they were done, they turned their attention back to me.

"Who is this?" Glasses asked.

"A witch," Angie replied softly.

"Obviously, but *who* is she?"

"I'm standing right here. You can talk to me," I said.

"All right," Punk Waitress said. "Who are you? Why have you interfered in the sanctioned work of Wardens?"

"I was bored watching Judge Judy," I replied, just as I implemented my next attempt at freeing myself.

This time I decided to push my shield outward until the sticky magic ripped apart. Maybe it wouldn't. Maybe it would stretch as far as I could push, but it would certainly become less stable and hopefully easier to shatter. I flooded my shield with power and shoved it outward. As an afterthought, I started spinning it so that their spells wouldn't be able to get a grip.

Another thought occurred to me, and I raised little blades all over the exterior of my spinning shield. At first, nothing moved. I might as well have been frozen. I shoved harder. A jerk and a fluttering ripple through the network of magic. Another jerk, and another, and slowly my shield started revolving and shearing through strands of the now taut spells encasing me until they popped completely loose.

I had another attack ready. I grabbed an end table with a tentacle of magic and whipped it at my two opponents. It crashed into Punk Waitress first, sending her sprawling, then toppled Glasses.

I didn't have much breathing room. Instantly a bolt of energy hit me, knocking me back a step. A half dozen more followed as the two recovered.

My back hit the wall. I had no place to go.

As much as I didn't actually want to hurt them, neither could I have them reporting back to their superiors about my existence. Angie wouldn't if doing so would compromise her twins, so I just had to free us both, then get her to put the same hex on them she had on me, only instead of keeping them from using their magic, she needed to make them forget about us. If she even could with those shackles on.

Another thing to add to the to-do list: pick the locks on the magical handcuffs.

Another blast of magic hit me, and this time it slammed me through the wall and into the kitchen. I landed half on the island and dropped to the floor. I swore while tears ran down my face. I was pretty sure I'd broken at least a couple of ribs and fingers, and my brain felt like it had been shaken in a paint mixer. My shield protected me from getting stabbed by debris, and had probably saved me from a broken back, but the rest of me felt like I'd been thrown off a rodeo bull and then trampled into the dirt.

I pulled myself up using the island. A Beck sized hole gaped in the opposite wall about a foot from the door. Fuckers did that on purpose. So much for playing nice.

Aunty Mommy had done a lot of terrible things to me, many of them far more creative than anybody with an ounce of sanity could have thought up. It gave me a horrid little encyclopedia of ideas, which, for once, I was grateful for.

I didn't even think. I knew each of them was shielded, so whatever I did had to either destroy those shields so I could get to their gooey centers, or it had to seal them inside and make it impossible for them to escape.

I pulled power up from everywhere it would come. Part of me screamed to wait, to make sure this wasn't a horrible idea. The rest of me roared full steam ahead.

They zapped power at me. I roared my rage and thrust mine at them. I didn't try for finesse. I reached out and grabbed hold of their lashes of magic. Fire exploded inside me, but I just pulled their magic into me, adding it to my own. Before they could think of a response, I slammed my power down on them with all the weight of a mountain collapsing. I let it continue to pour down onto them, even as I sucked power from them. They fought my grasp, but I'd sent parasitical roots of magic up the lances of power they'd shot at me. I used them as conduits, pushing through to their bodies and spreading through every artery, vein, capillary, and nerve, until I planted a hook into every last cell of their bodies.

Aunty Mommy had done this to me once. I'd hidden my magic from her, but I'd always been more than ready to use my mouth. When she had me trapped in one of her snares, I did everything in my power to piss her off. I never could remember what I said. The whole thing was murky in my memory. Always had been.

I remembered thinking she'd exploded like a star going nova. She'd been primal in her anger. No, it had been more than that. Bigger. Deeper. And so, so wild. Out of control. Whatever button I'd hit, I'd let loose something I'd never expected and so much more than I could handle. I'd been delighted to make her lose control that way. That delight had lasted mere seconds, and then horror set in. It had been so bad that my mind had done its best to forget it.

Unfortunately, some things just couldn't be forgotten. Or maybe it was fortunate, because right now, I held dominion over them in a way they couldn't yet comprehend. I could tell them not to breathe. I could stop their hearts. I could explode every single cell in their bodies. I could cause them such pain that their brains would put them in a coma, if not stop working altogether.

I wasn't interested in torturing them. Nor were they interested in sitting back and taking their punishment the way I had. They hit me back and though I absorbed the power and fed it back to them through my attack, it took a heavy toll on me.

My skin felt like it was melting and my bones ached and softened under the onslaught. I had to finish this before I couldn't. I clamped down on my attackers, sending pulses of electricity through them. I felt them jerk and twitch as they lost control of themselves. Their bladders let go and they went into convulsions. Their thoughts lost coherence and their attacks fizzled. I reached inside and smothered their consciousness and put them into a deep sleep they would not soon wake from.

It took me several minutes to withdraw my power and settle it back into myself. I sagged down to the kitchen floor. The tiles beneath me had cracked and were scorched black. Heat from them charred my clothing and blistered my skin. I made myself crawl forward, nearly sobbing with relief when I touched cool travertine.

I took several breaths and reached for the counter to pull myself up. After several attempts, I managed to lurch to my feet. They screamed. I looked down. Everything below my knees was charred. The soles of my shoes had melted through. I winced. My shield was still functioning, so I made it thicker under my feet. At least if I stepped on something I wouldn't add insult to what was clearly serious injury.

I staggered into the next room. The walls and ceiling had cracked as had the tiled floor. Glasses and Punk Waitress lay in uncomfortable-looking heaps, their arms and legs twisted at odd angles.

"Are they dead?"

Angie sat hunched in a corner, her knees pulled to her

chest, her face pale, her eyes so wide I thought they might pop out and go bouncing around the room.

"No," I said. My voice rasped. My mouth was parched. In fact, my whole body felt parched. I desperately wanted a glass of water, but walking the distance back to the sink might as well have been miles. No way did I want to do that at the moment.

"They'll be out for a while, though. Are you okay?"

"How did you—?" She shook her head. "What did you do?"

"Desperation breeds desperate measures," I said, not wanting to explain.

"What will you do now?"

Just then Ajax let go another long howl. Because I'm clearly a masochist, I sent a filament of magic to find the garage door and open it. Seconds later it slammed open and Ajax came bounding through. Upon seeing me, he skidded to a halt and sniffed the air.

"It's okay," I told him, hoping I wasn't lying. My physical injuries were nothing. Well, not nothing, but definitely fixable with the help of a certain magic healing pool and any healing my mother or Mason might want to toss my way.

The real problem was Angie and this whole other witch world. If I spoke up about it, I had a feeling I'd be unleashing hell. On the other hand, I didn't really want to lie about it, especially to Damon, if he ever turned up again. I squelched that thought. Not the time.

"Come here, boy," I said to Ajax, patting my thigh. Big mistake. I gritted my teeth and grimaced.

Ajax came close and whuffled me. I stroked his head. "It's okay. I'm okay." Or I would be.

"What's going on?"

Matthew appeared in the doorway to the living room. Good timing. Make an appearance after all the shooting ended. Not that I blamed him for waiting until the shit-storm had passed. I should probably congratulate him for being brave enough to come out at this point.

"Your girlfriend has unpleasant visitors," I said.

His gaze fell on the Eyeglasses and Punk Waitress. He paled. "Are they dead?"

"Nope, though it might be easier all around if they were." I looked at Angie. "How long before someone comes looking for them?"

She shrugged. "I don't know."

"What about your grandfather?"

She gave a jerky swallow. "He was probably at his house on Victoria."

I rolled my eyes. Her specificity left something to be desired. "Victoria Island? Canada?"

She nodded. That gave me a few hours at most. The question was, what did I want to do with those hours? Whether or not I told anybody about this other witching world, Angie knew I knew, and so did her grandfather, Matthew, the kids, and the two Sleeping Uglies.

"Is he going to come after me?" I asked her.

"Come after you?"

Had someone hit her on the head?

"Yeah, hunt me down to shut me up about what I know about you and your existence."

She frowned, clearly trying to sort through her thoughts. "Maybe. Probably. He can't allow a war. Too many will die."

"Yeah, well if he comes after me, I can promise he'll get a war."

I rubbed my hands over my face. I didn't think magic was going to solve this. But it could help.

"Okay, first things first. We need to get those cuffs off you so you can do your Jedi act and tell them to forget all about you and me and what happened."

"There's no way to take them off without the key, and if you try to break them, headquarters will know."

And yet another complication. "Okay," I said, thinking aloud. "I get the feeling your gramps has the power to deal with freeing you and covering up this mess. Is that fair?"

She gave a reluctant nod. "I didn't want him to know about Toby and Melissa and Matthew."

"Sucks to be you, then."

She looked like she was going to cry. I snarled at myself for the sympathy welling up inside. No way was I going to pity her. She'd got me into this mess and didn't deserve it. Even if she had been dealt a crappy hand of cards.

"All right. Here's what's going to happen. I'm going to leave you to deal with your grandfather. Meanwhile me and my dog are going to leave. I'll try to call off the cops. If you get locked up, we won't be able to hide the fact that you exist from the witch world I come from."

Came from, but belonged to about as much as I belonged to the one Angie came from. Ironically, she and I both fit into our worlds about as well a drag queen at a convention for the Spanish Inquisition.

"Try to call them off? You won't just make them?"

I stared at her. Okay, the question wasn't entirely unreasonable. I imagine most witches went with using magic to make humans do what they wanted. If it came down to choosing between the two witch worlds going to war and using magic to make the investigation go away, I probably would use it. I'm nothing if not practical and saving countless lives outweighed the repulsiveness of manipulating people like puppets and forcing them to do my bidding.

But it would be my last resort. I'd start with reason, my least strongest suit.

Hopefully I wasn't doomed to fail before I even got started.

CHAPTER TWENTY

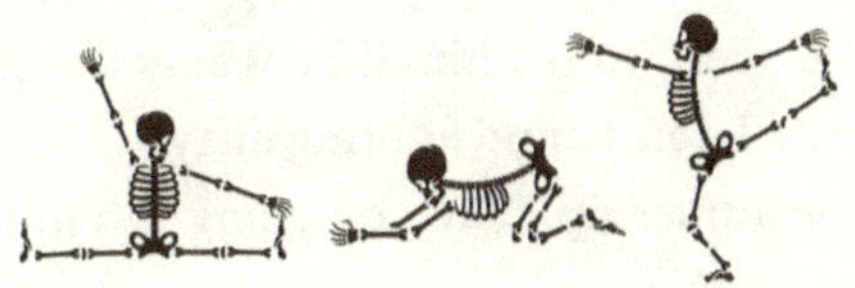

Before leaving, I sucked down so much water I should have sloshed when I walked. Hobbled, really. I didn't mess with my clothes or wounds. I'd do all that when I got to the pool. At this point I thought if I tried removing what was left of my shoes, I'd end up taking off chunks of flesh, too.

My stomach lurched at the thought and my mouth filled with sour bile. You'd think I'd be used to seeing my own wounds by now, but nope.

Ajax stayed glued to my side, maintaining an almost constant warning growl. The hair on his back stood straight. I gathered my purse and tucked it under my arm. My hands weren't eager to be holding on to anything at the moment.

"My grandfather will want to know who you are," Angie said, following me as I headed for the garage where she'd hidden my car.

I stopped and turned. Ajax move in between us with a not at all subtle *keep away* vibe. "Are you trying to say he's going to hunt me down and kill me? I'm not an idiot. I know that already."

She had the grace to flush. "I don't know what he'll do. He's powerful. Strong. Dangerous."

"Yeah? So am I. And I don't plan to play Good Samaritan again anytime soon, so tell him if he wants to come at me, I'll be ready and I don't mind fighting dirty."

She bit her upper lip. "Are you going to tell people we exist?"

"I don't want a war. Or a genocide," I said, which didn't answer her question, but I wasn't feeling in the mood to reassure her. That and I had no idea who I was going to tell. The girls, for certain. Damon....

I didn't even know if we were still together. My mind shied away from thinking of him.

"I'm sorry," she said as I reached for the door handle.

I looked back at her, my brows curved.

"For kidnapping you. For getting you involved."

I scoffed. "You're only sorry because you opened Pandora's Box, not for what you did to me."

I looked down at myself. I'd like to have said that I looked worse than I felt, but that was a laughable lie.

She flushed again. "I am sorry. I was desperate, but that's no excuse."

"No, it's fucking-well not."

"Thank you for wanting to help me. For stopping them from taking me."

"Sure. Anytime. Not sure you won't be landing in the fire with your grandfather, but at least you're out of the frying pan. For now."

"I'm better off with him." She seemed very certain.

"Only if he gets here before they wake up," nudging my chin in the general direction of Eyeglass and Punk Waitress.

"He will."

"Do you believe in the Easter Bunny, too?"

Angie frowned. "I don't understand."

"You've got a lot of faith and no facts tell you they won't wake up before your grandfather arrives. For all you know, they'll come to ten minutes after I get in my car and leave. What will you do then?"

She blinked. "*Will* they wake up that soon?"

"No. They'll probably be out at least until tomorrow."

"Then my grandfather will be here in plenty of time."

"If you say so."

I turned to leave, hesitated, turned back. "If he doesn't get here in time, you can call me."

Her eyes bugged. "Why?"

"Because I really am a fucking idiot?" I shook my head. "Let's just say I'd be doing it for the kids." Which would be true, but it would also be because I'm a total and complete sucker and I felt sorry for Angie. No way was I going to tell her *that*.

"I don't have your number."

Gritting my teeth, I thrust my purse at her. "Outside zipper pocket. Take one of my cards."

She did as told and returned my purse. She kept her eyes fixed on Ajax during the entire exchange. He'd started snarling and growling the second I handed her my purse. I made zero effort to settle him down.

A few minutes later I was in my car and backing down the driveway. Ajax stood on the passenger seat, unwilling to sit.

The clock on the car's dash told me it nearly six. I fished my phone out of my pocket, only to find the battery had melted right out of it. So much for calling Mikey and updating him on the situation and getting the search for

Angie called off. I'd short-circuited the spells connecting my phone to those of the girls, so I couldn't call them either. I sighed. What I really needed was to go to the pool and get some healing, and then I'd get working on the rest.

With a sigh, I put my car in gear and started driving.

I'd gone about two miles and had pulled out onto the main drag when I heard a siren. Whirling red and blue lights reflected in my rearview. For fuck's sake. I hadn't been speeding and I sure as hell hadn't run the stop light.

I pulled into the parking lot of a tire shop and stopped. The cop pulled up right behind me, blocking me into my parking spot like he thought I'd be making a break for it. I rolled my window down and waited, watching him in my rearview.

His cruiser door opened and out stepped Mikey. I groaned. *Mother fucker*. I was cursed. There was no other explanation for my day.

He stomped around to my window. "Where the fuck—" He wrenched open my door. "Jesus Christ! What happened to you?"

"Bad shit," I said. "Look, I'll tell you everything, but I need to get cleaned up first and call the girls."

"You need the hospital."

"I can do better."

He made one of those pissed-off faces like he wanted to strangle me, and shook his head.

"Okay, fine, but I'll drive you. You shouldn't be behind the wheel."

At that point, Ajax growled and stepped up on the console like he was going to leap over me at Mikey. He bared all his teeth and snapped at the man. Mikey had the brains to lurch back.

"Whoa!"

I rubbed a hand clumsy hand over Ajax's head, wincing at the pain. My fingers had swollen into purple and black sausages. My fingernails appeared to have melted away, leaving little puckered pockets where they used to be.

I drew a breath to settle my suddenly nauseous stomach. I'd been doing a really good job of not noticing how bad I was hurt to this point. Now I was starting to catalog it. I blamed Detective Douchebag.

"Ajax is feeling a little protective," I said. "And you sound threatening. You might want to take it down a couple notches."

Another one of those looks. "This is about the murder, isn't it? We've had a BOLO out for you since this afternoon."

I sighed. Might was well tell him. He wasn't letting me leave without at least some information.

"Murderer staged an accident. I stopped to help and they ended up kidnapping me. I got free and here I am."

His gaze narrowed. "That's not the whole story by a long shot."

"No, but I'd really like to get some medical care right now, so that's all you're getting."

"Fine. Get in the other seat. I'm driving."

"You can't leave your car."

"Yes, I can. Now get into the passenger seat."

I decided I wasn't winning. I tried flipping him off with very little success, then slid down off my seat. "I suppose you're going to be your usual asshat self and give me a ticket for not wearing my seatbelt," I muttered as I hobbled my way around to the other side of my car.

He got to the door first and opened it for me, offering me a hand. I hated to take his help, but leaned on his arm to steady myself as I climbed back in. He shut the door after me and a couple minutes later he'd parked his cruiser and gotten behind the wheel of my car. Ajax plopped himself on the console between us, just in case Mikey decided to stab me, I supposed. Meanwhile I tried to ignore my growing agony. Especially from my feet.

"Where to?"

I pointed him in the right direction. He drove quickly, surprising me by not asking any questions except for asking if I needed anything.

"Jen's been blowing up my phone," he said.

"Call her for me. Put it on speakerphone."

I wouldn't be able to hold the phone that well, much less tap buttons.

He did as told and set it my palm. Ajax snarled as he did. Jen picked up on the first ring.

"Well? Did you find her, Asswipe?"

"It's me."

"Fuck. Thank God. Where the fuck have you been? Are you okay?"

"I'm on my way to the pool."

Silence. Then, "How bad?"

"Not that bad."

"She's lying," Mikey said. "She looks like she got hit by lightning a couple dozen times. Extra-crispy."

I gave him a baleful look. "You're exaggerating. I could be a lot worse."

"If anything, I'm understating it. I should be taking you to the hospital."

"Should I call your uncle?" Jen asked. "Or your mother?" She actually sounded worried, which meant she was on the verge of going nuclear.

"No. Not before I talk to you, Stacey, and Lorraine. Something's come up."

"Something?"

"Yeah. I plan to come see you guys at the hospital as soon as I leave the pool. Meanwhile, nobody else can know what happened to me."

"They already know you disappeared," Mikey said, turning off the highway onto the road leading to the river. "They've been looking for you too."

"Shit. I *really* don't want to see them until I talk to you guys. How's Stacey?"

"She's fine. Freaking out about you in between her hits of morphine. I'll call Lorraine and we'll meet you at the hospital and hear the story in Stacey's room."

"I might be a while. The pool works, but it isn't instant and there's a fair amount of repair to be done."

The silence stretched. I could picture Jen biting back her fury.

"Please tell me that the person or people responsible for hurting you are worse off than you."

I thought about Eyeglasses and Punk Waitress. I had no idea how they were or how much they'd suffered in comparison to me. Anyway, I was the one who'd Betty Crockered myself, so me being fire-seared and overcooked was my fault. They just happened to be the reason why. Did that make my condition their fault?

The real culprit was Angie, but then she'd been driven by a desire to protect her children from an abusive asshole. And then there was the fact that Tweedle-Dee and Tweedle-Dum served some sort of government function and had shown up to take Angie into custody, so I could just as easily blame the witchy government they served, or I could go back to the prophecy and the fact that Angie's witch world were desperate to hide from genocide.

"It's complicated," I said finally. "Which is why I have to talk to you guys."

I could practically hear her grinding her teeth. Jen didn't handle frustration well. I could relate.

"All right, this is what I'm going to do," she said. "I'm going to check Stacey out of the hospital."

"No fucking way," Mikey declared hotly. "She's going to stay in that damned hospital bed until the doctor says she can leave. You are not going to fuck with her recovery."

Jen didn't deign to respond. "We'll meet you at the pool. The water will help her too, won't it?"

"Yeah, but everybody knows how bad she's hurt. If she's suddenly well, people are going to ask a lot of questions."

"She can suddenly be healed?" Mikey demanded, shooting me a caustic look.

I continued to ignore him.

"Let them ask. Anyhow, she can fake being hurt. She can stay at the house with you or at Luke's, and stay out of sight and have a miraculously fast recovery."

It wasn't the worst plan and it meant Stacey wouldn't be in pain, which was a big win in my book. "Okay. You'd better bring me some clothes. Shoes, too." I reached up to touch my hair. It was extra crispy along with the rest of me. "And a hat."

"What the hell did you do to yourself?"

"Do you think they'll let Stacey just walk out?" I asked, not bothering to answer.

"They have to. She'll just have to say she's going against medical advice. We'll explain there's been an emergency and she *has* to be there. Her favorite grandmother is on her deathbed or something."

"How are you going to get rid of her family?"

"I'll think of something."

"I can send Mikey to help."

He made a face like he wanted to argue, but he also wanted to be there for Stacey. Rock and a hard place. I was willing to bet Stacey would win out. He surprised me.

"You trying to get rid of me?" he growled.

"Can I?"

"Not a fucking chance."

"I'll be fine by myself at the pool. All I'm going to do is sit in the water, so you'll have time to go help and come back with them."

"And then what? You'll wiggle your nose at me so I have to leave? Or put me to sleep?"

I pretended to consider. "Well, now that you mention it...."

He growled again.

I chuckled and then realized that was a seriously bad idea. My muscles had apparently shriveled up and moving —laughing—was like having someone jam big roasting forks into my chest and lungs.

I broke off and sucked a couple shallow breaths, since deep breaths were entirely off the table. A coughing fit attempted to take hold. I clenched my teeth and braced my hands on the dashboard and made myself breathe slowly, counting through each breath.

"What's wrong? What do you need me to do?" Mikey demanded, swerving slightly as he glanced over at me.

"I need you to not get in an accident," I said, my voice scraping. "Get going, Jen. We're almost there."

"I'll stay with her," Mikey announced before Jen could order him to do just that. "Call me if you need help."

"You'd better stay put, asshole," she said. "Don't forget she wouldn't be in this mess if not for you. I'm willing to go to jail for ripping your balls off." With that, she cut the call.

"I think she's warming up to you," I said, pointing him to the turnoff for the pool.

He stopped in the road, eyeing the overgrown track. "Seriously? You want me to drive this car on that? Those ruts are like canyons. We'll break an axle or high center."

"It's not as bad as it looks," I assured him. Which is to say, magic hid the actual road, which was smooth as butter. Or at least as smooth as a dirt road could be.

He sighed. "If you say so. This is going to hurt, though. Don't blame me."

He turned off and drove through a tall clump of Johnson grass. The car rocked; I sucked in sharply.

"Told you so."

"Just drive," I said through gritted teeth.

The first ten feet *were* bad. That was the point. Nobody in their right mind would drive past that point. After that, it smoothed out. The ground continued to look rutted and car-destroying, but it was all illusion.

Mikey didn't say anything when it happened, just kept going until we dead-ended into a little parking area hidden from the main road by trees and a tumbled rock formation. He parked and turned off the car.

"Now what?"

"Follow the path," I said, reaching for my door.

"Stay put," he said, getting out and coming around to my side. He opened the door and extended a hand.

Ajax lunged forward, planting his front feet on my thighs and snapping at Mikey, who snatched his hand away.

"Ajax! Stop it. I'm okay. He's a friend. Of sorts." I stroked his head and made soothing sounds until he eased back.

Once again Mikey extended his hand and this time Ajax tensed but remained otherwise still.

"Thanks." I set my blackened hand on Mikey's up-raised palm and eased out of the car.

Pain rolled through me in waves that hit one side of me and rolled back in the other direction. I made a whimpering sound and grabbed the door with my other hand, which only caused another pain-quake to rage up my arm.

"How far?" Mikey asked in a clipped voice.

"Over that little ridge," I said. "There's a path."

"I can carry you. Ajax willing, that is."

Talk about humiliating, not to mention painful. I imagined any pressure on my skin would crack it apart. On the other hand, I'd be in the pool a lot faster, which would mean faster relief. I'd take it.

"I'd appreciate it," I said.

"It's going to hurt," he warned.

"Do you think I suddenly dropped a thousand IQ points? Of course it's going to hurt. Get the fuck on with it."

The corners of his mouth turned up. "All that politeness had me thinking you were possessed for a second. But you're definitely you. Put your arm over my shoulder."

"Easy, Ajax. I'm okay," I said. I did as told, clamping my teeth together. Mikey swung me up, one arm around my back, the other under my knees. I hissed and tried not to pass out. Ajax barked and jumped out of the car, lunging up and planting his feet on Mikey's shoulder as he sniffed at me. Mikey staggered, struggling to keep his balance.

"I'm okay," I told Ajax again. He dropped to the ground with a whimper and then gave a little moaning howl.

Mikey set off along the path, striding quickly and swearing as he stepped on a rock and jolted me. Ajax kept up a running commentary of moans, yowls, yips, and half-howls.

"Sorry," Mikey said as he turned me sideways to get between two trees.

"Shut up and keep walking."

"Jen's right. It's my fault you're in this shape. I shouldn't have pushed you into the investigation. You aren't a cop."

"You aren't a witch. If you had managed to find her, you'd have been worse off than me." Or not. Angie would just have made him forget. On the other hand, there's no telling what the two goon-queens would have done to him. For all I knew they might have killed him and dropped him into a deep hole and nobody would have seen him again, so yeah, he probably would have been worse off.

We cleared the trees at the crest of the ridge and he carried me down the trail to the little sandy spit beside my healing pool. A natural wall of rock separated it from the river, with a tunnel at the bottom connecting the two. Trees and bushes worked with the rocks to shroud the area from view and a fairy circle of mushrooms acted as the magical boundary and helped keep random hikers away.

The place had been made for me by a small yellow buddha. He looked like the laughing Buddha, but was only a couple feet tall, and came from a race of buddha people. So *a* buddha, not *the* Buddha. He'd never told my why he'd created the sanctuary for me, and I'd never pushed it after he'd made it clear he wasn't inclined to answer. I wasn't going to bite the hand that feeds and all that.

He'd also given me a carnelian healing ring, but I didn't wear it unless I thought I might need it. I should probably start wearing it all the time, given how often I seemed to be hurting myself.

Usually Banana Buddha didn't appear unless and until I talked to him, so I didn't think about warning Mikey, who squawked and jerked to a halt at the sight of a floating yellow buddha who popped into the air a couple feet away. He floated in the air, blocking the trail. Naked as usual, his rolls of fat managed to cover his male bits. He glared first at me, then Mikey, then back at me.

"What has happened now?"

"I cooked myself trying to fight off a couple attackers."

"Attackers?" Mikey echoed. "What attackers? Who were they?"

I ignored him, eyeing Banana Buddha thoughtfully. "Did you know about the other witching world?"

He tipped his head, his jowly face unreadable. "Other witch world?"

"You *did* know, didn't you?"

"What are you talking about?" Mikey demanded.

Clearly he hadn't gotten enough attention as a child.

"Who is this?" Banana Buddha asked.

"Mikey. Detective Mike Crowe. He's a...friend." Of sorts. "Mikey, this is ..." I looked at the buddha. I didn't know his name or if he even had one.

"She calls me Banana Buddha," he told Mikey.

I had the grace to flush a little. Not exactly the nicest name in the world.

"You may call me B.B."

I smiled. Had to love his doubling down on my rudeness. B.B. was my kind of guy.

"She's hurting pretty bad," Mikey said.

"Get her in the pool," B.B. said, gliding aside and then floating along beside us. "Dare I ask what happened? And why aren't you wearing your ring?"

"Because I wasn't expecting trouble, and I got into a fight."

"You should wear it always. Trouble finds you and will find you. You need to always be prepared," he admonished.

"I guess so," I agreed through gritted teeth as Mikey eased down the last few steps of the path and lowered me to my feet.

I hissed as my unhappy flesh met the sand. Ajax nosed my hands and made more worried sounds.

"Do you want me to help you with your clothes?" Mikey asked doubtfully as he gazed down at me.

"Not today, Hot Stuff," I said and stepped into the water. I'd take my clothes off when I didn't hurt so much.

I'd like to say the relief was instant, but the pool didn't work that fast. Still, the coolness felt good on my tender flesh. I went deeper until I could easily go under and I did just that. Of course, Mikey grabbed my collar and jerked me up.

"What the hell? Are you okay?"

To be fair, given how I must have looked, it's very easy to see how he could get the mistaken impression that I'd fallen down instead of deliberately dropping under the water. Especially since I did it in the least elegant way possible.

"Hands off, Detective Suck-juice," I said, twisting out of his grip with a yelp. "Fuck, that hurts!"

He obligingly stepped back, encouraged by the splashing arrival of Ajax, who darted between us, all the while barking and snarling. I sank back down into the water, this time stopping at my chin.

After a moment, Mikey spoke. "What now? How long does it take?"

"Bored already?" I asked.

"He's very impatient," B.B. agreed, floating around to face me. "Then again, so are you. Humans can be so exhausting. You should take more time to be quiet and relax."

I wondered how he propelled himself. The sudden image of fiery farts jetting him around made me snort, which made me inhale water, which made me start coughing. By the time I was done, I'd started crying tears of laughter and pain, and Mikey had begun to hover restlessly, clearly wanting to help me and not knowing what to do. I slung my arms around Ajax and gradually gained control of myself.

"I'm fine," I said after I caught my breath. I sounded like I'd tried to swallow a chainsaw.

"Sure you are," Mikey muttered, then sighed. "Can I get back in here if I leave? I think you need something to eat. Maybe a milkshake."

"You may if she permits it," B.B. said.

"I permit. A milkshake sounds divine. Thank you."

"Not doing it for you," he said sourly. "Doing it so Jen reconsiders killing me on sight."

"She won't. I told she's warming up to you. She'll only rip your balls off, not kill you outright."

"And that's an improvement?"

"If you're more worried about your life than your balls."

"I'm a man. I'm always worried about my balls. I'm leaving. Try not to drown while I'm gone, or I'll never hear the end of it."

"Ajax and I will take care of her," B.B. said.

"*I'll* take care of me," I said, yawning. "I always do."

Mikey turned back he was starting back up the path. "You know you don't always have to, right? Your girls would be the first to say so."

I stared in surprise and then my mouth curved into a grin. "Aw, look at you showing your soft and gooey center."

He snorted. "Fuck off. You know I'm right and the girls wouldn't thank you for saying otherwise. Hell, Ballard and Jeffers wouldn't, either. Speaking of whom, I need to let them know I found you."

"Might as well tell my Uncle Mason and my mother too. Just don't tell them anything else, please."

"I don't know anything else."

"A delightful combination: an empty head and a pretty ass."

He laughed and shook his head as he started away. "Enjoy the view." He wiggled his butt.

"I always do."

CHAPTER TWENTY-ONE

Mikey returned before the girls arrived. I spent the interim hour or so floating in the pool and occasionally dunking myself and sipping water. Ajax sprawled on the sun-warmed sand, watching me. I explained the situation to B.B. who had absolutely no advice to offer except to tell me again to wear the damned carnelian ring. I did learn that he had a sweet tooth but had never had cheesecake or flourless chocolate cake, or pretty much any other tasty baked good.

"I'll bring you some," I promised.

I heard Mikey coming before he appeared carrying a stack of five pizza boxes and a rolled-up grocery sack.

"Any word from Jen?" He asked as he set the food down. He unrolled the sack and reached inside.

"Nothing yet. I'm sure busting Stacey out of hospital jail will take a while."

He snorted. "This is Jen you're talking about."

He had a point.

"Here," he said, striding down to the water's edge and

holding out a big cold cup from my favorite coffee stand. "I had them make you a mocha milkshake."

I practically purred as I snatched it out of his hand. This time Ajax didn't react to him.

"If you're trying to buy my forgiveness for telling Jeffers and Ballard about me, it's totally working."

"Glad to hear it."

I tried to drink the shake slowly so I wouldn't get an ice cream headache, but I was too hungry, and it was deliciously cold and sweet. I nearly orgasmed the first time the coffee-flavored perfection hit my tongue.

"I brought one for you, too," Mikey said, holding a smaller cup out for B.B. "I didn't know what you like so I got you strawberry."

The little buddha snatched it and immediately started drinking. He let out a delighted squeal. "This is delightful! You are very kind to bring it to me."

"He's sucking up," I said. "He's got a thing for Stacey. She'll be happy with him if we're happy. It's very calculated."

"I don't know. I might just be doing it out of sheer guilt," Mikey said, digging in his pocket for a biscuit. He gave it to Ajax. "Stacey being happy might just be a bonus."

"Where did you get that?"

"At the gas station. Figured pizza wasn't the best dinner for him."

"See? Sucking up."

He shook his head. "I left drinks in the car. I'll be right back."

Right back turned into twenty minutes, and this time when he returned, he wasn't alone. Jen and Lorraine came down the path loaded with fat tote bags, followed by Mikey who was carrying Stacey. She still wore her hospital gown and a robe, and her leg was bandaged and in a brace.

Just from my position in the pool I could tell she was both drugged and in pain. She rested her head against Mikey's shoulder looking pale and wan. She had welts and scrapes crisscrossing her face and arms.

"You made good time," I said. "Did you sign any paperwork or just rip out all the IV lines and haul her out of there?"

"Pretty much the second one," Jen said without a hint of apology. "Once they realized Stacey was leaving whether or not they were ready, they got the paperwork sorted lickety-split. I snagged a wheelchair from the stand on the way in, so we escaped pretty quick."

"How are you?" Lorraine asked, squatting down at the edge of the pool. "Did you get burned or something?"

"Or something," I said. My skin had already gone from black to ugly red and the swelling had gone down. "Put Stacey in here," I told Mikey.

Miracle of miracles, he didn't argue and talk about how the water might be unsanitary for her wounds, or that her bandages would get wet. He just kicked off his boots and walked right in until she was neck deep.

"The water feels good," she said dreamily before yawning. She blinked slowly and looked around. "Beck. Are you okay? Jen said you needed...." Her face pinched in annoyance. "I can't remember."

"To talk," I said. "But first, I could use a slice of pizza," I said, my milkshake empty.

I started to get out of the water. Jen grabbed the empty cup.

"Keep your ass where it is. I'll get you a piece."

She brought me a slice of heaven on a triangle of bread. It was the thirteen topping special and my favorite pizza. I devoured it, and she brought more. After four pieces I was starting to feel a little bit like a fat tick and switched to sipping on a soda.

The others also ate, Mikey helping Stacey so she didn't drop her food, though she only managed a few bites before falling into a doze on his shoulder. B.B. had disappeared, no doubt to enjoy his milkshake in peace. I didn't doubt for one minute that he was listening, though. I'd fed Ajax my crusts along with bits of sausage and pepperoni.

"All right, spill," Jen said when I was done stuffing my face and Stacey had managed to wake up again. "What's going on?"

I launched into the story, starting with the accident. They broke in a couple times to ask questions and comment, but mostly sat silent as I spoke.

"What a fucking bitch," Jen said when I finished. "Assholes like Angie are why nobody stops and helps strangers anymore."

"Unless you're an idiot like me," I pointed out.

"You're not an idiot," Lorraine protested. "You're nice. That's not a crime."

"Angie said I was nice too. Complained it made her feel bad for being shitty to me. Anyway, it might not be a crime, but it sure isn't smart."

"And you're not going to change just because someone turned out to be a nutjob," Lorraine said. "Nor should you. You'll just be more careful."

"What does it say about me that I don't learn my lesson and keep trusting people to not be axe murderers, though?"

"That you're a good person," Stacey said, sounding a little more focused. She squinted and gazed slowly around at their surroundings. "This was a good idea. I feel better." She looked up at Mikey. "You can put me over by Beck."

His jaw tightened, but he did as told. She leaned against me and propped her head on my shoulder. I put my arm around her.

"I don't know what to do," I said.

"You have to tell someone, of course," Jen said.

Lorraine nodded.

"But it could start a war. A genocide."

"If you don't say anything, that makes you a loose end to be tied up and they will do exactly that."

"Probably along with all your friends and family," Mikey said, climbing out of the water. He peeled his wet uniform shirt off and propped himself against a boulder.

I did not drool, but it was a close thing. The man was almost as pretty as Damon, with a six-pack and those sexy pelvic lines that point right to the main stage between his legs. He also had a dusting of hair on his chest and a fine little treasure trail that also ushered the way to the man's playground.

He flushed, noticing us staring at him. I half expected him to try to cover himself up, but he remained still, his jaw flexing with embarrassment.

"You can't put on a show and not expect an audience," I said, trying unsuccessfully not to laugh.

"And you've got a lot to show off," Jen drawled.

"Damned straight," Lorraine said, eyeing him.

"He's teasing," Stacey said, rolling her eyes. "If you want to ride the ride, you've got to buy a permanent ticket."

"True," Jen said. "There are other fun rides. Maybe not as pretty, but with less commitment."

His cheeks darkened. "Can we get back to problem at hand? Genocide versus all of you getting murdered?"

"He gets so fixated, doesn't he?" Jen said. "One track mind. Bet that makes him great in bed."

"Probably," Stacey said. "Also makes him terrible at friends-with-benefits."

"Moving right along," Lorraine said, clearly taking pity on Mikey who'd gone even brighter red and had begun to scowl. "What are we going to do about this whole mess?"

"The real question is who can you trust?" Jen asked me.

"I don't know. I like Mason and I'd like to think I can trust him, but if he thinks he's saving the world by reporting the information, then he will."

"Damon wouldn't, though," Lorraine said.

I didn't say anything.

The girls stared at me.

"You think he would report the information?" Jen asked in disbelief. "He wouldn't. You know how I know? Because you'd never fall for a guy who would do that."

I stared at her, rolling that thought around in my head. The problem was I didn't trust my judgement. Angie was proof enough of that. And if not her, then Garret, the man who I thought was my friend and turned out to be trying to murder and then kidnap me.

"You're wrong," I said. "Look at Garret. I knew him for years and had no idea he was a psychopath. I *liked* him. I thought about dating him. If I trust Damon and he reports that information to the powers that be, then whoever dies because of it is on my conscience."

"And if you don't say anything, then you risk yourself and everybody you care about," Mikey pointed out.

"He's right," Stacey said. "Pretty sure Lorraine and Jen will back me up on this: you matter more than any hypothetical people who get killed out there. But even if you didn't, you aren't responsible for their choices. Not only that, it sounds like this secondary witch world is plenty prepared for the fight. They aren't going to be caught with their pants down."

"I agree," Jen said, wading into the water and plopping down on the other side of me and putting her arm around my shoulders. "And for what it's worth, I think you can trust Damon and Mason and even your mother."

"So do I," Lorraine said as she came to sit on the other side of Stacey.

With a little butt wiggling, we were soon sitting in a circle with Stacey's leg given all the room it needed so she wouldn't bump it. Ajax gave a little whimper and plowed into the water, nosing between me and Jen. I rubbed my cheek on his head and he licked my nose.

"In the end, you don't really have a choice," Jen said. "If you try to keep the secret, you put too many innocent people at risk. You've got all the people working at your house, everybody at your business, the gargoyles, us, our families, Ben, Mikey, and who knows how many others? If the cat's out of the bag, then everybody is safer than if you keep the secret."

I thought about that. "You're right."

"Start with Damon," Lorraine advised. "He will have ideas on how to handle it."

I sighed. I guessed that meant I'd have to call him again. Since he wasn't planning on coming back anytime soon, I'd have to tell him on the phone. I could just imagine how awkward that was going to be.

"What's the matter?" Lorraine asked, all too quick to notice my lack of excitement at the prospect.

I grimaced and looked down at the water. "I, um, might have both told Damon I was in love with him and broke up with him."

It's not often that I can strike all three girls dumb at the same time, but that confession did it. They all stared at me. Jen opened her mouth and then shut it. Wow. It took a lot to strike her speechless. I ought to be taking that as a win. It didn't feel like it.

"Maybe you should explain," Lorraine said finally, because one of us had to be the voice of reason and she generally took on the role.

I sighed. "It happened last night. Or this morning. After everybody left, I called Damon and things took a turn."

"Clearly. Care to get more specific?" Lorraine again.

I had one arm around Ajax. Stacey grabbed my free hand and squeezed it. Her face had lost its pinched look and she was fully awake now.

"I told him about what was happening and he started in on how dangerous it was to go looking for the witch and that I should take Mason or my mother with me."

"Which he was right about," Jen pointed out.

I rolled my eyes. "Yeah, he was."

"What a dick," Stacey said.

"Right? It would have been so much more polite for him to be wrong and let me rub it in his face."

"Totally rude," Lorraine said, nodding. "Maybe even unforgivably so."

I giggled. I might be totally in the wrong, but at least my girls had my back.

"Feel free to get to the good part," Jen said, poking a finger into my thigh. "Anytime now."

"I might have gotten a little testy and changed the subject. I asked about his day and he said it's complicated. I told him I missed him and asked when he'd be back and he said it's complicated. I may have lost my temper a little bit and said fine and hung up on him. He called back and asked me to be patient with him. I told him I'm not that good at patience and then asked how he was doing. He said he was stressing and I wasn't making it any easier, so I up and told him that I knew that falling in love with him would be a disaster and I never should have done it and I hung up on him again. He didn't call back."

Several moments went by as the girls considered.

"Okay, his reaction or lack thereof is seriously weird," Jen said finally. "The guy loves you a lot. He pretty much worships the ground you walk on."

Tears burned my eyes and I blinked them away. "Maybe he changed his mind."

"Bullshit," Stacey declared. "That man is crazy about you."

"Then how do you explain him not responding?" I asked.

"I don't know. Maybe he didn't hear it. Maybe a meteor struck his house. All I know is that he wouldn't give up that easy."

"Maybe he just came to his senses. He's been gone weeks. Absence doesn't always make the heart grow fonder. It also makes for out of sight, out of mind, out of heart."

"Out of sight, out of mind, out of heart, isn't a thing," Stacey countered.

"Close enough."

"So what are you going to do about it?" Mikey asked suddenly. "Are you going to just give up? You're finally in love. Are you going to let him get away without putting up a fight? Or are you going to roll over like a coward?"

I glared at him over my shoulder. "I don't remember asking you."

"Good. That means your memory is intact," he shot back.

"Stacey, can't you control him?" I groaned.

"If I can't get him into bed without having to put a ring on my finger, what makes you think I can make him do anything at all? And no, I'm not going to agree to marry him just to shut him up. I love you, but not that much."

"You wound me."

"I'm sure," she said, putting her head back on my shoulder.

I leaned my head against hers. "Are you feeling better?"

"A lot. I can practically feel my leg knitting together."

"I'm not wrong," Mikey said from his perch.

"Yes, I know," I told him. "It's not endearing, either."

"I'll make a note."

"So that you annoy me more later, is that it?"

He chuckled. "Of course."

"Has anybody else noticed that he stopped despising us for corrupting poor little Stacey?" I asked. "I think we're starting to grow on him. Like fungus, maybe. Or mold," I added, before he could say it.

"You're changing the subject again," Lorraine said.

"Fine. Damon. I should fight for him. How and when? Because I have no idea where he's staying and no idea when he's coming back."

"Call him."

"My phone's a little bit destroyed at the moment."

"Get a new one."

I glared at Lorraine. "You have to have an answer for everything, don't you?"

"Of course. Most of them are even good ones."

"All right. I'll tell him about Angie and all the rest," I finally conceded, my stomach twisting. "I'll tell Mason and my mother too. And the gargoyles. They have to be prepared in case grandpa or the goons attack."

"Good," Jen said. "Now are there any other world problems we need to solve or can we eat some more?"

"I'm hungry," Stacey said plaintively.

She hadn't been awake enough to eat previously. I discovered I was back to starving. I fed Ajax some of the now-cold pizza and promised a real meal when we got home.

WE DIDN'T LEAVE THE POOL UNTIL CLOSE TO TWO IN THE morning. I was pretty much back to normal except for head-to-toe pruniness. After sending Mikey to put stuff in the car, I slipped on the skirt and blouse Lorraine and Jen had brought along for me, along with a pair of flip-flops. I brushed out my hair, which had also been restored by the pool.

Meanwhile, Jen and Lorraine stripped Stacey out of her hospital duds and put her in a bright blue maxi dress.

"Underwear or no underwear?" Jen asked.

"I don't think I can get it on over the brace."

"We can take that off for you," I said. "You probably don't need it anymore."

"Everybody will expect it though," she replied. "I need to look the part."

"So we'll put it back on."

"The bandages will get my panties wet, so there's not much point."

"It hurts to walk, but I can do it," Stacey said with a bemused smile as she limped in a little circle. She stretched out her arms and rolled her shoulders. "I think the bruises and scrapes are gone, too."

"There are definitely going to be questions," Jen said. "Maybe you shouldn't have stayed in the pool so long."

"Don't care. Totally worth it."

"Agreed," Mikey said, returning from his trip to the car.

"Says the man who doesn't have to deal with the fallout," I said. I looked at Stacey. "How much you want to bet your mom is going to parade you in church as having been given a miracle cure?"

Her nose wrinkled. "Ugh. You're right."

"*And* you have to explain to your parents and the rest of your family horde why you left the hospital," I pointed out. I frowned. "How did you even get out without them stopping you? It should have been trying to get through a minefield."

"We got lucky. If I didn't know better, I'd say it was supernatural. Most of the family had gone home for the night and the rest went to eat," Jen said. "The nurse had sent them away so she could check Stacey's wound sites. We got there just in time for her to finish her check and then escaped. In fact, her parents were getting off the other elevator right when we were getting on. I did text them when we left and told them Stacey was safe."

I snorted. "I'm sure that calmed them right the fuck down. Delusional much?"

"Can you use magic and make her look bad again?" Lorraine asked, focusing on solving the problem at hand.

I yawned, my jaw cracking. "I should be able to. Maybe you should all come back to the house and do it after we get some sleep. Plus, you'll be safer there if Angie's witch-friends start stirring up trouble."

"I've got a surgery first thing in the morning," Lorraine said. "I need to be getting things ready by five-thirty.

"Okay, then. Let's see what I can do now."

"Are you sure? You just made some pretty big magic," Jen said. "You've barely been healed."

I shrugged. "We'll find out, won't we?"

"Do you have a death wish?" Lorraine asked, brows arching.

"You'd think so, but no. Anyway, I've been through a lot worse. Besides, what if someone decided Stacey needs to be a saint or something? We'd never see her."

"Me, a saint? As soon as I opened my mouth they'd know better. They start calling me a demon and burn me at the stake."

"Demons don't get burned. They get exorcised," Lorraine said.

"And witches. You know that sooner or later someone is going to start noticing weird stuff happens around you, you know," Stacey said. "Maybe not with this injury, but something else."

"You know what they say. I'll burn that bridge when I come to it," I said. "Right now I want to focus on burning today's bridges."

"Very Zen of you," Lorraine said, unsuccessfully biting back a smile.

"I like to think of it as living in the moment," I said.

"Or more accurately, putting your head in the sand," Mikey said.

"Your glass is always half empty, isn't it?" Jen retorted.

"Just calling it like I see it."

"And you wonder why Stacey doesn't want long-term with you. The light at the end of the tunnel isn't always a train, you know."

He folded his arms and glared at her. "It is more often than not, and anyhow, just because it's not a train doesn't make it sunshine and roses."

"It must be exhausting living in your head. Seriously, how do you stand yourself? I mean, Beck has lived through years of torture and abuse and she sees the bright side more often than you do." Jen propped her hands on her hips and returned his glare.

"If you don't mind, I'm just going to get started." I didn't wait for them to quit arguing, but turned to Stacey, picturing her appearance when she'd arrived. I pulled up gentle strands of power and wrapped her in them, weaving a glamour around her. I was certain I wasn't getting the details right, but I had to hope it was close enough.

"Too bad we didn't take before pictures," I muttered.

"I did," Jen said.

I flicked a startled look at her. "Seriously?"

"They were more like future blackmail pictures, plus I snapped a few of our getaway," she said. She pulled out her phone and scrolled to the pictures before handing it to me. I flipped through them and adjusted Stacey's appearance.

"I'll have to adjust the illusion every day or two as the bruises and scratches heal. You're going to have use your crutches. You might want to put tacks in your socks for a while. I could give you a pain spell you could trigger that would hurt when you need to be sure you act the part."

Stacey wrinkled her nose. "As sadomasochistic as that sounds, it might be a good idea."

"Give me your ring for a second." I held out my hand.

"I don't have it. It's in my hospital bag with whatever's left of my clothes."

"Here, use this," Jen said, removing a gold chain with a pearl pendant and handing it to me.

I closed my hand around it and concentrated. When I was finished, I fastened it around her neck.

"Activate it by saying 'Marco.' Deactivate it by saying—"

"Polo. Yeah, I got it. You couldn't have come up with something more interesting like maybe dick and vagina? Or drag and queen?"

"First of all, I'm tired. If you're not nice, I'll make it so everybody else can activate it, too. I did you a favor. Given how often you say dick, vagina, or drag queen, you'd be randomly activating and deactivating it every couple of minutes. Then you'd be whining to me to make it something completely unusual."

She laughed and pulled me into a hug. "That's so true. I give in. You're the best and I am so grateful you came and found me in that stupid ravine. I knew I could count on you."

My throat knotted it. "Always."

We gathered up the rest of our things and made sure we'd cleaned up all our garbage before heading out. Ajax bounded ahead, more than ready to get home.

"Thanks, B.B.! I owe you," I called out. "I promise to repay you with all the tasty things, starting tomorrow."

The little yellow buddha popped into view. "Another milkshake?" he asked hopefully.

"Absolutely."

His chubby smile widened and he practically glowed. "Delightful."

I drove Mikey back to his cruiser before returning home. The girls headed to Lorraine's where they planned to spend the rest of the night.

"I'll follow you back to your place," Mikey said as he got out of the car.

I'd refused to let him drive.

"You don't have to. I'll be fine."

"Still going to do it, and if you try to race away before I can, I'll give you a ticket."

"That's rude. What's going to stop me from throwing a magic bomb at you?"

"I promised Jen I'd make sure you got home safe."

My brows rose. Jen and not Stacey? "Did she threaten you?"

"When does Jen *not* threaten me?"

He had a point. Since this was Jen's idea, I decided not to fuck with him. Given my day, I wasn't all that much in the mood anyway, though I would have stepped up to the plate just on principle.

"Fine."

I waited for him to get settled and back out, then proceeded on my way. Ajax crawled up into the front seat and curled into a tight ball, his nose tucked under his tail.

Mikey flicked his lights and continued on as Marlen waved me in at the gatehouse entrance of the drive. He was Joseph's son, and they switched off duties along with Joseph's daughter, Manique. I'd gone about halfway up the drive when gargoyles divebombed, two of them landing in the road just ahead. I slammed on the brakes. My heart just about exploded out of my chest. Ajax lunged into the air, all four legs stiff. The hair on his back stood on end and his head dipped down. A threatening growl rolled through him, loud enough to vibrate the windows.

"It's okay, boy," I told him, running a hand down his back. I tried to catch my breath as I watched the two gargoyles pace around to my window, which I rolled down.

"You scared the shit out of me," I said.

Ajax growled again, his lips curling from his teeth.

"Peace, little brother," the second gargoyle said to Ajax. "We mean no harm."

That one had a sort of cat-like face with a bristly mane running down the back of his neck and over his shoulders. The other one had a longer face with a snubbed nose like a hyena and a pair of long, spiral horns protruding from his forehead. Both had wings, though they seemed more furry than leathery. I didn't know either of their names and hadn't tried to find out. If they wanted me to know, they'd tell me.

Horn-head bent down to look in at me. "We have been waiting for you. We sensed you were in danger and we could not find you."

I couldn't tell if there was any reproof in his tone. I wouldn't blame him if there was. I had promised to find a way to free him and the rest of his companions, and if I died, I couldn't do that.

"A witch attacked me. Kidnapped me, actually. I managed to escape, but she and her, um, friends, might come looking for me. I was going to warn you about that now that I'm home."

I didn't know if I should go into detail about who the other witches were and why they might be coming after me. Did the gargoyles know about the prophesy? Would they even care?

"What did the witch want of you?"

Now that was a good question. "She killed someone and I was close to finding out who she was and reporting her, so she got to me first."

"Are you injured?" His orange eyes scrutinized me with clinical detachment.

"I was. I'm better now."

"That is good." He gazed around behind me and up into

the sky then back at me. "We will keep watch. Someone waits for you."

Before I could say anything, he and his silent buddy launched into the air. For flying rocks, they sure went fast and quietly. They disappeared quickly into the darkness.

I started back up the driveway. Someone was waiting for me? Who? The gargoyles weren't exactly concerned, which meant my mother or Mason. Probably Mason, since they knew him better.

I groaned. What in the hell was I going to tell him? That I had decided to take a quick trip to Disneyland and forgot to tell anybody and oh, yeah, my phone died. That was totally believable. Maybe I could crash my car into the house and distract him that way. Take a handy dose of cyanide? *Damn, must have left it in my other purse.*

I drove as slowly as possible, but still hadn't come up with any ideas by the time I parked the Highlander in the garage. Another delaying tactic. I never parked in the garage, which was closer to a barn in size. That would probably change during winter, if I was still living here, but until then, I preferred parking near the door.

I closed the garage door before getting out. I gathered my purse and the tote full of papers I'd been carrying for the two meetings I'd missed thanks to Angie.

Ajax followed me out the side door. I paused on the threshold. I could sneak in the house and up to my suite. Of course, Mason had no doubt seen my car drive up and would probably come knocking on my door. Either that or he'd sleep in a spare room and be waiting for me at breakfast.

"Can't win for losing," I muttered to Ajax. "Let's get this over with. Oh, I know. Laryngitis. That's the answer. I'm suddenly mute as a board."

"I hope not. I was thinking we should talk."

My whole body went white hot, then glacial cold, then back to white hot. My mouth went dry, opened and closed. I must've looked like a stoned goldfish. Always a good look. Then, finally, I managed to push words through my constricted throat. Unfortunately, they were not happy words of welcome.

"Damon? What the fuck are you doing here?"

CHAPTER TWENTY-TWO

I managed to close my mouth, mostly because I couldn't come up with anything more to say. Instead, I just looked at him, letting his presence sink into me. Every single one of my nerve endings exploded with excitement. Or maybe trepidation. Or terror. Could have been any of those.

He looked as gorgeous as ever, with his chiseled jaw covered in a closely-trimmed blond beard, blunt nose, broad shoulders, and powerful legs. His scent wrapped around me and I had to stop myself from just closing my eyes and breathing deep.

"Like I said, I think we need to talk," he said, his voice rumbling through me, sending my hormones ping-ponging around like marbles in a blender.

"I thought you were busy back wherever." I waved my hand at an imaginary place. "Too busy to come back."

I couldn't bring myself to say *home*. Given the weeks since he'd been gone and his lack of communication, I'd gone back to feeling like he didn't think he belonged here. That he didn't belong with me. And that didn't even take into account the discovery of another witching world. For all I knew he'd go racing off to deal with that and I'd be left dangling in the wind. Again.

"Home," he said, stepping forward. "Come back *home*."

He stood a foot away. He was dressed in one of his cashmere shirts, the arms stretching tight over his biceps and lovingly shaping his chest. I dropped my hand to stroke Ajax's head. Better than petting Damon. Well, not *better*, per se. Just a lot less embarrassing at this point.

I shrugged as if to say 'if you say so.' His mouth tightened and he scowled.

"We could have talked on the phone. You didn't need to make a flight out."

"I think I did. Where have you been?"

"You didn't call Mason?"

He shook his head. "I landed around nine and caught an Uber from the airport."

"From San Francisco?"

He made an exasperated sound. "Yes, from San Francisco."

"You didn't rent a car?"

"No."

"Why not?" Like it mattered.

"I was in a hurry and the Uber was faster. Plus I had some things to take care of on the drive."

"What things?"

"How about we talk about you? Where have you been?"

"Visiting with Stacey, Jen, and Lorraine."

"Until two in the morning? The hospital doesn't allow visitors that late."

"Jen and Lorraine broke her out. We were at the pool."

"What happened with helping the police find the

kidnapper/murderer? You said you were going to do that today."

I rubbed one of my eyes. "I didn't quite get around to helping, exactly."

He just looked at me, waiting. I sighed.

"Maybe we should talk about this inside."

He looked like he was going to argue and then gave a sharp nod. "Fine. Let's go inside."

Damon stepped aside to let me pass. I crossed the breezeway and entered through a side door. The house was quiet with a few lights left on. Others came on automatically as we walked through.

As we reached the main living area, Deirdre rose from a chair where she'd been reading.

"Good evening," she said. She scanned me up and down. "I was worried. Your mother and uncle both called, as did Jennifer, Lorraine, and the police. The gargoyles came awake during the day." Her voice held a hint of reproof, that I should have thought of them worrying about me.

Damon jerked to look at me. "Why were they all looking for you? What happened?"

I set my stuff on a side table and spoke to Deirdre. "I'm fine now, but I had to go to my sanctuary pool and heal up a bit."

"What?" Damon grabbed my wrist and turned me to face him. "How badly were you injured?"

"Somewhere between extra-crispy and char-broiled." I looked over my shoulder at Deirdre. "There may be some trouble coming. I don't know, but I've warned the gargoyles."

"Beck, I'm getting really tired of you ignoring me,"

Damon said in a hard, flat voice, his stormy blue eyes gone hard as diamonds. "What the fuck is going on?"

I looked back at him. "I'm not ignoring you. I just want to get settled in private to have this conversation."

He flushed and flicked a glance at Deirdre, whose expression was a mask of impassivity. I wondered if my obvious dismissal annoyed her. Not that I could really keep secrets in the house. I'd never directly mentioned the sanctuary pool, but she clearly knew what it was. Anyway, if the witches from Angie's world were going to attack, my entire household would need to know who they were facing.

Just not yet. First, I had to consult Damon, and that had to be done without an audience.

"Would you like anything to eat or drink?" she asked.

"No, thank you. Please don't bother with me. I've kept you up late enough."

"It is no trouble."

I snorted. "It's a lot of trouble and you deserve a raise for putting up with me and all the shenanigans I get up to."

She smiled, her teeth pearly white against her Indian skin. "You are certainly not boring, and your aunt required far more of us. You are less stringent."

"That's an incredibly polite way of saying she was a huge bitch," I said.

Her smile widened slightly. "Have a good night. I'm glad you're home safe. It is very nice to see you as well, Damon."

With that, she withdrew.

"I have to feed Ajax really quick. Then we can talk."

I took him into the kitchen and found his gourmet meal in the refrigerator. It was chopped unseasoned chicken with mashed sweet potato, carrots, and green beans. I removed the lid and set his bowl on the floor. He devoured it in nothing flat, then drank from his bowl.

"Let's go upstairs," I said, patting my leg.

Ajax trotted over. I scratched his head before leading the way to the staircase.

It was not lost on me that not only had Damon not kissed me hello, he had also not hugged me. In fact, he'd barely touched me. I couldn't seem to scrape up the courage to initiate contact. I'd told him I loved him. The ball was in his court and he seemed to be ignoring it.

I trotted up the stairs to the third floor. I had a large suite with a giant bedroom and a separate sitting room and a small office. I'd redecorated, despite the fact that it was not the same suite Aunty Mommy had occupied. There were four suites on the third floor, each equally as spacious as the other. I'd chosen the one furthest from away from Aunty Mommy's former digs.

I still didn't want to live here. I had totally been planning to return to my apartment once the rebuilding of my shop and apartment were complete. That was looking less and less like a good idea the more enemies started to crawl out of the woodwork.

Staying in Aunty Mommy's House of Torture was ironically the safest place to be, given all the wards she'd installed to protect the place, not to mention having the gargoyles on watch.

I grabbed a bottle of iced tea out of my mini-fridge. "Want anything?" I asked Damon. "I've got water, the usual juices, iced coffee, beer, and tea."

"Orange juice, please."

I handed him a bottle and then took a seat at the end of the couch, curling my feet up under me. It wasn't entirely a defensive position, but it didn't encourage cuddling, either. Mostly because I doubted he wanted to cuddle, and if I put off the go-away vibes, then I could blame myself and not feel hurt. In other words, I was acting like an idiot. Knowing that, however, didn't stop me. Ajax chose his favorite over-stuffed chair, circling himself twice before flopping down and curling into a ball.

Damon sat on the coffee table facing me, his knee touching the edge of the couch. His eyes were hard with intent. I sighed inwardly.

"What happened?"

I took the tale up from when I left the house. I was sort of shocked to realize that that was only eighteen or nineteen hours ago.

"I thought it was just a regular accident, but then she drugged me at her home. It turned out she was a witch. The witch who killed Arthur Chapman and kidnapped the husband, Matthew Chapman, and their children, Melissa and Toby. Only it turns out that wasn't quite the reality."

"How so?"

"For one, Angie was the kids' biological mother. She'd given them up when they were born and wanted to get back in their lives. Then it turns out that Arthur was an abusive bastard and Matthew was the one who killed him. In self-defense. So, Angie used her magic to cover it up and was hiding them in her house. She panicked when she realized another witch was looking for her. I was dumb enough to leave my spell active at the murder house and she used it to follow me here."

I sipped from my tea. "I don't know that she had a plan for after kidnapping me. While I was drugged, she spelled me to have to obey her and somehow kept me from accessing my magic. I don't know if that was an actual block, or just her telling me I couldn't, but suddenly it felt gone. I couldn't feel it at all."

Damon scowled. "That's an unusual power. Not many can do that. I wonder what family line she's from."

"Well, that's sort of where things get interesting," I said, teasing the fabric of my skirt between my fingers.

His brows rose. "*That's* where things get interesting? Because I was thinking the entertainment levels kicked up when she kidnapped you."

"I can see how you'd think that. I thought so, too, but turns out we're both wrong."

I took another sip, trying to formulate how to reveal the next bit. He took a swig of his juice and replaced the cap as he waited.

"Well?" he prompted finally.

"I don't exactly know how to tell you," I admitted, then shrugged. "We got to talking and she made me tell her about Aunty Mommy and how I grew up and meeting you and Mason and pretty much everything." I paused, remembering the feeling of being out of control, of being unable to stop myself. I shuddered. "That might have been the worst thing anybody's done to me," I said, and I meant it.

Sure, I'd been physically hurt and Aunty Mommy had done her best to humiliate me and tear me apart, but having someone else taking control of me so that I was mentally and physically enslaved—that was far, far worse.

I hardly finished saying it when Damon set aside his juice and shifted to the couch beside me. He tugged me into his arms, pressing me against his chest and stroking my hair. His scent enveloped me, and I closed my eyes, letting the electric bliss of his touch wash through me. It was like silk and fire on all my senses. Flutters rippled through my chest and stomach.

"I'm sorry that happened," he said, his voice rumbling through his chest. "I wish I'd been here."

I could hear the real pain and guilt in his voice. Part of me stamped its foot and said *damned straight, you should have been here and not off doing* complicated *shit that you refuse to talk about.* The more rational side of me gave a slight shake of my head.

"There's nothing you could have done. I'd have gone to work and fallen into her trap even if you were here."

"You don't know that for sure."

"Just like you don't know that being here would have changed a damned thing," I said and pushed myself away. "Anyway, that's all over."

He let me adjust myself back into my seat, but kept an arm around the couch behind me and refused to let go of the hand he'd captured.

"That sort of thing doesn't just go away because it's over."

I shrugged. "I'll deal with it. Anyhow, we've got a bigger craptastrophe to deal with."

"I'm listening."

"A while back, Ben told me about how the whole breeding program started. Something about a vision some old witch had on her deathbed and everybody believed her."

He frowned, nodding. "The ruling families of the witching world fell out and starting fighting. It went on for a couple decades and then it looked like all-out war was going to break out and one side—"

"*Your* side," I interjected.

His brows rose. "Our side," he conceded, "though I wasn't born yet, and neither were my grandparents."

"That's what I meant."

He gave me a side-eye look but continued. "Our side cursed the others so they'd never have children and their side would die out. Everything calmed down and the threat of out-and-out war died. That went on for many years, and then Olivia Siddiqui had a deathbed vision. She'd always been a powerful witch and had such a power for foretelling the future that she went blind."

"Ouch. That sucks. Was she always right?"

"There was always truth in her visions, though whether she or anybody else understood them correctly, I don't know."

I chewed my lip, thinking. "So, she could have a vision of you with a knife trying to kill someone, but the part of the story where you're doing it to protect somebody else might not make it through?"

"Basically. Context matters and visions don't really give that. Of course, one of the things that made her so powerful was that her visions generally lasted minutes and had a great deal of detail. Many seers only catch glimpses or fuzzy suggestions of what might happen. Some hear voices or experience smells. Olivia Siddiqui experienced hers as if they happened to her."

"What was her death bed prophecy?"

"That's always been somewhat problematical. By that time, she was quite old and had been ill. She raved about the return of those who'd been cursed. She said that we hadn't really destroyed them and that they'd rise up."

"With a lot of blood and destruction, if I remember correctly. And so the breeding program started to create witches powerful enough to withstand them."

"That's the story, though I'm pretty sure it was really somebody's project and the prophecy conveniently gave them an opportunity."

I cocked my head. "So, you don't think the prophecy was real?"

"I think she was old and likely had dementia and her family certainly grew more wealthy and powerful because of it. Why?"

No way to say it but just rip off the bandage.

"Because Angie freaked out when I didn't know certain things that were standard among her, um, people."

His brows rose. "Her people?"

"Yeah. Seems like the cursed ones didn't die out but are alive and well and living in the suburbs."

His eyes widened and he sat back as if to get a better look at me. "You'd better explain."

I went on to tell him about Grandpa, and my fight with Eyeglasses and Punk Waitress. When I was done, I sipped from my tea as he processed all that I'd said. At least I expected him to process it.

He cupped my face in his palm. "How badly were you hurt?"

I lifted one shoulder. "Like I'd been left on the barbecue a couple hours too long. As you can see, the pool worked. For Stacey too."

I then explained what had happened after I'd left Angie's.

"I don't know quite what I did, but I probably shouldn't have ended up so hurt. The more power I used, the more I seemed to hurt myself, but it worked in the end." Another half-shrug.

He pulled me against his chest again, lifting me so I sat across his lap. He buried his face in my neck, his breath hot on my skin.

"I almost lost you again. Godammit, Beck. You can't keep doing this. I don't know what I'd do if I lost you."

I wanted to debate that. He'd been MIA for weeks and weeks and refused to talk about what was going on with him. Surely if he really wanted me, if he wanted to be with me, he'd have come back or been a little more forthcoming on the phone.

I pushed back a little, looking into his eyes and ignoring the hot flush of emotion through my chest. I was so damned grateful to be looking at him. I might have died today or been taken off to some secret prison in the Himalayas, and I'd have never seen him again.

He must have read something in my eyes because he slid his hands up from my hips, over my ribs, arms, and shoulders and cupped my face. He pulled me to him and touched my lips lightly to his.

His lips moved slowly over mine, the tip of his tongue sliding across the seam of my lips. Amazing how such a tiny gesture could light such an inferno. I gave a little gasp and gripped his wrists, my fingers digging into his flesh as the rest of me exploded into sizzling sensation. How was this even possible? He'd barely kissed me. His lips were featherlight against mine.

My gasp gave him the opportunity to deepen the kiss. His fingers slid behind my neck, pulling me in. His tongue dipped into my mouth in little teasing darts, almost like asking permission for more. It reminded me we had not talked about us or my confession and that he'd not called me after it.

But he came home.

Sure, he hadn't looked all that happy to see me, and he hadn't kissed me hello, but he was kissing me now and I wasn't about to stop him to complain.

I touched my tongue to his and tilted my head to keep from smashing my nose. He made a noise of approval that curled my toes. He slid one hand down around my hip and tugged me so I was half laying across his lap. He had one arm around my back and the other came back up to wrap the back of my neck as he abandoned his careful flirtation and went for full-on romantic assault. His mouth widened over mine, his tongue tasting me deeply.

I'd managed to get my arms around his neck and pulled myself sideways so that I could deepen the kiss further. He made a growling sound in his throat and jerked me closer. His body was hard against mine, his pulse pounding. My breasts had begun to ache for his touch. I wanted his hands on me. I wanted his mouth, teeth, and tongue on my skin. I wanted to touch him, run my fingers over his hard muscles and I wanted to finally...*finally*... hold his cock in my hand and watch his expression when I took him in my mouth.

It was my turn to make sounds. Hungry ones. I slid a hand beneath his collar. His skin was hot and begging to be tasted. Not at all interested in denying myself, I pulled from his kiss to replace my fingers with my lips, only to have a bucket of ice water dropped on my head.

"Wait, Beck," Damon said, pushing me back.

I felt myself recoiling and retracting. Self-defense.

Don't do it. He's here, and he's clearly wanting you. Give him the fucking benefit of the doubt, why don't you?

I curled my fingers into his shirt, less to keep him from pushing me away and more to make sure I didn't end up across the room in a hurt little rejection ball. Or raving violently like the woman scorned.

"We need to talk. We can't—" He swallowed and his eyes flared. "We need to talk," he said again, after a long moment.

He eased me up but didn't push me off his lap. He anchored me down just in case I planned to go somewhere.

I was tempted to wriggle back and forth a little. Damon Junior was hard as marble and poking at the back of my thigh, telling me to do something about it. I decided to shift my weight and pretend to adjust myself on his lap. He sucked in a breath and squeezed his eyes shut. I hid my entirely-too-pleased grin.

Surprisingly, I was more than willing to skip the talking and head right to the fucking. Out of the blue, all my reservations had evaporated. That probably wasn't a healthy sign. I'd been really paranoid about taking the next steps since both of us knew that sex meant more than just pleasure. For us, it had to mean real commitment. I had to let myself be too vulnerable and exposed for it to be anything less than that. Damon was the same. So was Detective Mikey, but he could just stay right out of my head.

Damon might think I had a screw loose if he knew I was eager to throw caution to the wind and jump in way over my head and comfort zone. But I was horny and I had been getting regular abject lessons in the fact that life is short and you have to live it while you can. Plus, I'd finally admitted to myself that I'd fallen in love with him. He'd already told me he loved me, so really, there was nothing left to do but get on with it. *Now* would be good.

Sadly, it looked like he really did want to be all adulty and hash things out.

"What do you want to talk about?" I asked, sounding like I'd run sandpaper over my vocal chords. "The fact that there's a whole other witch world out there and if we tell anybody there will probably be another attempt at genocide? Maybe a big war, too? Or maybe the weather? How do you feel about cilantro? Yummy or tastes like soap?"

The corners of his mouth flickered. He cleared his throat. "As important as the first topic is—and we do need to sort out what to do—and as engrossing as a conversation about the weather would be, and let's face it, cilantro is one of the most controversial subjects on the planet, I think we should talk about us."

His smile faded and his eyes went deadly serious.

"Oh? Do elaborate."

That smile again, but also a hint of wariness in expression. Like he wasn't sure what I was up to. Made two of us. No, that wasn't true. I was up to no good, as usual, and he should know that much about me.

"I've not been very forthcoming about what I've been up to overseas," he said.

My brows went up. I'd thought he'd dive right in with a 'I noticed you said you loved me on the phone last night,' conversation. Color me surprised, and a little bit peeved. Peeved is a step or two below pissed, for everybody following along.

"I did notice that," I said, deciding to play along.

"I didn't want you to know." He paused, clearly waiting for me to say something.

I cycled through my various reactions. Annoyance, hurt, anger, curiosity.

"I'm not sure how to respond to that," I said finally. "Why didn't you want me to know?"

"Because you'd have up and jumped on a plane and put yourself in danger."

My gaze narrowed. "Just what the fuck has been going on? Do I need to get off your lap because we're about to have a fight?"

His hands tightened. "If we're going to have a fight, I want you right where you are."

"I might get violent and punch you in the jaw."

"I'll risk it."

At that moment, Ajax whimpered and lifted his head, staring over at us.

"It's okay," I told him. "We're just ironing out some stuff." I looked back at Damon, my voice developing a hard edge. "Like why you'd ever try to shut me out."

"I'd say it was complicated, but it isn't, really." He sighed. "Your father is putting pressure on my family. He figures he can force me to break things off with you if he makes it impossible for my family to make quality birthing contracts, so he's been out threatening everybody who even thinks of contracting with us. He's using every bit of leverage he has, from money to political capitol to genetics."

"And you've been trying to stave off that pressure?"

"That's part of it. As soon as I got back, I was put to work salvaging contracts along with a whole cadre of family attorneys. It didn't do a lot of good. Your father wields enormous power."

"And you didn't want me there to help you? Why not? Am I a liability?"

He caught my face between his palms and waited until I met his gaze. "Never. But you'd have been in a lot of danger there. Garrett's not the only one who'd be willing to take you against your will and using you as a broodmare. Your father would, too, along with a host of others. I wouldn't have been able to protect you, not even from my own family."

I stared at him, letting the meaning of his words sink in. Angie's little trick of forcing me to obey her had scared the shit out of me. What if a whole family of witches had ganged up on me to do the same thing so I could pop out litters of babies for them?

The idea made me want to both puke and commit murder. A lot of murder.

"Okay," I said, pulling his hands from my face. "What happened then?

He grimaced. "So, then things got a little ugly."

I scowled. "Ugly, how?"

"Some of my family thought it would be a good idea to put me under house arrest until they could force me to break things off with you."

I made a sound of pure fury.

"There were also those who thought this was a fabulous opportunity and that I should lock you into a contract for a whole host of children. Certainly, I could father one or two, but then others would have to have their opportunities, and all would have to be taken into the Montrovani family umbrella. Many of those supported bringing you there and forcing you to cooperate if you refused."

"Fucking assholes," I said, barely able to get the words through my clenched teeth. My fingers had fallen into my lap and curled into claws. I'd have been ripping out eyes and throats if those assholes had been near enough. "I'm sorry, but I don't think I like your family."

"You'd like a few, particularly the ones who thought this whole thing was a load of bullshit. My sister, Nora, for one. She and some cousins helped me escape and return here."

"Escape? Your family seriously had you locked up? I am so going to go nuclear on their asses."

He covered my hands with one of his, rubbing the back of my neck with his other.

"I wasn't really locked in. I had watchers who kept an eye on me every time I left my home. Which is why it took me so long to get back here after you hung up on me last night and I realized what you'd said. I had to lose them before I could get on a plane."

He brushed away the hair shielding my eyes.

"Did you mean it? *Do* you love me?"

His voice had softened and turned uncertain.

I looked down at our hands, suddenly feeling bashful. "I'll be honest. I hadn't actually been able to decide when I blurted it out."

He sagged. "Oh."

"I didn't know how to be sure, you see. I kept chewing on the question, especially after you didn't call me back, and I realized that yes, I do love you. A lot. At least I think it's love. Either that or I have wicked indigestion, a serious heart problem, brain lesions, and someone's been breeding butterflies in my stomach."

His smile came back as I spoke, his eyes brightening with joy.

"You're sure? I really need you to be sure. I'd understand if you weren't. It would hurt, but I'd understand. This has been really fast—"

I lost patience and kissed him.

CHAPTER TWENTY-THREE

This time there was no taking it slow. Fire erupted between us. I don't even know how it happened, but one second I sitting on his lap kissing him, the next I was lying full length underneath him, the hard ridge of his cock pressed intimately against me.

The heat of his body wrapped around me, and his mouth devoured me. It was all I could do to keep up. I was feeling so many things. All my nerves were sending me messages of delight and pleasure and I couldn't sort them all out.

Abruptly he tore his mouth from mine. I made sounds of protest and tightened my arms to keep him from moving away as he began to push himself upright.

"What's wrong?"

"You've been through a serious ordeal in the last day, you've been wounded and healed, and it's only a few hours until dawn. You don't need me mauling you right now. You need some sleep."

My first instinct was to tell him to shut up and get back to business, but then I had an idea. A little romantic torture never hurt anyone, *and* I could get a shower before rubbing around all over him.

I yawned. "Well, now that you mention it, I am a little sore still. And tired. I wouldn't mind a shower, either."

He instantly looked solicitous and jumped to his feet. "I'm sorry. I'm an asshole. I shouldn't have been pushing."

"I don't know. I was enjoying myself, and I hear pushing can be a lot of fun." I flicked my eyebrows up and down.

He snorted and pointed to the bedroom door. "Go shower. I'll unpack."

I looked around. "Where's your suitcase?"

"In the bedroom."

"A little presumptuous, don't you think?" I asked as I headed in that direction.

"You said you loved me. I was hoping I'd heard right and you hadn't changed your mind."

"I am known to be wishy-washy like that." My entire body felt full of happy bubbles. "I won't be long."

I zipped into the bathroom and back out into the massive closet and dug out a lacy pair of red panties and a matching camisole. Within a few minutes I was in a steamy shower. I stayed in there longer than necessary. I wanted Damon to get bored and get horizontal on the bed. With any luck, he'd be napping.

I chortled happily to myself as I made plans. I fully expected him to run the show once we got started, seeing as how I had no idea what I was doing, at least beyond what I saw in movies and heard from the girls. Porn wasn't my thing, so I couldn't say I'd seen every virgin's guide-to-sex manual.

Eventually I left the shower and dried off and dressed in my sexy lingerie, then blew out my hair. Last of all I brushed my teeth, then went through the closet, donning my fleece robe as I did. As I'd hoped, Damon lay on top of the bed, sleeping. He hadn't removed anything but his shoes and socks. Ajax sprawled beside him.

That wouldn't do. I snapped my fingers and pointed to the giant cushion beside the bed. I'd bought it just for this eventuality. Sharing the bed with him and Damon was fine until we decided to get down to business. Then Ajax needed to be elsewhere. He wagged and hoisted himself off the bed and padded out the doorway into the sitting room. I tiptoed over to shut the door. He was in the process of making himself comfortable on the couch.

I went to the foot of the bed and looked down at Damon. Muted light from one of the lamps cast its glow over him, highlighting his blunt, masculine features and burnishing his blond hair and beard. Nervous anticipation tickled through me. I unbelted my robe and let it slide to the floor. I approached the bed like I was sneaking up on a lion.

I almost giggled. Damon wasn't dangerous, and if he wanted to bite me, I was all for it. At the foot of the bed, I contemplated my next move. I'd been hoping he'd have pulled off his shirt at least, maybe undone his belt. No such luck. Meanwhile I was doing my best to look sexy in very little red lace. I wondered if I could get his zipper down without waking him up. I could just get into bed and wait for him to figure out I was there, but all the parts of me that ached wanted his attention *now*.

I gave myself a mental kick. I was overthinking this. I flicked a little magic out and dissolved all the seams of his clothing. Instantly strips of his legs, ribs, and shoulders appeared. I could work with this.

I eased onto the bed and slid the front of his shirt away,

exposing his chest. His rippled abs were utterly lickable, so I did just that. I ran the tip of my tongue from just above his belt up to his nipple. His stomach tensed at my touch. Before he could figure out what was going on, I straddled his hips and grabbed his wrists, holding them to the side. I tongued his nipple, swirling around the hardened point. He groaned and his hips undulated beneath me.

"Beck? What are you wearing?" he asked in a strangled voice, his voice deepening as he took in my pushed-up cleavage and red lace cami. Really it was more on the corset side of things. "You're fucking beautiful. And I'm not complaining even a little bit, but I thought you were tired."

I switched to his other nipple, delighting in the shudder that ran through him. "Turns out I just needed a shower."

"Fuck," he said, drawing out the word as I bit him gently. Once again he bucked under me. It felt divine.

I did it again on the other side.

"You're killing me, Beck. What happened to my clothes?"

"They had terrible seams," I murmured, nibbling up his neck to suck on his ear lobe. "Terrible quality, really." I still had a firm hold of his wrists but knew that wouldn't last long. His entire body had gone rigid. His arms and chest flexed. His eyes had narrowed and he looked like the lion I'd imagined him to be, only very hungry. I was his prey.

I gave a shiver and didn't fight when he wrenched free of my grip. In one move, he rolled me under him and began kissing me. Intense sensations spun like a firestorm inside me. Everywhere he touched felt impossibly hot and throbbing and my body ached for *more*.

Most of his shirt had been left behind in the roll, not to mention his pants and underwear. His belt had chosen to not quite go away, and I couldn't help but wrap magic around it and fling it away.

Damon chuckled, the sound vibrating through his chest and into mine.

"Impatient, are you? I like it." He said the words against my throat as he kissed and licked along the sensitive cords of my neck.

I shuddered and ran my hands up his ribs, feeling my way across the dips and rises of his muscles. My fingers traced to his back and spine and slid lower, exploring the curve of his ass. His muscles tightened and his hips pushed into mine. The hard ridge of his cock slid over me.

I gasped. Electricity shot through me like someone had tossed a match into a box of fireworks and they all went off at once.

He continued to move his hips, all the while kissing me. I got hotter and hotter even though he stayed above my shoulders. I bent my knees and squeezed my thighs against his hips, whether to stop his sensual rocking or beg for more. My insides had drawn tight and continued to tighten. It was too slow.

I started to grind against him for relief and he lifted away.

"Not too fast," he admonished. "You want to enjoy this."

"I am enjoying it," I said, tilting my hips into his again. "I want to enjoy it faster."

"Uh uh," he said. "It'll be better if we go slow."

"Says you. We can go slow later. Fast now." I'd begun to sound more than a little whiny and I could tell from his smile that Damon was enjoying my neediness. If I hadn't been teetering on the edge, I'd have told him where he could stick himself. Actually, maybe that's exactly what I should do.

"I want you inside me."

He shook his head. "Be patient. This is pretty much your first time. I want it to be good. Better than good."

"It is better than good. You're driving me insane."

"It's going to take time. I don't want to hurt you."

He gave me a long, drugging kiss that only served to stoke the flames burning inside me. When we came up for air, it took me a second to remember what I meant to say.

"You won't hurt me. The girls made me get a dildo to help with that."

He froze, staring down at me. My mouth went dry. Did I just kill the mood?

"You have been playing with yourself," he said slowly. "With a dildo."

"Is that bad?"

He sucked in a breath, closing his eyes. "It's fucking hot and if you want to go fast, I may have already just beaten you to the finish."

A smile curved my lips. "I didn't mean that fast."

"Between you wearing this lacy thing and knowing what you've been doing, I might need a minute."

"Go right ahead," I said, deciding to nibble on that soft spot where his neck ran into his shoulder. "I have things to keep me busy."

He groaned. "You do not play fair."

"This is news to you?"

"I guess that means I don't have to play fair, either, right?"

And then I couldn't respond because he rolled us back over and sat up so my knees were on either side of his hips and my breasts were in his face. He ran his hands over them, cupping them and circling his thumbs over my nipples.

I clenched my thighs on him, my mouth falling stupidly open as sensation zapped through me. Pleasure zinged around and settled into throbbing heat between my legs. I grabbed his shoulders to keep from flying off into outer space and he took advantage of the moment, his mouth closing on my right breast. His tongue flicked my nipple through the silky lace of my cami and the tightness inside of me clenched harder. I moaned and curled my fingers into his flesh.

He repeated the gesture on the other side, then sucked harder.

"I don't think I can wait," I gasped.

"No? Maybe just a little longer."

He slid his fingers under the cami and gently pushed it up, stopping when he exposed my breasts. His eyelids drooped and lit with lambent hunger.

"You're beautiful," he said in a hushed voice, lifting away the cami and settling his hands on my hips. He dipped his head and took me in his mouth, sucking deeply. Meanwhile he rubbed his thumb over my other nipple.

I rocked my hips forward against his cock. His fingers on my hip tightened and he made a gravelly sound. I did it again, abundantly pleased at the affect I was having on him. I didn't want to be the only one losing my mind. He dropped his other hand to my hip and pulled me tight against him but kept licking and sucking. I tried to rub on him some more, but he wouldn't let me. My head fell back and I gripped his shoulders, my body straining to tip over the edge.

To no avail.

I was stuck teetering and Damon refused to let me fall.

He wound me tighter and tighter, inching me closer and closer. I was making incoherent sounds and starting to claw his shoulders. He pulled away from my aching breasts and kissed me, another one of those long, sensuous kisses.

"Are you ready?"

"Are you stupid?" I replied, entirely too revved up for his teasing.

He chuckled. "Is that a no? Should I go back to foreplay?"

"I will kill you."

Another chuckle. Smug bastard. He deserved to be. I had never felt anything like this before and it was only going to get better. Soon, if he knew what was good for him.

His fingers teased along the edge of my panties, sliding under to follow the curve of my ass.

"You're overdressed."

"You're a witch. Fix it."

"But I like these panties. A lot. You look amazing in them."

"I'll buy more."

"Promise?"

He didn't let me answer, pulling me back for another kiss. Only now he grabbed the back of my underwear and ripped them, pulling them away and tossing them aside.

"You're getting your cave man on," I purred. "I like it." And I did. That small violence made me feel feminine and desirable, as did the way his hands stroked me from shoulder to ass, his fingers dipping tauntingly between my legs.

My insides quivered like jelly and his hot length felt velvet-smooth against my slick heat.

"Are you ready?" He asked in his smokey voice. "I want this to be good for you. We can take all the time you need."

My answer was to tilt my hips and slide myself up and then back down his cock. "If you don't get on with it, I swear that when I have you in my mouth, I will torture you. Or bite you. Maybe both. Probably both."

At my words, his body shuddered and his arms contracted around me. He gave a groan that seemed to come from down in the ground. "Jesus, fuck, Beck. You're going to make me blow before I even get inside you. God, just the thought of your lips on my dick...."

He didn't finish the thought. Instead he lifted me, angling so that his blunt thickness nudged against me.

"You're in control," he said, his body clenching like it was taking all he had not to start thrusting. "Damn. I forgot to ask if you wanted a condom."

"I'm on the pill, and I'll go to a witch doctor if you give me herpes." I almost couldn't find enough coherence to speak.

Sensations cascaded through me and I was losing the ability to think. Actually, I didn't want to think. I just wanted to feel and not let it end too soon.

"Let yourself slide onto me slowly," he said against my throat. "Let yourself adjust as you go. Relax as much as you can."

He had to be kidding. Relax? I was coiled tighter than a torsion spring about to blast a rocket into space all by its lonesome. He kept sliding his hands over my back and butt while alternating his mouth's attention between my breasts. My head had dropped back and while I'm sure my eyes were open, I'd just about gone blind.

I relaxed myself and began the excruciatingly and intensely pleasurable journey of impaling myself on

Damon's cock. More than the physical sensation, I was caught up in the intimacy of the connection. Suddenly, I felt the need to look him in the eyes. I lifted my head and bumped my forehead against his, locking eyes with him. His hands stilled, resting on my hips, and the only movement was my slow, delicious descent.

All I could hear was my heart pounding in my ears and both of our ragged panting. Down, down, down, until I was fully seated back on his thighs. Inside, his hot length pulsed and throbbed. I felt full in a way I had never imagined, not even using the practice dildo the girls had given me. It was glorious and so very intimate. I was open and vulnerable in a way I'd never been with anybody before.

This was me without defenses, without pretenses, without walls, without words. Reflexively, my inner muscles clenched, sending a shivering quake of exquisite pleasure through me. I gasped and his fingers dug into my flesh, his eyes squeezing shut.

"Fuck but you feel good," Damon said hoarsely. "Are you okay?"

"Uh huh," I said, barely able to answer.

"Start moving when you're ready."

He still held me upright, so I wasn't sure how much I could actually move. First I tried rocking myself back and forth. Sensation erupted from inside me, spiraling outward in thick, lazy coils. I moaned and bit my lower lip. Instantly Damon kissed me, holding my head where he wanted it as he wiggled his hips. My brain short-circuited and I lost all sense of physical control.

I began to move, lifting myself slightly and bottoming out against him. The tightening pressure returned, this time like a powerful whirlpool pulling me down into a syrupy vortex of glorious sensation.

My orgasm gave me little warning. Suddenly it hit and my entire body seized around him as pleasure exploded, boiling through me and energizing every cell with bliss so luscious and thrilling I might have stopped breathing just to focus on feeling. I was twisting and rocking and grinding, making mewling sounds and repeating Damon's name along with a lot of curses. It felt so good my eyes got in on the action and I teared up.

The orgasm started to subside and I felt like melted butter, all my nerve endings, especially my nipples and clit, electrically sensitive.

When my shuddering slowed, Damon rolled us over so he was over me. He pushed my knees up and hooked them over his arms, holding me open.

"Ready for me?"

"There's more?" I asked. "I don't know if I'm capable. I might die."

"You won't die. I'll show you." He bent and kissed me and started a slow slide out, followed by slow slide in.

I flung my head back and my back arched without any orders from me. I was stunned at the new build of deliciousness coiling in my belly. My hips lifted as he thrust back in and I moaned again. Damon chuckled with masculine triumph and repeated the movement. He set a slow, deliberate pace, his arms keeping from clasping my legs around him and increasing his speed. He lowered his head to kiss me and then to attend to my aching breasts. My fingers dug hard into his shoulders, but nothing I did changed the relentless slowness of his pace.

I was no more prepared for my next orgasm than the first. This time it unrolled slowly, picking me up on its back and rising to a leisurely crest. I felt it far more powerfully. My body shook and quivered, and at some point I felt like I could barely move. I couldn't breathe. All of my awareness was focused on that slowly spreading detonation.

Damon kept up his gentle thrusting all the way through, his face pulled into a mask as he fought to keep himself from joining me.

That wouldn't do. I wanted him out of control and as mindless with pleasure as I was. I ran my hands down his back, and then I had a wicked idea. He still held my knees wide, which gave me precious little ability to do much more than play with his nipples. I did, lifting myself to tease them with my tongue. He sucked in a breath and his careful rhythm stuttered.

"If you keep that up, I'm going to lose it," he said.

"Good. It's about time, don't you think?"

"I want your first time with me to be something you'll never forget." He'd begun to pant.

Sweat slicked his skin and I looked down between us at the muscular ripples of his chest and stomach, and lower to the blond curls surrounding his cock and oh, the sight of him moving in and out of me was almost more than I could take. I felt quivers beginning again and this time I wanted him on this glorious ride with me.

I slipped my hand down between us to palm his balls, gently massaging him. That did it. All of a sudden, he switched into high gear. He leaned forward, tipping my hips at a better angle, and drove into me harder and harder.

I'd thought I'd felt good before, but this time the crescendo he was thrusting me toward was beyond my imagination. Harder and faster and then it was his turn to slide his hand between us. He brushed his thumb over my clit and that was it. My mind went blank. Feeling overwhelmed me. I tipped over the cliff and found myself in freefall. Damon's face was planted in the crook of my neck and he'd thrust home, grinding himself against me, his dick twitching and pulsing as he came.

When he was done, he rolled back over, leaving me sprawled boneless on top of him. Both of us were panting. It took a little while before coherence set in. His hands skated lightly up and down my back

"Wow."

His arms tightened at my incredibly articulate response and he brushed his lips against mine.

"I've wanted to do that since I met you. Next time will be better."

"I don't think that's possible, but of course I'm willing to try. As many times as necessary."

His laugh rumbled through his chest and through me. "It will be." He tipped my chin so he could look me in the eyes. "I love you."

I smiled at how easily and naturally the words rose to my lips in return. "I believe you. I love you too." I yawned and my jaw cracked. "I may have to stay in bed all day tomorrow. Or today, actually."

"Sounds like a plan."

"I meant in order to sleep."

"We'll sleep. And then we'll play."

He kissed me again, leaving me no doubt about just what he had in mind.

CHAPTER TWENTY-FOUR

I woke around one o'clock the next day. My body felt deliciously sore and relaxed, like I'd just been through a week of spa treatments. As Damon had promised, we'd slept and played several times over. I stretched, realizing I was alone in bed. Or rather, I was in bed with Ajax.

I turned on the bedside lamp, noticing that the shower was running. I kicked the covers off. I could definitely use another shower, and one with Damon sounded like a very good idea. Unfortunately, the water shut off before I'd swung my feet to the floor. A few moments later, he came through the door. He rubbed his hair with the towel, the rest of him damp, clean, and looking very, very tasty.

"You're awake," he said, noticing me, and veered away from the dresser where he'd stashed his clothes, making a beeline for me instead.

Just seeing him in all his muscular glory started getting me hot and bothered again. I eyed his cock and licked my lips in an effort to be seductive. He hadn't given me much chance to give him the kind of pleasure I wanted to, and I was ready to do some teasing of my own. Anticipation burned in my belly. He clearly noticed my intention because little Damon sprung to attention. Unfortunately, big Damon decided to be an asshole and stopped short of me.

"Christ, Beck. You can't go looking at me like that." He proceeded to wrap the towel around his waist, which looked very silly given the large bump sticking out in front.

"How am I looking at you? And why are you being so rude and putting a towel around yourself that I'm just going to have to take off?"

I might have also shimmied a little bit and made my boobs bounce.

He groaned and looked up, fingers gripping the towel like it was a safety rope. "You are not making this easy."

"But I am. I'm so easy. Look how easy I am!" I flung myself backward and bent my knees so my feet were flat on the bed and he had a great view of my goodies. "How much easier do you want?"

That did it. He dove on top of me, whisking the towel out of the way as he did. No foreplay, just sliding all the way inside, just the way I wanted it. I might have squealed and thrust upward to meet him, but my brain switched to autopilot. We went into feral mode, touching and licking and biting. He lifted me further on the bed so he could get a knee down for better leverage. I vaguely heard Ajax give a grumpy growl and depart.

Then I was flying again and part of my brain continued to marvel at how powerful the sensations were and how good it was, and part of me wondered what had taken so long for me to get Damon between my legs. What a waste of time.

We both hit orgasm fast. He held me against him as I

went into uncontrolled spasms of delight, his own body jerking and grinding as we went nuclear together.

After, he held himself on his elbows above me. A sign of true love, I decided, was when he kissed me despite my undoubtedly serious case of morning breath.

"You're everything," he whispered against my lips before kissing me again. But then he lifted himself away, reaching again for the towel that head fallen on the floor and handing it to me to clean up. "We've got company. They've been waiting downstairs scarfing down food and apparently driving Deirdre slightly insane by frequently asking when you'll be down. She continues to stuff food down their gullets in an effort to shut them up, but it's starting to look a little dangerous."

I frowned. "How do you know?"

"I took Ajax out before I showered."

"Who's here?"

"Mason, your mother, Ballard, Jeffers, that other cop— Mike Crowe?— plus Jen, Stacey, and Lorraine. And someone named Luke."

"Shit. What am I going to tell them?" I sat up. "I really don't want to start something terrible, but I don't know how I can keep Angie and her whole world a secret."

He sat beside me and pulled me against him, his skin warm and damp. I rubbed my cheek against his shoulder, inhaling his scent.

"We'll tell them the truth, but I think we need to go further than that."

I frowned. "What do you mean?"

"I was thinking about it in the shower. You're not safe from attack from either side for different reasons. I'm not safe, even from my own family. There's a good chance

Mason and your mother will get targeted for not trying to force you into the family fold or for helping to protect you. Ben is in the same shoes. Hell, this Angie, much as I'd like to rip her head off for kidnapping you, is in danger from her people."

"Okay, I'm getting a theme here. We're all up shit creek. What do you want to do about it?" But I already had an inkling. I'd given the idea a little bit of thought here and there too. I just didn't know how to make it real.

"We create our own family," he said, using air quotes around *family*. "We make Sweetwater our domain and we make it a refuge for people who want to escape the family dictates of enforced breeding, or who just want to live their lives the way they want. We make rules for being included and we expel anybody who breaks them.

"What kind of rules?"

"For one, we have each other's backs—mutual protection—and nobody gets to be an asshole. We'll draw up a contract and make it binding. You and I can be in charge, or we can have a board. Personally, I think there should be an advisory board, but all final decisions should come down to you."

"Me? Why?" That job sounded like the worst one on the planet. I didn't want to be responsible for anybody else.

"Because you aren't greedy, you aren't selfish, and you care about people more than you care about yourself. You're also fearless with a strong sense of justice and fairness. You'll make good decisions for the benefit of people and any magical people—like the gargoyles—who might end up wanting to be a part of this. And yes, I know, they don't want to be a part of this, but for now, they are and deserve the consideration and rights of everybody who comes by choice.

"My only caveat is that I want the right to have a say when you decide to put yourself in harm's way. I want it in writing that you have to at least listen and consider what I have to say."

I drew back to look at him. "You don't want veto power?"

He didn't smile. "I want it, but I won't get it. You're going to do what you think you have to, no matter what I think. But if you have to listen to me, then I get a chance to help figure out a safer way to do it, or I get to come along for the ride. Either way is safer for you."

"That's fair. It's kind of eerie how well you know me."

He shook his head. "I know that much about you, but it's going to take a lifetime for me to actually know you."

My brows rose. "A lifetime? That's a long time to put up with me. I can be annoying."

He kissed me. "I'll start with a lifetime. We can negotiate for after that. Now shower and get dressed and I'll go calm the seething masses. The faster we deal with everybody and kick them out, the faster we can go back to bed."

"You're beginning to sound like Stacey."

He stood and pulled me into his arms, his forehead resting on mine. "I imagined what being with you would feel like, but my imagination didn't begin to capture reality. I'm addicted. I feel no shame in admitting I want a whole lot more of last night."

If I'd been wearing panties, they'd have melted. "Counter offer," I said. "How about we let the masses seethe and you come help me in the shower. I'm very dirty."

"I love the way you think."

And with that, he swung me up into his arms caveman-style and took me into the bathroom, where we spent a long time getting ourselves clean. The good news was we made it downstairs in time for dinner, and Deirdre hadn't killed anybody.

The End

READ A SAMPLE FROM THE INCUBUS TRAP
(FORMERLY KNOWN AS THE INCUBUS JOB)

I got the fish-eye stare from the concierge when I walked past him into the lobby. I passed through the security net, feeling it ripple across my skin like seeking fingers. My lips tightened smugly. I could go out and come back again and totally change my aural signature. It might remember this version of me forever—and it probably would—but it wouldn't do it a damned bit of good if it never saw this me again.

Effrayant was a mash-up of the Bellagio and the Bates Motel, with a little dash of old-school English castle for flair. Brick and ivy smothered the outside and gave it an air of age. The mansard roof that rose up six or eight stories on top gave it the eerie, death-is-going-to-get-you vibe. The central tower stood a good forty stories high, with four wings sprouting like spokes from its shoulders. Their flat rooftops boasted pools, clubs, restaurants, and helipads, all for the comfort and diversion of the rich, powerful, and supernatural. From the ground, the central rooftop resembled a big green afro, with lush trees billowing up in a thick forest.

If it weren't for the fact I was on a job, I wouldn't be caught dead there. Or maybe the opposite was more true: if I weren't on the job, the only way I'd end up here is dead, though why anybody would want my dead body around was open to debate.

Inside the lobby, elegant dark wood surrounded me. Polished marble and thick carpets, modern furniture, soft lights, and museum-quality art added to the luxurious ambience. Muted opera music wandered through the cavernous lobby. The staff all wore Italian wool uniforms in gray, burgundy, and navy, while customers dressed in designer glitz and blue-collar chic.

I couldn't blame the bellman for looking at me sideways. Wearing Levi's, a gray, long-sleeved cotton shirt from the Goodwill; a pair of tennis shoes that had seen better days; and a blue ball cap, I looked neither glitzy nor chic. I didn't even look like I could afford to work its elegant halls.

Given the fact that my luggage was nothing more than a ratty backpack, I was more than a little surprised that the security guards inside didn't try to stop me—with force. Sure, the ghosts make people want to turn and head the other way and let me be someone else's problem. Security guards ought to be better trained. They shouldn't let the heebie-jeebies get the better of them, especially working for a joint like this. I get that it's not every day that you get the ghost push-off from someone made of flesh and blood, but Effrayant liked to brag their security was the best of the best, so these jerks ought to have been all over me like flies on juicy roadkill.

I walked in and all six of the thick-necked best-of-the-best got busy picking lint off their coats, making me the check-in clerk's problem.

Poor thing. I could tell she wanted to be anywhere else.

That's Tabitha's fault. She can put the fear of Jesus into just about anyone without trying.

Tonight she was trying.

If I were to say my little teenaged monster didn't want to come inside Effrayant, it would be about the same thing as calling Hurricane Katrina a slight rain event. Somewhere on my latest job tracking down the incubus, she'd started acting out. When we reached the doors of Effrayant, she went from mild temper tantrums to full-on nuclear meltdown. Apparently she thought the job was too dangerous.

I wanted to tell her to suck it up and settle down, it was just a retrieval job, but she was only a thirteen-year-old girl, and dead or not, her hormones were raging. Stir in a dose of inexplicable terror, and there was no way I was going to get her to listen to reason.

The irony was that she was at least as dangerous as the incubus I was tracking. She still had a lot of PTSD issues from how she got killed. Not that I had any idea how it had actually gone down. I only knew she was pissed as hell and she had nightmares that occasionally leaked into my dreams. If any of what happened in those nightmares had actually happened *to* her, she had a right to her attitude. Hell, she had a right to have gone completely over the edge into insanity-land. I didn't think she had, but it's not like she talked to me. She didn't talk to anybody. Anyhow, all that meant was that when she got scared, she killed first and asked questions later. Or rather, never asked questions.

So here I was, looking like a hobo with an angry, terri-fied, homicidal teenaged poltergeist in the nicest hotel on the east coast trying to finally corner an incubus with a stolen box full of who knows what sorts of valuables. That was the job; I was supposed to get the box back.

The chances of this going badly were growing by the second.

Tabitha's a pretty good killer when she wants to be, which is why I was glad the security guards hadn't bothered me. I might not have been able to hold her back without serious force, and I didn't like doing that. It would hurt her. Plus, it reminded her and all the others that I could snuff them out without much effort.

That's me—Mallory Jade, former exterminator. In the bad old days, if you wanted something or someone killed, for a fee, I'd kill it—from ghosts to banshees to terrorists to disgruntled employees. I don't even know how many final deaths I'm responsible for; I don't want to know. I quit that life, left it behind like dust in the rearview. I don't kill anymore. I'm a fixer now. If you've got a problem, I'll help you fix it, so long as I don't take anybody's life or half-life or dead-life. The money's decent and I get to sleep at night.

Unfortunately these days I sleep with ghosts. They like to attach to sorcerers, which is usually guaranteed suicide. Most of us with enough power to attract ghosts also have enough power to send them off to the final death. It's a moths-to-the-bug-zapper situation. I'm the rare exception since I've sworn off killing. I don't even like binding them off so they can't come near me. It's not like they take up space or weigh anything, and they do have their uses.

Like helping me to fake my aural signature and making unfriendly types look the other way. Unfortunately the desk clerk looked like she wanted to pee her pants. I sighed and pushed down on Tabitha slightly. The other ghosts pressed in on her too, trying to reassure and calm her. The girl-ghost recoiled and struck back. Lightning arced through me. I turned my grimace into a tight smile and leashed her as tight as I dared. I didn't need her flinging furniture and blowing up computers. Not that I could stop her if that's what she really wanted to do. Or rather, not that I would.

Stopping her would violate my no-torturing policy. On the other hand, I didn't want her killing people either. That put me in a bind because no matter what, I wasn't going to exterminate her and that might be what it took to stop her if she went on a rampage. That meant I'd have to protect any innocent lives and reveal what I was, which would completely defeat the point of being here. On the other hand, with its particular clientele, Effrayant no doubt kept an exterminator on staff. If Tabitha went wild, she risked extermination. I wouldn't protect her. This was her decision. Choices have consequences. You pay your money, you take your chances.

I could tell that every step I took inside Effrayant only fed her fury and panic. She clawed at me. I could feel things tearing on a metaphysical level. I was getting close to cutting her loose. Had to if I didn't want to get torn to shreds. Inwardly I groaned. This was so not going to end well.

I glanced back at the door and away. I'd come this far. No turning back now.

"Can I help you?" the clerk murmured, directing the question to the floor as she edged away.

I'm not sure she even knew what her feet were doing. She was small, smaller than me anyhow. I'm compact: about five foot six and carrying about a hundred and forty-five pounds of lean muscle. And boobs. I've got what people call an hourglass shape—big boobs and child-bearing hips. I've got thighs that could knock down trees. The clerk—Yun Chee, according to her name tag—was maybe five feet tall, though I doubted it, and probably wore a size zero. She had no hips and no boobs and probably never would without the help of a plastic surgeon.

"I've got a reservation," I said as Tabitha slammed against my inner shields. I flinched as a sensation of not-quite-pain frizzled through my nerves. The bottoms of my feet prickled with needles, and gray fuzz billowed across my eyes. Twitches ran through me, making me look like a tweaker in need of a fix.

"Um. Let me look . . ." Yun Chee said, her voice trailing off as she realized that she had backed up against the cabinet behind her. She was leaning back like she wanted to climb up on top of it. All the same, she kept herself together better than the security guys had. "What's the name?"

"Carson. Mary Carson."

She finally scraped up the nerve to actually look at me. Her gaze took in the scar running down my cheek, the half-healed black eye, and the Walmart quality of my clothes. Her back stiffened and she lifted her chin. "Really?" she asked, her brows meeting in disdainful scorn.

You've got to love snobby waitstaff. I was willing to bet I had a lot more money in the bank than a lot of her other patrons, and anyway, judging a book by its cover in a place like this could get your head ripped off—literally. You never know who or what you might be talking to.

"Really," I said firmly. In other circumstances I'd have kicked up holy hell at her attitude—I really enjoy that sort of thing—but occasionally I have enough sense to know better.

"That's . . . let me see," she said and inched forward, stretching her fingertips out to the keyboard. If Tabitha hadn't been wired to blow on a hair trigger, it would have been funny.

"Could you hurry?" I asked. "I need to get settled as soon as possible." Let her imagine why I *needed* to.

Once in my room, I could set up wards and let Tabitha loose. She'd shred the place, but I figured that was a basic hazard of hotel ownership, particularly for the sort of clientele Effrayant catered to. All I had to do was get there before she totally melted down.

Unfortunately Yun Chee was not all that quick at her job, and Tabitha was way off the reservation. Before the clerk could finish typing my fake name into her computer, Tabitha launched herself at me again, this time no holds barred. The fury of her panic and rage added to her already substantial strength. I grabbed the edge of the counter, an electric jolt streaking fire through me and turning my legs to Jell-O. Heat flushed through my body. I gritted my teeth, rapidly considering my choices. All of them were bad.

Tabitha hit me again, and I pretended to cough, bending over so the clerk couldn't see me talking to myself.

"Shut it down or you're on your own," I warned the ghost. "Your choice."

She shrieked inside my head. I swallowed bile as my stomach lurched in reaction. Blood started to trickle from my nose. I sniffed and blocked it with the back of my hand.

"All right, then," I said, straightening. "If that's the way you want it."

I wondered if all thirteen-year-olds took this long to grow up. Tabitha had been with me for the past four years. I don't know how long she was wandering around before that. Her clothes were pretty modern, but she could have been from anytime in the past forty or fifty years. Nothing about her gave any defining clues, and she never spoke a word to me. The only reason I knew her name was she'd spilled my orange juice one morning and scrawled it on the table. I'd been calling her Squirt. She didn't like it. She also didn't like rules and sure as hell didn't like it when she didn't get her own way, making her a fairly typical teenager. I didn't know how much her life and death played into her obnoxious behavior. At the moment, I didn't care.

I'd warned her and just because her ghost was stuck in hormone hell didn't mean she didn't have to follow my rules. After four years with me, she knew I wasn't going to kill her or bind her, but neither was I going to let her kill me. That meant she was about to be somebody else's problem and my fixing job was about to get a lot more complicated.

I felt the clamor from the other ghosts as they quadrupled their efforts to settle her down. They knew what was about to happen.

I focused on Tabitha's aural signature and wrapped it in a loose web of power. I pushed it out of me, beyond my shields, but still holding her in a bubble. She still wasn't visible. My magic protected her. The moment I withdrew, everybody in the lobby would get a show. A spectacular one, since she was doing her version of Mount St. Helen's.

Ready or not, here she comes . . .

I let the web unravel, and Tabitha exploded. Electricity arced through the lobby in crackling blue-white cables. Wind blew up out of nowhere. Furniture dragged across the floor toward the spinning center, and various bits of horrendously expensive artwork whirled into the air. Tabitha hung in the air, her long curly blonde hair a halo around her head. She glowed with transparent light, and her eyes had gone completely white. She was totally out of her gourd.

The impressive thing was that despite the arcing electricity and wind picking up the debris, the rest of the lobby was relatively unscathed. Nothing had caught fire, and the computers remained anchored to the counters. That was a damned good security web.

The clerk had begun to float up off her feet and clutched the counter for dear life. The guards pulled out weapons, though what Tasers or guns were going to do to a poltergeist, I didn't know. I wanted to tell them to put them away before Tabitha got ideas about using them herself, but I figured they ought to know better and if you're stupid enough to give artillery to a poltergeist, then you deserve what you get.

I used loops of magic to anchor myself down, and my other ghosts protected me from the flying debris. My hat went flying off into the maelstrom. Damn it. I'd just broken it in. Plus now the undyeable and all-too-memorable white streak was revealed. It hooped from my hairline above my left eye around my left ear. Evidence of my encounter with an Ammit demon. Didn't matter, I supposed. White streak or not, nobody at Effrayant was going to forget me anytime soon, not with Tabitha doing a floor show.

I hit the ground when I heard the first gunshot. I wrapped myself in thick shields. More shots. My mouth dropped open. The guards were actually *shooting* at a poltergeist. A six-headed electrical hydra snapped at the six idiots. They went rigid and their hair stood on end. Tabitha didn't let them go.

"Don't kill them," I admonished softly, knowing she could hear me. To my astonishment, she listened.

The cables of electricity dissolved and the six guards collapsed to the floor, flopping and jerking. The smell of burning hair made my gorge rise.

"C'mon, Tabitha," I murmured. "Pull it together. This is not the place, and this is not the time."

Apparently she wasn't open to more advice because a chair smashed into me. It bounced off my shields, but the force of it slammed me against the stub wall holding up the counter. I was going to be sore later.

The surge of suppression magic came without warning. It rose up and dropped down like a curtain on closing night of a Broadway show. Tabitha vanished. All the crackling snakes of electricity dissolved. Debris dropped out of the air to hammer the floor. Papers drifted down more slowly, like oversized ticker tape. It looked like a tornado had hit.

I stood. The suppression lay heavily over me. It thickened the air into syrup, making breathing an effort. At least my shields held. I looked around. The guards remained incapacitated on the ground. They smelled like a sewer. Electrocution wasn't good for bladder and bowel control. Guests hunched stunned against the walls or sprawled like crash-test dummies on the floor. I leaned to look behind the counter. Yun Chee had crawled down to the end and sat with her knees against her chest, her face pressed into her knees.

I sighed. I wanted to be safely out of the way before their exterminator arrived on the scene. I needed to find my mark before he vanished. I didn't want to spend another three weeks tracking him down.

Underneath the counter was the button to call the housekeeper. Despite the rather menial name, he or she would be in charge of Effrayant. Though I expected the housekeeper was already on the way, I walked around and pressed the button anyway.

The suppression magic didn't lift. It wouldn't until the exterminator reset it and got rid of any lingering poltergeists. Tabitha wouldn't have long between the lifting of the suppression and the exterminator's summons to make her escape. If she got back to me, I could protect her. If not, she'd be toast. It wouldn't matter if she ran to China, once the summons was done, without protection, she had to answer.

I hoped she'd make it. She was a pain in the ass, but she was scared, not evil. She deserved to live whatever life she had left.

A heavy wood door swung open to the right of the counter, and a woman who could only be the housekeeper strode through. She was tall and wearing four-inch spike heels, a pencil skirt, and a tailored silk blazer. Her sleek ash blonde hair was shorter in the back with long wings on the sides to frame her porcelain face. She glanced down at the clerk before surveying the lobby. Finally her blue gaze settled on me. Her brows rose in disbelief of my existence in her auberge.

"May I help you?"

"I was checking in. Do you get poltergeists often?" I asked, letting a note of disapproval color my tone.

Her pink lips firmed, her eyes narrowing. "I must apologize, Ms. . . .?"

"Carson. Mary Carson. I have a reservation."

That caught her up short. She *really* ought to have known better. I could have pointed out that most people took Howard Hughes to be a vagrant. Not everything was what it seemed. Especially me.

She tapped on the keyboard, her fingernails the same color as her lips. She blinked at the screen and looked up at me. "I have your reservation right here, Ms. Carson. Everything is already taken care of." All the distrust in her expression was gone, replaced by benevolent welcome. "I'll show you up myself."

She led the way across the lobby to the main bank of

elevators, stepping around bodies and strewn furniture as if like it happened every day. Already a small staff army was pouring in, helping the injured and straightening the room.

I followed the housekeeper into the elevator with relief. Thank goodness Ivan had made the reservations. He was my current employer and had more money than god. What he wanted, he got, and he'd wanted a room for Mary Carson in Effrayant.

I was to be housed in the main tower, apparently, just below the residence floors. Of course. The priciest rooms. I should have told Ivan I wanted something closer to the ground floor and exits. Not that I couldn't manage a quick escape with magic, but I preferred not to rely on it more than I had to.

"To answer your question, Ms. Carson, we do try to keep the ghosts out—this *is* a quality establishment, after all—but occasionally they do find a way. Our exterminator is quite good. Lawrence will have the situation well in hand within the hour," she said, preening as she delivered the news.

I blinked at her, more than a little surprised. Unpleasantly so. "Stanger?" I asked before I thought to keep my mouth shut. "Law Stanger is your exterminator?"

Both of the housekeeper's artfully plucked eyebrows arched. If she'd been a cat, her ears would have flattened. She was possessive about him. I wondered if she was screwing him. I wouldn't be surprised. She was damned beautiful, and I'm sure men panted after her like dogs after a meaty bone.

"Do you know Mr. Stanger?" she asked.

Biblically. Not to mention he used to be my partner when I was still working for Acadia.

"We've met," I said. I wondered if she'd keep the fact I

was staying at the auberge a secret if I asked. Discretion was part of her job, after all. It was worth a try. The last person I wanted to see was Law. "I expect he'll be busy with your little haunting. I'd just as soon not disturb him," I said as the elevator doors opened.

She gave me a sidelong glance. "Of course. I've put you in the Ronce suite on the corner. I'm sure you'll be very pleased with it."

Her gaze slid down to my feet then ahead down the hall. I bet it twisted her hard that she didn't know a damned thing about me *and* I knew Law. I wondered if her curiosity would win out over discretion. If so, it wouldn't take him long to put two and two together and come up with the fact that I was Mary Carson. Law was many things. Stupid was not one of them.

I'd better come up with a plan fast. This job was already half derailed thanks to Tabitha; I didn't want Law to push the train all the way over.

The housekeeper scanned a card over the door lock. The light turned green, and an electronic pad slid out.

"Put your left thumb on the pad please," she said.

I did as told. Magic flowed over my thumb, and my body pulsed hot. It was over in an instant.

"The lock is now keyed to your aural signature. No one else can enter without your permission, including staff. When you want your room cleaned, simply press the service button inside. All the information on our services is listed in the notebook on the desk. Please do not hesitate to call down if you need anything. My name is LeeAnne Watson. I'll be happy to look after any of your needs."

She handed me a linen card embossed in blue and gold. "Enjoy your stay at Effrayant, Ms. Carson. Please do note that all your meals will be comped during your stay as compensation for your difficulties checking in. We have several doctors on staff if you would like to consult anyone, at our cost, of course. Effrayant values your patronage."

"Thank you," I said. "You're very generous." She wasn't. It was bare minimum compensation for me nearly getting killed by a poltergeist in the lobby. It's not as if LeeAnne Watson knew Tabitha being in the auberge was my fault. All the same, I'd take it with a smile and get on with my business. With luck, I'd be gone by tomorrow.

Unfortunately, I've never been very lucky.

AVAILABLE NOW!

TO MY READERS

Thank you for hanging out with me, Beck, Ajax, and the gang! If you enjoyed *Putting the Ice in Nice*, consider leaving a review on your favorite book-buying site. Also, read excerpts from my other books on my website and sign up for my newsletter to hear more about upcoming releases at: www.dianapfrancis.com

ACKNOWLEDGMENTS

No good deed ever goes unpunished, and this is where the punishments happen. Or in this case, inadequate but heartfelt thanks.

I've had a lot of help with making this book happen. From having the support of my amazing family, to my cover artist and copy editor, to my writers support friends (I think I need to get Writer Support Friend shirts for them), to my beta readers, to my fans, to strangers answering random research questions, to the internet, and everything in between. That all said, I need to call some people out in particular.

Thank you to my family. Love you to bits and especially my husband for all he does. Thanks also to my puppies for all the cuddles and walks and otherwise giving me joy.

Thank you to Tiffany Trent, Lyn Forester, Jen Stevenson, Pat Rice, Devon Monk, Christy Keyes, Melissa Sawmiller, Kim Antell, the members of BVC, and Diane Barker for tech and creative support. Thanks also to Rainforest Writers and the Trash Panda Squad.

Thank you to Barb Cass and Nancy Marie Tice, patrons extraordinaire.

Thank you to all my readers and fans who find and read my books. Thanks to those of you, too, who go the extra mile to give reviews, tell your friends, and share my books. You mean everything to the career of a writer and especially to me.

ABOUT THE AUTHOR

Diana Pharaoh Francis is the *USA Today* and Amazon Bestselling writer of fantastical, adventurous, and often romantic fiction. She holds a Ph.D. in Victorian literature and literary theory. She's owned by a corgi, a mini blue heeler, and a blue-eyed corgi mix. She spends much of her time gardening, airbrush painting, herding children, and avoiding housework. She likes rocks, geocaching, horses, knotting up yarn, and has a thing for 1800s England, especially the Victorians.

For more about her books and to sign up for her newsletter, visit her at www.dianapfrancis.com or:

Patreon: www.patreon.com/dpfrancis
Instagram: www.instagram.com/di_pharaoh_francis/
Facebook: www.facebook.com/Diana.Pharaoh.Francis

BOOKS BY DIANA PHARAOH FRANCIS

From Book View Café

Everyday Disasters
Putting the Fun in Funeral
Putting the Chic in Psychic
Putting the Ice in Nice

Mission: Magic
The Incubus Trap
The Elf Deception
The Giant Riot

The Path series
Path of Fate (Forthcoming)
Path of Honor (Forthcoming)
Path of Blood (Forthcoming)

Hunger Pains

The Quick and Dirty Guide to Character Creation
(Forthcoming)

Diamond City Magic series
Trace of Magic
Edge of Dreams
Whisper of Shadows
Shades of Memory
Shatter of Light

Crosspointe Chronicles
The Cipher
The Black Ship
The Turning Tide
The Hollow Crown

Horngate Witches series
Bitter Night
Crimson Wind
Shadow City
Blood Winter

Magicfall series
The Witchkin Murders

ABOUT BOOK VIEW CAFÉ

BOOK VIEW CAFE

Book View Café is a professional authors' publishing cooperative offering DRM-free ebooks in multiple formats to readers around the world. With authors in a variety of genres including mystery, romance, fantasy, and science fiction, Book View Café has something for everyone.

Book View Café is good for readers because you can enjoy high-quality DRM-free ebooks from your favorite authors at a reasonable price.

Book View Café is good for writers because 90% of the proceeds goes directly to the book's author.

Book View Café authors include New York Times and USA Today bestsellers, Nebula, Hugo, Lambda, Chanticleer, National Reader's Choice, and Philip K. Dick Award winners, World Fantasy, Kirkus, and Rita Award nominees, and winners and nominees of many other publishing awards.

Book View Café's Newsletter includes new releases, specials, author news, and event announcements.